GREAT
Canadian
MURDER
and
MYSTERY
Stories

Other Quarry Press Anthologies of Fiction & Poetry

Spirits of the Age: Poets of Conscience
Edited by Mona Adilman

Canadian Christmas Stories in Prose & Verse
Edited by Don Bailey & Daile Unruh

The Naked Physician: Poems about the Lives of Patients & Doctors
Edited by Ron Charach

Poets 88: A New Generation of Canadian Poetry
Edited by Ken Norris & Bob Hilderley

Engaged Elsewhere: Short Stories by Canadians Abroad
Edited by Kent Thompson

Open Windows: Canadian Short Short Stories
Edited by Kent Thompson

GREAT
Canadian
MURDER
and
MYSTERY
Stories

EDITED BY
Don Bailey and Daile Unruh

Quarry Press

The publisher acknowledges the financial assistance of The Canada Council and the Ontario Arts Council in producing this book.

Canadian Cataloguing in Publication Data
  Main entry under title

   Great Canadian murder & mystery stories

ISBN 1-55082-019-2

   1. Detective and mystery stories, Canadian (English) I. Bailey, Don II. Unruh, Daile

PS8323.D4G73 1991   C813'.08720   C91-090439-1
PR9197.35.D48G73 1991

Cover art entitled ``Church and Horse'' by Alex Colville, reproduced by permission of the artist.

Design by Keith Abraham.
Type and imaging by Queen's Graphic Design Unit.
Printed and bound in Canada by Hignell Printing,
Winnipeg, Manitoba.

Published by Quarry Press, Inc., P.O. Box 1061, Kingston, Ontario K7L 4Y5 and P.O. Box 348, Clayton, New York 13628.

CONTENTS

Preface
Acknowledgements

MURDERS

MYSTERIES

PREFACE

According to my old Webster's, "mystery is anything that is kept secret or remains unexplained or unknown."

This collection of stories by authors from all across the country shares the common theme of mystery. As Daile Unruh and I waded through the 263 submissions we received in response to our advertisements, I was intrigued by the diverse approach different writers brought to the subject.

I have always been fascinated with mystery. I grew up as a ward of the government and spent most of my early years in Toronto being shunted back and forth between the orphanage and various foster homes. At a very early age I became aware of adults discussing my future in hushed whispers behind closed doors. I would put my ear to the wall and try to listen in on these conversations. All I ever overheard were snatches of this secret, grown-up talk. I learned only enough to frighten myself. I would then retreat to my room with the clues I had gathered, the small fragments of a puzzle that I would then attempt to assemble into a picture that was clear. In my mind anyway.

Such an exercise is unnerving. Mystery in our own lives can often trigger fear. To live in an atmosphere where we feel certain secrets are being kept from us, information critical to our well-being is being withheld, can cause excruciating anxiety.

And yet most of us develop an appetite, even an addiction for mystery. As a child I turned not-knowing into a game. I became a secret detective ever vigilant for clues to solve the mysterious plots that seemed to swirl around me. By casting myself as a character in a mystery story and speculating about how events would unfold, I was able to experience a titillating pleasure. To this day, when I pick up a newspaper and read a story that is more suggestive than revealing I enjoy trying to figure out what the "real" story is behind the vague text. The truth.

Truth, however, is subjective. It is an elusive commodity that has the allure of a bright light shining in the dark. We are drawn to it like moths and each of us must decide for ourselves what we believe the truth to be. Depending upon our imaginations, truth can be horrific, hilarious, or harmless.

In the 1950s when I began to read murder and mystery novels, the only books available in the stores were by British and American authors. To my knowledge there was no such creature as a Canadian mystery writer. I plowed my way through a dozen Agatha Christie novels but soon wearied of the fastidious style that she and her many imitators used. I wasn't terribly interested in the rather pompous characters that peopled British whodunnits. But then in 1956 I read a novel called *The Man with the Golden Arm* by Nelson Algren. I suppose there are those purists around who might say this book is not authentically of the mystery genre, but I remember being caught up in the suspense, tension, and terror of the world the main character inhabited. This was what I was looking for, not only good plot and character but a strong sense of the environment where the story took place.

The Man with the Golden Arm led me to Dashiell Hammett and Raymond Chandler's gritty novels set in Los Angeles. These guys conveyed the street smells, the music that drifted from windows, and they documented the decay of American cities long before urban planners began to sound warning bells.

In the 1960s I was preoccupied with being a bank robber and didn't read that much, but a sudden forced retirement to the penitentiary for almost nine years led me back to the library. I discovered John D. MacDonald and was delighted with Travis McGee's commitment to a form of morality that was neither black nor white. He was a character I could relate to, someone who lived and operated in the gray shadows.

In the 1970s when I had regained my freedom, I began to write and publish, figuring it was a safer profession than being a thief. Never did it occur to me to even attempt a book that dealt with murder, crime, or mystery. I was a Canadian. We didn't do that sort of thing.

In 1978, Howard Engel was the producer of an important CBC weekly radio series that broadcast poems, stories, and commentary by writers. I sold to this show regularly, and one day Howard suggested we have coffee together. Flattered, I agreed and we wandered across Jarvis Street in downtown Toronto to what was then the Four Seasons Hotel. In a hushed voice, Howard revealed that he was writing a mystery novel and said he wanted to pick my brain for certain underworld details. I was amused but complied, thinking who is going to be interested in reading about a Canadian detective? Nobody I concluded. We were not a nation who had mysteries intriguing enough to write about. No one would read about us. Of course, I was wrong. Benny Cooperman with his chopped-egg salad sandwiches has found a permanent place of affection in the hearts of mystery fans, not just in Canada, but all over the world.

The 1980s ushered in a parade of new authors who dazzled us with a variety of literary heroes all struggling to solve the murders that took place in our very own Canadian streets. We now have William Gough and L.R. Wright firmly established as chroniclers of west coast crime, while on the east coast Kenneth Langdon sets a murder in Saint John. Toronto is bursting with writers like Eric Wright, Howard Engel, and Medora Sale who are steadily taking over book shelf space from the likes of big American guns like Robert Parker.

As a fan of good mystery writing I wonder how this new popularity came about. Did Canadian authors suddenly wake up one day and declare to themselves that they were capable of producing good murder stories? No, I don't think so. The answer that makes sense to me is that Canadians have been writing and publishing mystery stories for years. The most successful ones like Sinclair Ross's *The Painted Door* were not identified as such and were appreciated simply for their good writing. Suddenly, though, the appetite that has always existed among readers for good mystery writing is out in the open. Particularly the hunger for stories that originate in the imaginations of our fellow countrymen. And women.

The popular Canadian mystery authors who have emerged in the last decade or two write with original voices. They are so unlike the British and Americans that readers and fans have developed a certain pride in the writers and the characters they have created. It would not surprise me to see Charlie Slater's name on the candidate's list in the next election for mayor of Toronto, or the beaming image of Benny Cooperman's face silk-screened on a T-shirt sold to rich teenage girls at upscale stores in suburban malls.

The writing of mystery, murder, and crime has become so respectable in Canada that there are now authors who actually earn as much money from this activity as, well, a postman. That's progress.

One of the great joys that Daile and I took in assembling this collection of stories occurred when after a long cold winter day, we'd light a fire in the grate, turn out the livingroom lamps, and read aloud one of the stories by the flickering light of the flames. Sometimes our fifteen-year-old son Daniel would join us in the dark and shiver as he listened to a tale of intrigue that would leave us all teetering precariously on the edge of an emotional cliff.

Would the main character in Donna Gamache's story "The Perfect Plan" get away with murder? The scenario that plays itself over and over again in a variety of different ways in the story "Dress Rehearsal" by Stan Rogal suggests an ominous situation that gave me the creeps, but there was no mutual agreement among the three of us as to what exactly is taking place. Is Margaret Atwood inviting us all to take part in a deadly game that she outlines in her story "Murder in the Dark?"

But not all these tales are concerned with crime or the dynamic of evil. Some explore the mysterious territory of love, as you will find in "That's the Island and These Are the Stones" by Charles Wilkins, and the poignant story "Red Barn, Interior" by David Helwig.

Humor is also present as the reader will discover in the mad-cap yarn " Ah, Sweet Stewart" by Ann Walsh, or "The Shanghai Noodle Killing" by Ted Plantos.

We hope this anthology will provide the reader with a satisfying opportunity to experience the fine writing being done in the shadowy arena of mystery. I know I will be going back to these pages again and again to experience the vicarious thrill of participating in the unknown.

This is a book that can be read alone in bed, in the dark with a flash light, the covers pulled up over your head, or it can be enjoyed read aloud in the company of family and friends sitting around an open fire. Whatever way makes you feel safest.

Don Bailey

ACKNOWLEDGEMENTS

"Murder in the Dark" by Margaret Atwood is reprinted from *Murder in the Dark: Short Fictions and Prose Poems* (Coach House Press) by permission of the author. "Crime of Passion" by Bill Dodds previously appeared in *Aphelion*. "The Mikveh Man" by Sharon Drache is reprinted with changes from *The Mikveh Man & Other Stories* (Aya Press) by permission of the author. "Becoming" by Jake MacDonald is reprinted with corrections from *Two Tickets to Paradise* (Oberon Press) by permission of the author. "The Little Black Knife" by Scott Mackay previously appeared in *Ellery Queen's Mystery Magazine*. "Invitations" by Carol Shields is reprinted from *Various Miracles* (Stoddart Publishing) by permission of the publisher. "Penalty for Misuse — $20" by J.J. Steinfeld is reprinted from *The Apostate's Tattoo* (Ragweed Press) by permission of the author. "That's the Island and These Are the Stones" by Charles Wilkins previously appeared in *Border Crossings*.

MURDERS

1
Margaret Atwood
MURDER IN THE DARK

T HIS is a game I've played only twice. The first time I was in Grade Five, I played it in a cellar, the cellar of a large house belonging to the parents of a girl called Louise. There was a pool table in the cellar but none of us knew anything about pool. There was also a player piano. After a while we got tired of running the punchcard rolls through the player piano and watching the keys go up and down by themselves, like something in a late movie just before you see the dead person. I was in love with a boy called Bill, who was in love with Louise. The other boy, whose name I can't remember, was in love with me. Nobody knew who Louise was in love with.

So we turned out the lights in the cellar and played *Murder in the Dark*, which gave the boys the pleasure of being able to put their hands around the girls' necks and gave the girls the pleasure of screaming. The excitement was almost more than we could bear, but luckily Louise's parents came home and asked us what we thought we were up to.

The second time I played it was with adults; it was not as much fun, though more intellectually complex.

I heard that this game was once played at a summer cottage by six normal people and a poet, and the poet really tried to kill someone. He was hindered only by the intervention of a dog, which could not tell fantasy from reality. The thing about this game is that you have to know when to stop.

Here is how you play:

You fold up some pieces of paper and put them into a hat, a bowl or the center of the table. Everyone chooses a piece. The one who gets the x is the detective, the one who gets the black spot is the killer. The detective leaves the room, turning off the lights. Everyone gropes around in the dark until the murderer picks a victim. He can either whisper, "You're dead," or he can slip his hands around a throat and give a playful but decisive squeeze. The victim screams and falls down. Everyone must now stop moving around except the murderer, who of course will not want to be found near the body. The detective counts to ten, turns on the lights and enters the room. He may now question anyone but the victim, who is not allowed to answer, being dead. Everyone but the murderer must tell the truth. The murderer must lie.

If you like, you can play games with this game. You can say: the murderer is the writer, the detective is the reader, the victim is the book. Or perhaps, the murderer is the writer, the detective is the critic and the victim is the reader. In that case the book would be the total *mise en scène*, including the lamp that was accidentally tipped over and broken. But really it's more fun just to play the game.

In any case, that's me in the dark. I have designs on you, I'm plotting my sinister crime, my hands are reaching for your neck or perhaps, by mistake, your thigh. You can hear my footsteps approaching, I wear boots and carry a knife, or maybe it's a pearl-handled revolver, in any case I wear boots with very soft soles, you can see the cinematic glow of my cigarette, waxing and waning in the fog of the room, the street, the room, even though I don't smoke. Just remember this, when the scream at last has ended and you've turned on the lights: by the rules of the game, I must always lie.

Now: do you believe me?

2
Ted Plantos
THE SHANGHAI NOODLE KILLING

H E DIED as he had lived. His face in a bowl of noodles. This would not be written into his obituary. Only the standard words would apply. A good father to five children. Lily Lee's beloved husband. You understand. Nobody'd believe it. They'd think it was made up by someone who trifles with honesty.

Nobody dies with his face in a bowl of noodles. In a bowl of pasta done *al dente*, yes ... with blood mixing into oregano seasoned tomato sauce, yes. But at Queen's Noodle House on Queen Street, who could predict it?

"Shanghai noodle ... the thick one," Lo told Elizabeth, who took notes for a story in *The Gazette*.

"He liked them best, did he?"

"Ben very particular how noodle cooked. A few minute before the shooting, he complain they too chewy."

Elizabeth thought this stuff about the noodles would have plenty of human interest. "He was a perfectionist about how they were cooked," she said, and wrote it down when Lo agreed.

Lo was under the table when the gunmen opened fire. He tried to warn his friend. But you have to eat at Queen's Noodle House to understand that bedlam and not noodles or sizzling pork or anything on the menu or written in Chinese on the walls is the order of the day. There are thirty-five tables and each is surrounded by voracious stomachs and teeth that mash down into steaming plates of flesh and greens with chopsticks clicking, tongues salivating ... and under the din there is a low growl, a murmur, if you will, that emanates from the intestines of the eaters. Close your eyes and you are transported to Hong Kong. Open them in the mist of hot and sour soup and you see faces shifting like one hundred and forty four mahjongg tiles. In the mystifying sweat of the moment, laced with oyster sauce, hunger is an addiction you can afford at these prices.

Lo explains. "I shout to Ben when I see those hoodlum come through door ... *Duck, Ben.*"

"Did he hear you?"

"Yes."

"What did he say?"

"He say, *You order duck?* They his last word. *You order duck?* Then the noise. It deafen me. People screaming, little children shrieking. I stay down, my head on the floor until police come. Then I get up, see Ben's face in the bowl. Blood all over. Ben's eyes open. But Ben dead."

Elizabeth puzzled over how she could work these lurid details into her story without offending anyone. This was her first gangland slaying. All the other stories were about natural deaths. He died in his sleep. She suffered a stroke. The kind of deaths you come to expect. Elizabeth had never heard about anyone being gunned down while eating a bowl of Shanghai noodles. She knew the editor would say *Change this ... change that* until it sounded nothing like the way Ben Lee died on that Saturday afternoon in the Queen's Noodle House. How could the editor blame her? She was told to interview this man, Lo, because he and Ben were good friends. Didn't she ask innocuous questions? The kind she was expected to ask? Was it Elizabeth's fault that Lo wanted her to know all the sordid particulars?

"Ben owe money to wrong people," Lo told her.

Elizabeth tensed. She hoped Lo would say Mr. Lee owed money on something normal, like a bank loan. Anything but drugs. How could she write in her story that Mr. Ben Lee had a drug addiction?

"Gambling," Lo said.

Elizabeth felt relieved. Gambling is not as bad as drugs. She would have to change Lo's words though. She would have to distort. Lie. Her story could explain that Mr. Ben Lee was a speculator. He was dining with a business associate, Mr. Lo Chen, at a downtown restaurant when he was cut down ... no, slain by a gang that had tried wrongfully to extort money from him. She didn't have to mention the noodles — although it might lighten the story for the readers. Elizabeth believed that her readers came first. If you can't be explicit about the truth, offer an amusing side to it — at least.

"Gambling his big trouble," Lo continued.

Elizabeth thought for a moment before writing: Mr. Lee was dedicated to his business.

"Gambling like drug for Ben."

Elizabeth wrote: When Mr. Lee was not at home with his family or working at his business, he enjoyed recreational games of chance with his friends.

"Ben was marked man," Lo explained. "I warn him, don't go to Queen Noodle. The mob know he love noodle. Too bad his last meal chewy."

This comment challenged Elizabeth's inventiveness. She tried: Mr. Lee was known to frequent this restaurant because of its excellent noodles. With his final breath he courageously defied the criminals who would steal money from an honest citizen.

"His family suffer because he gamble."

Elizabeth would have to lie: Mr. Lee's family had supported him through some recent business difficulties.

"He take money for his children education. Gamble it. No good."

Elizabeth stopped writing. She knew how hard her parents had worked so she might have an education. She believed no decent parent would gamble with their children's future. "Is this true?" she asked Lo.

"It is tragic truth about Mr. Ben Lee. I am sad for him. Sad for his family."

Elizabeth believed Lo, who seemed like a sincere man. She had heard about people like Ben Lee. She too was sad. The true story could never be written. The censors would kill it. Perhaps the censors are also responsible. Who would a lie protect? The family, or the people who are afraid of the truth being exposed? Elizabeth didn't know, and she wanted to. She decided to ask Lo. "Do you want me to write the true story?"

Lo laughed. "True story?"

"What you have told me about Mr. Lee."

"What I say about Ben Lee are the rumor, lie, and shameful gossip you'll hear from other people."

Elizabeth could not believe that a friend of the deceased would be so cruel as to repeat these rumors. He had taken advantage of her, and lied to her. "You were his friend. How could you act as if these lies were true?"

"Why wouldn't I?"

"No, you answer my question first."

Lo explained. "Ben owed me money. Lots of money. What's truth or lie matter no more. We meet at Queen Noodle to discuss payment he miss."

"Why are you telling me this? I could expose you."

Lo leaned forward and whispered. "But you won't."

Lo was right. The editor would laugh her out of the office. It would never see print. But the gossip, the exaggeration? That's another story. Elizabeth didn't know what to believe. Lo saw to that.

3
Scott Mackay

THE LITTLE BLACK KNIFE

MIRIAM Lancaster instantly recognized the black man sitting over by the piano. Paper crepe ribbons arced from corner to corner, a few nurses stood by in case the excitement became too great for the old people, and Mrs. Hutchison, the activities director, fretted over the buffet table while giving directions to a member of the Oceanview Towers kitchen staff. The newcomers' party had been marred by the late arrival of the caterers.

Miriam took another sip of her coffee, looked once more at the man, put her styrofoam cup down, and approached him, trying to get unobtrusively nearer. Could it really be, she wondered? From so long ago. She stopped by the Chinese print of the butterfly hanging on the wall above the fireplace. The pleasant cafuffle of the Strawberry Social Welcoming Party for New Residents disappeared, and she sat in a circle with seven other teenage girls, shaded by euphorbia trees, the wind rippling the wheat fields nearby. She studied his face more closely.

The man, now noticing her, stared back, annoyed, gave her a gruff look, then turned away. He didn't recognize her. How was he to recognize her, she thought? She had been eighteen at the time. Now she was fifty-one, in a white lab coat, the nurse practitioner for Oceanview Towers, a little chubby and hair going gray. Those were his eyes, she thought — bloodshot, the irises a concentrated black, the eyebrows short and wiry, more like steel wool than hair. He gave her another look, a peevish old man, and turned in his chair, showing his back, then continued to eat his strawberry shortcake.

Why did they have to overheat seniors' buildings, she wondered? She never perspired yet now her forehead was moist. She turned away. She worked her way through the wheelchairs, past the old people with their canes and glasses — rich old people who had done well enough to live in the luxurious Oceanview Towers — and continued towards the buffet table. She took Elaine Hutchison by the elbow.

"There's more than usual this time, isn't there?" she said.

Elaine Hutchison was thirty-five, had brown hair, and wore a brown outfit with a name tag pinned to her lapel. Her movements were quick, precise, and efficient, fueled by her daily intake of eight cups of coffee.

"Five or six more," she said.

"Do you find it hot in here?"

"No, not really."

Miriam lifted a shortbread cookie from the table and nibbled. She felt as if her hands needed something to do.

"You wouldn't happen to know who he is, would you?"

"Who?"

"Over by the piano."

Elaine Hutchison looked at the man.

"That's Mr. Ngala. Thomas Ngala. I don't know much about him, only that he owns a chain of import stores here in town."

"What kind of import stores?"

"Oh, I don't know. African odds and ends mostly. Masks, carvings, ornamental spears — that kind of thing."

That night, while Miriam had her ten o'clock cup of tea and muffin in her private quarters on the ninth floor, she couldn't help thinking of Thomas Ngala and his little black knife. Was he a Mau Mau, a member of the political cult made up of Kikuyu tribesmen, was he the man with the little black knife? She took a sip of her tea, then put it aside. She needed something stronger.

1956. At the height of the Mau Mau Rebellion in the Kenya Highlands. Sitting in a circle surrounded by Kikuyu tribesmen, and Thomas Ngala asking who shall be next for his little black knife. But tell him where units of the King's African Rifles were and there would be no more little black knife.

Miriam stopped halfway to the liquor cabinet. She saw the little black knife, the blade about a foot and a half long, floating before her, covered with blood.

Please. The King's African Rifles. We know they were here last night. No? Who shall be next for my little black knife?

They untied her and brought her to the center of the ring where the ground was soaked with blood. Now only Heather, Barbara, and Camilla were left in the slowly diminishing circle.

She shuddered, even though she was hot, crossed the floor, and pulled a bottle of Courvoisier out of the liquor cabinet. Dead ghosts from long ago, she thought. She poured a double tumbler of cognac.

The next day she tried to watch Thomas Ngala, but she was busy and had only two opportunities. As a nurse practitioner in a senior citizens' building she was always busy, mainly with minor complaints. And she had to give routine physicals to the newcomers, twenty-eight in all.

She was able to observe him in the games room playing shuffleboard with one of the other residents for fifteen minutes snatched from her lunch hour. To think that they were both here, in Canada, so far away from where it had happened in 1956. The Tana flowing nearby. The thornbush, acacia, baobabs billowing in the breeze, a bowerbird coo-cooing in the branches above them. He was the man with the little black knife. Here after all these years, like a bogy. Like a ghoul, haunting her. She was getting the third degree, as the girls used to say on those giggling nights at the farm in Kenya before the King's African Rifles had requisitioned their compound for a command post, before the Kikuyu had moved in afterward to find out what they could, before they incidentally killed three young women. She was about to be the fourth, but then there was a lot of shouting, gunfire, and Thomas Ngala took a bullet in the back as five troops of the King's African Rifles came through the baobabs to save them.

At dinnertime she observed him as he ate the marinated chicken with a roll and salad in furtive bites, as if he were suspicious of everything around him. He sat alone, made no attempt to fraternize with the other residents, watched everyone closely as if he were waiting for something to happen. He was black-black, true African black, and his phrenological contours screamed Kikuyu.

Kikuyu. The name would always frighten her. Yet now, thirty-three years after, she had come to understand the Mau Mau ends if not exactly their methods.

Thomas Ngala came for his physical the next day. Beforehand, she read his medical file thoroughly. Thomas Ngala. Born, 1915, Embu, Kenya. Languages: Bantu and English. Occupation: merchandising. Next of kin: none. History: three myocardial infarctions since the age of seventy-one, skin cancer of the ear successfully treated three years ago, angina, a salt-reduced diet. But nothing at all about the thing she wanted to know. Nothing about the gunshot wound. She read further. He suffered from chronic arrhythmia, hypertension, and occasional breathlessness. Prescriptions included propranolol, glyceryl trinitrate, and digitalis.

When he entered the examining room, she grew nervous, fearful, stalked by the things that had happened thirty-three years ago. He wore a colorful African short-sleeved shirt and a pair of red running shoes. He looked at her suspiciously, and she could see that he neither liked nor trusted doctors. She tried a few pleasantries but he was disinclined to talk. She put the sphygmomanometer cuff around his arm, inflated it, and took his blood pressure. High but not unmanageable. She looked into his eyes with the ophthalmoscope, checked his ears, nose and throat — they were, for his age, in good shape. Then she asked him to take his shirt off. He did so reluctantly.

There was a circular scar on his back about the size of a bullet hole.

The examining room disappeared and she was back on the banks of the River Tana, seeing Thomas Ngala running away, blood streaming from his back, his arm twitching and his legs stumbling before his friends grabbed him and hurried him into the bush. She looked at the scar, a light tan color against his prune-black skin, and tried to swallow. Her mouth had gone dry.

"What's this?" she said. "Your medical file doesn't say anything about this."

"Gunshot wound," he said in his deep resonant voice, the same voice that had asked who shall be next for my little black knife. "World War Two. North Africa."

Her muscles hardened with hatred. Liar, she thought.

"It says here you're from Kenya."

He nodded.

"I spent a summer there back in the Fifties," she said. "On an agricultural exchange project from Britain. It was during the Mau Mau Rebellion. Were you there then?"

He shrugged, as if he wanted to go. "I spent the Fifties in Egypt," he said.

Liar. She listened to his heart and lung sounds through his back, so overwrought she could hardly hold the stethoscope. When the examination was over, and she was left alone in the room, she had to sit still for a long time. She saw the little black knife slicing into Jennifer's throat, tearing through her windpipe, and Jennifer's shocked eyes turning glassy as the life seeped out of her.

The previous night they had felt so safe, with the King's African Rifles using the farm as a command post. She saw the flies collecting around Elizabeth's dismembered limbs, heard sudden gunfire as the King's African Rifles emerged from the dense bush near the river's edge. Liar, she thought. Murderer. Her stomach heaved and she felt as if she were going to be sick.

She took a few deep breaths, then walked to the dispensary for some anti-nausea medication. She was just washing two of the small blue pills down with water when her eyes settled on the second shelf where the digitalis, digoxin, and heart-related prescriptions were kept. She picked up one of the tiny vials of digoxin, a drug that increased heart muscle contraction, could actually cause heart attack if the patient were given too much, then put it back on the shelf. She had to do this, she thought. She would have to do this for Jennifer, Helen, and Elizabeth.

She got her chance two weeks later. While Thomas Ngala was playing shuffleboard with one of the other residents, he suffered heart failure. Two staff members rushed him on a stretcher to the infirmary. As a nurse practitioner there were only a limited number of things she could do. His skin had lost its sheen, had become the color of a dusty old puck. Her assistant, Marjorie French, a young woman in a white nurse's uniform, stood by, unsure of what to do.

"Go phone an ambulance," said Miriam Lancaster, "and wait for them in the lobby."

When she was left alone with Thomas Ngala, she examined the Kikuyu once more. His eyes, though open, were pale and unseeing. His breathing was shallow. The veins in his neck were engorged, and edema had occurred. He looked as if he were suffering from cardiogenic shock as well.

"You thought you were going to get away with it, didn't you?" she said.

He was semi-conscious, unable to comprehend.

"But I know who you are," she said. "Oh, I know who you are, all right."

She acted quickly, with firm resolution. She filled a syringe with a triple dose of digoxin, the exact medicine heart failure required, and held it up before his eyes. "You see this?" she said. "This is my little black knife."

She rubbed his arm with alcohol and gave him the full injection. Three minutes and forty-six seconds later Thomas Ngala died of a heart attack.

There was never any suspicion. The doctor, when he came three hours later, was satisfied with her explanation. None of them could ever know there was any connection between herself and Thomas Ngala. Two staff members wheeled the body to the freight elevator which led down to the morgue in the basement. The undertakers were called and so were the lawyers.

It was eight o'clock the next morning, with the body still in the morgue, when the lawyer reached her at the infirmary extension. He said the sole beneficiary would like to see the body and look after the funeral arrangements personally.

"Sole beneficiary?" she said. "But I thought there was no family."

"There isn't," said the lawyer. "This is an old friend. A man by the name of Michael Tboya. When should I say he can come?"

Miriam Lancaster felt numb. She hadn't expected this.

"Tell him to come any time he likes," she said, her voice high. "I'll be here."

Michael Tboya was a short man, as black as Thomas Ngala, and she tried to place him in that group of Kikuyu tribesmen on that hot Highland day so long ago. But he looked unfamiliar.

She took him to the morgue. There was a weak smile frozen to his face. He was upset but he was doing his best not to show it. "So you and Mr. Ngala were friends," she said. "I'm very sorry. I know how hard it must be."

"Good friends," said Mr. Tboya. "We have known one another for a long, long time."

In the morgue he lifted Thomas Ngala's sheet and looked at his dead friend's face. After some moments, he let the sheet drop. He lifted his eyes, looked at Miriam. "Where are the papers?" he said.

"They're upstairs. Would you like some coffee? I have a pot brewing in my office."

"I don't like coffee," he said. "Would you have any juice?"

"Yes, I could get you a juice."

On the elevator ride up they stopped at the third-floor snack-bar to get Michael Tboya a carton of orange juice.

She was going through her files looking for the appropriate forms when Michael Tboya, sipping his juice, began to talk about Ngala, how they had known each other since 1931, and how they had been business partners.

"So you were in on this import business, then," Miriam said.

"Yes. Since the very beginning. Ever since our days in Egypt. We started in Cairo."

Miriam stopped looking for the form.

"Egypt?" she said.

"Yes. That is where we got our business started. In fact, most of our contacts are still there and Cairo is where we get most of our merchandise."

She continued looking for the release forms, and when she found them she realized she had gone past them at least three times. She pulled them out, clipped them to a metal clipboard, and presented them to Michael Tboya.

He began filling them out slowly. "We go back such a long time," he said. "We were in the war together."

"War?" she said. "What war?"

"The Second World War. King's African Rifles. We fought outside Tobruk. As a matter of fact, Tommy was wounded there. He got shot in the back."

"Did you say he was in the King's African Rifles?"

"Yes," said Michael Tboya. "Why? Of course, today they're known as the Kenyan African Rifles." His eyes narrowed and he leaned forward. "Are you all right, Mrs. Lancaster? You don't look well. Is there anything I can do?"

"No," said Miriam. "No, nothing at all."

4
Fraser Sutherland
THE BLACK DAHLIA

I USED to see her every now and then when I worked at the Biltmore in Los Angeles.

A barkeep's got to remember faces.

No trouble remembering hers.

Her face was a long oval with high cheekbones, the crow's wing black brushed back, and her skin the glowing white you never see in California and seldom see anywhere, as if lighted from underneath.

Her full mouth was a slash of red, her teeth when she smiled had the pearly pallor of her skin.

Her eyes had lights in them also, as if caught in a photographer's flash, the irises the greeny gray a flat sea takes on a cold windless day.

Long straight lines of eyebrows over her eyes, tiny mole on her left cheek.

She dressed in black.

Black sheath dress, black stockings, black underwear, black patent leather shoes, black ring on the wedding finger of her left hand.

The Black Dahlia.

She wasn't just pretty, she was beautiful, but she was not a beautiful person.

Her real name was Elizabeth Short, but her name didn't match how she looked, or the way she was.

Once she spread her birth certificate, her social security card, her address book across the bar.

She wanted to show me who she was.

"If you pasted every prick that's been inside me on the outside of me," she said, "I'd look like a porcupine."

I didn't like that kind of talk.

We got a respectable crowd at the Biltmore.

"I'm the Black Dahlia," she said.

I'd see her with all kinds of men.

The long, the short, the tall.

Dark, blond, red-haired.

Rich, poor, average; young, old, middle-aged.

They all kept company with the Black Dahlia.

You want to know her story?

It's a short, nasty story.

I got some of it from her.

The rest I heard later.

She was born in 1925 in a place called Medford, Massachusetts, a small town, one of five kids.

When she was six her father took one of the kids and went off to California, leaving his wife, Mrs. Phoebe Short, to work and raise the others.

She didn't do too good a job with the Black Dahlia.

The Black Dahlia couldn't wait to leave home, start a new life, but the way she started was to get herself a record as a juvenile delinquent.

Juvenile delinquent is just one of those words people use.

She was a tramp.

She took a bus way down the coast to Miami, sun city, sin city, 1942, the Black Dahlia seventeen, and airbase boys making time on the weekend beaches.

She worked as a waitress, found a man but he got shipped overseas and was killed there.

So the Black Dahlia hit the bottle and the soldier boys came marching in, left, right.

She got known all over Miami.

A steak and a drink, you could *have* the Black Dahlia.

The police picked her up chatting up some soldiers, bought her a ticket, gave her grub money, and packed her on the train back to Medford, Massachusetts.

She got off the train before it reached Medford, returned to hustling chow, and nobody checked to see if she'd ever found home.

Took up with a good-looking blond boy with a dimpled chin, U.S. Army Air Force Major, wings all over him.

He was sent to the Far East, and the Black Dahlia went back to Medford to wait for him.

On August 22, 1946, she answered the door and it was a telegram from the boy's mother and the telegram said that her son had been killed in an air crash.

The Black Dahlia crumpled the telegram into a small tight ball and walked straight out to the nearest bar.

She told the barman she had a hex on her and that was what she told me, too, and she was right, I guess.

Now the Black Dahlia really let herself go to pieces, and as everybody knows, if you really want to go to pieces the place to go is California.

The idea was to get into movies.

The Black Dahlia figured that the best way to get into movies was to sleep with anybody whose second cousin was a friend of the producer's ex-wife.

That was when I first saw her.

She'd come through the door, tall, elegant-like, and every eye in the place would track her to the bar and I wouldn't need to ask, she'd want a Black Russian.

If she was going to do something she was going to do it whole hog.

So she was butchered like one.

On the cold windy morning of January 15, 1947, a sobbing, screaming woman flagged a passing patrol car and what she was sobbing and screaming about was what she saw in the vacant lot of that Los Angeles suburb, the garbage on it, and among the garbage the Black Dahlia.

They didn't know it was her just then.

It was only what was left of a young woman.

The young woman was nude and sawn in half, each half bound with rope, and there wasn't any part of her that wasn't cut and hacked and carved, and carved deep into her thigh were initials.

BD.

They figured that most of it was done while she was strung up by the ankles while she was still alive, maybe even the big cut.

It was so bad that the cops had trouble getting a fingerprint.

But they matched it up with one the F.B.I. had, dating back to the days when the Black Dahlia was a juvenile delinquent.

It was so bad that Mrs. Phoebe Short had trouble identifying her daughter.

Phoebe Short gave the police a letter she'd gotten from the Black Dahlia a few weeks earlier.

At that address the cops found out that she'd taken no luggage when she'd left there six days before they found what they found in the vacant lot.

What they also found at the address was a note from one of her boyfriends.

"You say in your letter that you want us to be good friends.

"But from your wire you seemed to want more than that.

"Are you really sure what you want?

"Why not pause and consider just what your coming out here would amount to?

"You've got to be practical these days."

Poor, practical sap.

Somebody had spotted a tall red-haired man talking to the Black Dahlia in a San Diego bus station a few days before her death, I guess you'd call it.

They tracked down the guy and he said he'd gone on a binge with her and taken her to a motel and then dropped her off at the front entrance of the Biltmore Hotel.

She told him she was going to meet her sister.

That was the last that anyone saw of the Black Dahlia to remember except, of course, whoever did it to her.

And they couldn't hold the tall red-head because he was with his wife visiting friends when it happened.

All the papers had it plastered on their front pages and then every loony, crazy, loopy man and the occasional woman who was lost in the woodwork and cement cracks of the Greater Los Angeles area came briskly stepping forward to confess.

One of them said his wife had deserted him so he killed the Black Dahlia to make himself notorious and have his picture in the papers so his wife would come back to him.

Another man, a U.S. Corporal, claimed to know the Black Dahlia well. He got turned over to the psychiatrists.

Another man said he hadn't murdered her, but he had helped somebody else cut her up.

A woman said she'd killed the Black Dahlia after she had stolen her man.

I guess a lot of women wanted to.

But none of them, man or woman, knew enough about the size, extent, and nature of what was done to the Black Dahlia.

The papers didn't print all the details.

It was that bad.

Besides, the police thought they could get somebody that way.

The woman angle persisted.

A couple of bartenders reported that they had seen the Black Dahlia talking to a woman a few days before she died.

I don't know who that was, and they never found her.

The next thing was a newspaper got a postcard postmarked January 24 with pasted-on words and letters:

Los Angeles Examiner and OTHER Los Angeles PAPERS
HERE! IS *Dahlia's* Belongings LETTER to FOLLOW

The police had gotten lots of those before but this one was different, this one had with it the Black Dahlia's address book, social security card, and birth certificate.

Also dark fingerprints all over the card but they didn't check out with anything the F.B.I. had.

Nor were the many names in the address book of any use.

One leaf of the address book was torn out.

No letter ever followed.

There was a picture of the Black Dahlia's burial in the newspaper.

Masses of white flowers on, above, and beside the grave dug into the steep slope of the cemetery, a row of folding chairs and people sitting on them, men in overcoats, women with hats on bowed heads, bare trees, and two cars parked down on the highway far below, two men standing between them.

The police never found the Black Dahlia's clothes though they searched in almost every drain and sewer in Los Angeles, and talked to just about everybody except me, maybe.

They still don't know who killed the Black Dahlia.

I do.

5
Donna Gamache
THE PERFECT PLAN

A LIGHT drizzle was falling as I silently slid the back door shut. "Good," I said to myself. "Anyone who's still out, will go inside now."

I put down my duffel bag and stood for a moment on the sagging step debating whether to go back for a raincoat, but decided against it. The coat was a light beige, more noticeable than the dark gray jacket I was wearing. And I had no desire to be noticed.

Besides, Tim was asleep, and I mustn't chance waking him. He was a light sleeper, nervous about many things, and he didn't like being left alone in the house at night. Not that it was my custom to go out at 2:00 a.m.

Picking up the duffel bag, I headed east at a brisk pace. I didn't want to risk taking my old Ford car. The muffler had a hole in it, and starting the car might rouse Tim, or the neighbors. I didn't want it noticed, either, if I parked close to Broadview Street.

The walking eased the cramped muscles of my legs, but my stomach was still a tight ball. "Nerves," I told myself. "Take it easy. Nobody will see me. One hour should be long enough. And Tim won't even know I've been out."

The street lights shed dull yellow circles on the wet pavement as I hurried along. The elm trees were in full leaf now, and they glistened in the rain, but under the trees, the sidewalk was still almost dry.

"Please let Tim stay asleep," I said to myself. "I don't want him to know I've been out."

Tim was twelve now, tall and wiry, but whenever I looked at

him I still saw a blond, curly-haired toddler thrusting a pudgy hand into mine. "Daddy," he'd say, "let's play." He called me Daddy, in those days. But that was before Rita's long illness, and her death. It was after that I told Tim to call me "Jasper" instead.

Two blocks away a car turned the corner, its lights cutting the darkness. I stepped behind the trunk of a large elm until it passed. No need to advertise my presence at 2:00 a.m. There was nobody else on the street and the houses were all dark. I hoped mine was, too, that Tim was still sleeping soundly and hadn't missed me.

The boy didn't use to be so nervous. When his mother was still with us, he was confident and sure of himself, not afraid of the dark, or of shadows. But since Rita's death, he'd changed.

I'd changed, too, of course. Two years with a sick wife and two years as a single, unemployed father were bound to affect anyone. I liked to think I'd managed okay, but I knew there were many times I'd failed Tim. Especially when I tried to drown my sorrows. But I shouldn't think of those times. They were over, and I wasn't about to fail tonight.

The warehouse was over a mile away. I'd counted on twenty minutes fast walking to get there, twenty minutes or less to do the job, another twenty back. Tim would never need to know what I was doing.

It was for *him* that I was doing this, for him that I wanted to leave behind the old house with its sagging back step, and walls that needed painting, and postage-stamp sized back yard. The new beginning was for his sake, not mine.

The drizzle was easing when I turned onto Broadview Street. I headed down the back alley to the rear of the warehouse. It was dark there, and I stood silently for a few minutes until my eyes adjusted.

Fifteen years ago when I married Rita, this was a well-run business — a warehouse for a Montreal-based manufacturer of children's clothing — though even then, the building was old. Her father owned it and, though he wasn't happy about Rita's choice of husband, she was his only child, and he'd hired me to work in the storeroom. Over the years, he grudgingly gave me more authority, and when he died, Rita owned the building, and I was in control.

"That's when the trouble started," I muttered to myself. "I should have known I didn't have a head for business."

Even then, I might have managed, with Rita's brains to help me, if only she hadn't fallen sick. The business went rapidly downhill, and I knew it didn't help any when I started on the bottle. The business folded, just one month after Rita died.

But that was all water under the bridge now. The warehouse had been empty for nearly two years, and it was no use to me. No use standing there, at least, and nobody seemed interested in buying it.

Gradually my eyes adjusted to the dark. Unzipping my duffel bag, I felt around until I found the gloves. I pulled them on and took out the brick. I still had a key, but it would look better if the building had been broken into.

The window splintered with a loud crash. I huddled against the warehouse for a full minute until the pounding of my heart eased. Nobody appeared. There were no houses close by, just other old buildings in various stages of deterioration.

With my gloved hands, I shoved the remaining glass inside and pushed my bag through. It landed with a thump on the floor, and I pulled myself through the empty frame into what was once my father-in-law's office. I fumbled in the bag for the flashlight and switched it on. It had two levels of intensity, bright and dim; I kept it on dim.

Dust layered everything. Otherwise, the room looked the way it had fifteen years ago. There was a big oak desk, two chairs, even pictures on the wall, one of them a family picture with six-year-old Rita and her parents. I knew Tim would like to have it, but I couldn't chance taking it home. He'd know where it came from; and he wasn't to know I'd been here.

I hooded the flashlight with one hand to dim the light more, and started down the hallway, my steps echoing loudly in the empty building. I glanced into a couple of rooms, then decided on one at the back, in the far corner from where I'd entered. I put down the duffel bag and took out my supplies.

In only a few minutes the rags began to smoulder. Had I used the right amount of gasoline? I'd never done this before.

"Needs more air," something inside me said. "Open a window."

The windows locked from the inside, and I forced one up a few inches. Cool air mingled with the musty inside air, and light flickered in the rags.

Suddenly, from the far end of the building, I heard a faint, muffled noise, as if something had dropped onto the floor. My heart fluttering, I doused the flashlight and eased myself through the door and down the hallway. Could there possibly be someone in there? There were no more sounds, but I *knew* I'd heard something.

I reached the office door. Then, from the room across the hallway, I heard a light rustle. Putting down my bag, I took a fast breath, shoved open the door, and switched on the flashlight.

Orange eyes glared at me, and a gray and white streak dashed past and through the still open door of the office. Cat!

There was a loud scrabbling noise, and I followed it just in time to see a gray tail disappear out the broken window. I started breathing again. I didn't know how a cat had got inside, but I was glad it was out. It wasn't my intention to burn animals, too.

Retrieving my bag, I switched off the flashlight and packed it away. My eyes took a few minutes to readjust, and by then the smell of smoke was seeping down the hallway, and I could see flickering from the far room.

I'd debated starting a second fire to speed things up, but that might spell "Firebug" to the inspectors. And this mustn't look suspicious. The building might be old, but it was still insured, and that was all Tim and I needed for a new start. Add that to the value of the house we lived in, even though it was small, and we'd have it made. It was the perfect plan.

I dropped the bag outside and squeezed through the window. The rain had stopped, and the air was fresh and cool after the dead warehouse air. Taking a deep breath, I started for home. "Nobody will be hurt by this," I told myself. "It'll be better for everyone, with this old place gone."

There was one more thing to do, but I'd planned for that, too. I'd brought a garbage bag with me, and after a few blocks I stopped in a dark alley and put all the items I'd used into the garbage bag — gloves, lighter, flashlight, duffel bag, everything that might have a gasoline odor. Not that I expected much of an investigation, but just in case.

I followed the back alley to the Sunny-Vee Apartments, then added my garbage bag to the five others already piled at the rear. Nobody would notice an extra one, and tomorrow was garbage pickup day. I'd planned everything. Nothing could go wrong.

It was 3:20 a.m. when I let myself in the back door — an hour and twenty minutes. Without putting on any lights, I hung my jacket in the front closet and slipped downstairs to leave my shoes in the cupboard there.

There was no sound from Tim's room when I peeked in. I could see the dark shape of his body, but he didn't move. I was sure he'd never missed me. For his sake, I was glad everything had gone well tonight. He was the only thing in the world I cared about anymore. Undressing, I slipped into bed, and surprisingly, I slept.

The telephone shrilled at 6:30 a.m. I hurried to answer it, but it rang four times first. The voice was official, and male. I was careful to sound sleepy and surprised.

"Burned?" I repeated his words. "Completely?"

"Not totally. The outside is mostly intact. The inside is gutted. It's just under control now. The firemen will check the inside shortly."

"What would start it?" I asked.

"Maybe the wiring. It's old, isn't it?" He paused. "Could you come down here, do you think?"

"All right," I hesitated. I hadn't expected to be called there, but maybe that was the way they worked things. "I'll be a few minutes. I'm not dressed yet."

"I'll be waiting at the back," he said, hanging up.

Rain was falling again, harder now, a steady drum on the roof. I'd need my raincoat this morning. But first I went back to the bedroom to pull on jeans and a shirt.

There was still no sound from Tim's room, and I was surprised the telephone hadn't wakened him. "I'd better tell him where I'm going," I decided.

I switched on the hallway light, thinking that would rouse him, but he still didn't budge. I went into his room and reached to shake him gently.

The bed was empty. What I'd assumed in the night was the shape of his body was merely the blankets where they'd been tossed to one side.

My legs collapsed onto his bed. Where could he be? He'd gone to bed at 10:00, as usual, and he wasn't one to go visiting friends at any time, especially in the night. Had he awakened, discovered me missing, and gone to one of the neighbors? But we weren't that neighborly with anyone here, and surely, if he was at somebody's house, they'd have telephoned me.

Or had he got up early to go for a walk? It was light before six, these days. But he'd hardly have gone out in this rain!

Turning on the bed lamp, I felt the bed. It was cold; he'd been out of it for some time. I checked the pile of dirty clothes by his door. The jeans and T-shirt he wore yesterday weren't in it, and I couldn't see his runners.

I hurried out to the backdoor, but his runners weren't there, either, and the blue plaid jacket he wore everywhere was not on its usual hook. Where *was* he?

My watch read 6:45, and the policeman was waiting. Grabbing my raincoat, I hurried out to the car. Tim's whereabouts would have to wait until I returned. I tried to shove that problem into the back of my mind and concentrate on what to say at the warehouse.

By car it was only five minutes to Broadview Street. I saw the smoke before I got there, but there were no flames now. At the front, two fire trucks were still hosing water, one onto the roof, the other through a window. The windows all gaped holes where they'd been knocked out, and the front door swung open.

I slowed to turn into the back alley, but a third fire engine and an ambulance blocked my way. Ambulance! My heart sank.

Parking my car farther along the street, I scurried back, just as the ambulance pulled out of the alley and screamed away east on Broadview, its lights flashing.

A tall policeman, about thirty-five, his face gray with fatigue, stopped me as I hurried up. "You Mr. Calendar?"

I nodded. "Why the ambulance? Is somebody hurt?"

"Yea," he said abruptly, then looked at me sharply. "There was an intruder. Did you know there was a broken window at the back?"

My stomach turned. "They're all broken," I said, pointing to the gaping holes.

"Yea, now. But one was broken before."

I felt hot inside my raincoat. "They were all okay, the last time I checked."

"The window on the far corner was broken," he said. "Somebody got in. Maybe the fire was set."

"Set??" I asked weakly. "You said faulty wiring on the phone."

"Yea. Maybe I was wrong. I didn't know anyone was in there, then."

The ball in my stomach tightened, and my voice faltered. "Even if someone did set it," I managed, "why didn't he get out afterwards?"

"Looks like he put his foot through a rotten place, and couldn't get it free," the policeman said, looking at me closely. "Too bad, though. Just a boy. Maybe he went inside to get out of the rain."

"Just a boy?" My voice was a whisper now. I swallowed hard.

"Just a kid," the policeman said. "Can't be more than twelve or thirteen. Just a kid in a blue plaid jacket. Somebody's going to be awful upset."

6
Helen J. Rosta
FEATHERS

L AURA unfolds the newspaper clipping that Betty has enclosed with her letter, scans the letter — as usual, names of long-ago children, Edith Coleman, Andrew Wilson, Gerald Shaw. It's like Betty to keep in touch, gathering information where she can, embellishing it, dispersing it.

Laura pictures Betty on a hilltop as "The Village Gossip." Does Betty recall that story in their Grade Five Reader?

The Village Gossip, having done much harm to her neighbors, is brought before a wise judge. The judge hands her a bagful of feathers and orders her to scatter them afar. The Gossip, rejoicing in the lenience of her sentence, climbs the highest hill in the neighborhood and flings the feathers into the wind. Sir, I have done your bidding. I have scattered that bagful of feathers to the four corners of the earth. Now go, the judge commands, and gather up each of those feathers. Bring that bagful of feathers back to me. Sir! cries the Gossip in despair, it is impossible for me to bring back those feathers. And the wise judge replies, those feathers are your gossip.

All the denizens of Fairvalley Community people Betty's letters. Fairvalley School, smell of farm boots, lunch pails, chalk dust. Laura's fingers cramping on the scrap of chalk, scrawl of words on the blackboard, Mr. Damion's angry voice. Laura has never forgiven him. Or Edith. Edith Coleman and her sanctimonious child-face. Does she still wear that expression?

The picture of Edith and Gerald in the clipping is too smudged for Laura to make out the features. "THE BRIDE (capitalized — who writes these things?) walked down the aisle to the strains of the Wedding March. She wore a lovely dusty rose *peau de soie* afternoon gown and carried a nosegay of white roses caught with a lace ribbon."

White roses! Betty has scribbled in the margin. No blue for-get-me-nots! Ha, ha.

For-get-me-nots. That's for Andrew Wilson, Edith's first husband.

Betty had sent Andrew's obituary. "Deer season," she wrote in her round, schoolgirlish hand. "A stray bullet right through the heart."

Andrew was shot in late November — trees bare, dead leaves underfoot, a crust of snow. But Laura sees him falling — red hunting jacket — falling, falling against an autumn of turquoise sky, golden sunlit hills, bluffs of yellow aspen and scarlet saskatoon.

"Historic Fairvalley Church, banked with masses of white and mauve chrysanthemums, was the perfect setting for the quiet elegance of the wedding party."

Fairvalley Church. You walked past the church on the way to school. "Our church" Edith called it. On Sundays, the yard filled with buggies and Model T's. If you opened the car window as you passed, you might hear singing, Mr. Damion's voice louder than the rest.

Laura's father once said, "They're trying to cheat the devil."

"Don't talk like that," Laura's mother scolded.

"T'is no sin to cheat the Devil."

Fairvalley School is a one room building — just like the school Laura attended before her family moved to the river. But back in Laura's old school, teachers came and went; Mr. Damion has been at Fairvalley forever. "Since before I started," Betty told Laura.

Mr. Damion assigns desks. "You, the new girl, over there. Stand until I say you can sit down."

He opens a large, black bible. "Woe onto them . . ." His voice rattles the windowpanes. "O Assyrian, the rod of my anger." The rod. That's his teacher's strap.

"Be seated." Mr. Damion picks up a chalk and writes his name on the blackboard. "That's for the benefit of the new girl."

Everyone stares at Laura.

Mr. Damion lays down the chalk, brushes off his hands and grabs the pointer which he jabs in Laura's direction. "Come here. Write your name on the blackboard and tell us something about yourself. Bring me your report card on your way up."

Laura walks slowly to the front, hands over her report card to Mr. Damion, and waits for him to praise her good marks.

"Grade Five. Edith Coleman and Betty Bowes will be your classmates. Well write your name, Girl."

"Laura Peevy." Beside Mr. Damion's name, Laura's looks pinched. She leaves wet finger marks on the blackboard. Her voice won't come; she stands head down, wiping her palms on her skirt.

Mr. Damion taps the pointer against his desk, tap tap tap. "Well, Laura Peevy."

It comes in a rush. "We live by the river and my dad has a great big garden and we used to live by Clintin but we rented out our land 'cause my dad said maybe it'll rain this year but he'll put his faith in a vegetable garden and irrigation so we rented down by the river and my dad sells vegetables in town. And Howard Rogers rented our land and he's got a great big dog that pulls his kids on a sleigh."

Laura glances at Mr. Damion.

"What did you do this summer?"

"I helped my mother pick saskatoons and we canned them and made jam and jelly. It was a lot of work."

"That's good. Satan finds mischief for idle hands. I want you to understand, Laura Peevy, there will be no idle hands in my classroom. You may return to your desk."

Years ago, Betty wrote that Mr. Damion had died and that the Fairvalley Community was setting up a scholarship in his name. "We feel that a scholarship fund is a fitting tribute to his years of service at Fairview School. It will hold his name in our thoughts as well as in our hearts." She asked Laura for a donation.

Laura sent a card. "I'm sorry," she wrote, "that a scholarship is necessary to keep Mr. Damion's name alive in Fairvalley's collective mind."

Fairvalley Community. A collective mind with a huddle of shabby buildings for a heart. Church, school, post office.

Church days, school days, mail days.

Mr. Damion is strict about mail days. "One child from each family may pick up the mail during the last recess. There's to be no loitering at the post office."

As soon as Laura drops her parcel on the long bench at the back of the classroom, Betty pokes the brown paper wrapping.

"Don't. You'll tear it."

"What's in it?" Betty asks, drilling with her finger.

"I don't know."

"How come?"

"It's from my Aunt Mabel in the city."

"She must be rich."

"Yes," Laura says, "she is."

Betty's plump arm lies warmly on Laura's shoulder. "You have so many clothes."

"The Bride's gown, accented with antique lace at the bodice, was complemented by matching satin slippers. Her jewelry consisted of diamond earrings and a diamond and pearl pendant on a gold chain."

Peau de soie, antique lace, diamonds and pearls. Not the Edith that Laura remembers, the Edith of the pinched face, faded print dress and sagging, thin-at-the-elbows sweater. The Edith who, each morning, cast sullen glances at Laura's fresh dress and matching hair ribbons.

Now, Edith's too old for hair ribbons. But her gown and slippers match. Slippers. Like in Cinderella. Edith as Cinderella. Will her *peau de soie*, diamonds and pearls vanish at midnight and will Gerald turn into a rat?

Betty's arm is heavy on Laura's shoulder. "You have such pretty clothes. That dress is pretty enough for church even." The arm closes on Laura's neck. "Why don't you come to church?"

Laura wipes her palms on the skirt of her pretty dress.

"I've been saved." Betty removes her arm. "Have you been saved?"

"Dad saved me from drowning. I fell in a pothole in the river and he pulled me out."

"Saved. Like in church."

Laura doesn't answer.

"Why doesn't your family come to church?" Betty's dimpled

face is friendly, her blue eyes innocent.

"We're ag ... agnostics," Laura blurts out.

"Ag ag — what? I never heard of it."

"My dad says if you don't know the meaning of a word, go look it up in the dictionary."

"How do you spell it?" Betty asks.

Gerald Shaw always was a rat; Edith will have no surprises on that score.

Andrew Wilson was the surprise. For Laura. She can't imagine what he saw in Edith.

Laura fingers Betty's letter and tries to call up an image of Andrew Wilson, the boy. Quiet. Standing on the edge of the pack.

The minute Mr. Damion closed the bible, Edith's hand shot up. "Mr. Damion, Sir, what's an agnostic?"

"Where did you hear that word?"

"Laura Peevey, Sir. She bragged that's what her family is."

"An agnostic is an abomination in the eyes of the Lord." Mr. Damion's voice is like a roll of thunder. "He is a fool and a tool of the Devil."

Andrew, head down, standing on the edge of the pack.

"Laura Peevey is a fool and a tool of the Devil. An abomination in the eyes of the Lord."

Bully-rat Gerald Shaw.

Laura sees Andrew's face as he helps her up, feels his gentle hands as he brushes the dirt from her coat. And to think he married Edith. Now Andrew's dead and Edith's a bride again — Gerald Shaw's bride. At least, they deserve each other. A rat and a bitch joined in holy matrimony.

"That bitch," Laura says aloud. "Edith, the bitch!" She wishes Mr. Damion could hear her. "Edith, the bitch."

Sometimes Laura marvels that the years have not decreased her rancor.

"I stopped off at the farm," Laura's father says. "Howard's bitch just whelped a litter of pups. As soon as they're weaned, you can pick out one."

    "John! Don't use that word."

    "What word?"

    "You know what word."

    "Bitch? Laura, get the dictionary."

That sanctimonious expression, the same one that Edith is probably wearing in this newspaper picture of her and Gerald Shaw, and Andrew scarcely cold in his grave. That's how Betty puts it — "scarcely cold in his grave." Well, every hunting season someone is mistaken for a deer. Why not Andrew Wilson?

"Guess what!" Laura is excited. A pup is more important than agnostics and abominations. "Howard Rogers'...*bitch*" — the word comes out louder than she had intended — "just whelped a litter of pups and I can pick one out when they're weaned."

Mr. Damion is standing behind Laura. "Class dismissed," he says. When Laura starts to rise, the pointer taps her shoulder. Mr. Damion's voice is low and harsh. "I want a word with you."

    Laura cringes in her desk.

    Betty calls, "Aren't you coming, Laura?" There is tittering at the back of the room.

    "You girls run along now." Mr. Damion moves to his desk and sits down. "Laura Peevey, you know why I've kept you in."

    Laura shakes her head.

    "Speak up."

    "I don't know."

    "Don't lie to me."

    "I'm not lying."

    "Come here."

    Laura's legs tremble.

    "Edith told me you called her a bad name."

    "I didn't."

    "The father of lies is the devil."

    Mr. Damion rises, takes a fresh piece of chalk from the box on his desk, and slowly, in block letters prints BITCH on the blackboard.

    "That's what you called Edith."

"I didn't."

"Liars don't enter through the gates of the heavenly city. 'For without are dogs . . .'"

"That's the word for the mother dog!" Laura exclaims. "The one with the puppies."

Laura is writing lines on the blackboard. "All liars shall have their part in the lake that burneth with fire and brimstone." Over and over. Her arm aches and her fingers cramp. Through the window, she glimpses turquoise sky, golden sunlit hills, bluffs of yellow aspen and scarlet saskatoon. Sunlight is caught in Andrew's hair. Edith and Betty, arm in arm, walk blithely into the vivid landscape. Going home.

"All liars shall have their part in the lake that burneth with fire and brimstone."

Edith is doomed.

Why doesn't she look sad?

"He was wearing a red jacket but some of those fellows from the city will take a shot at anything that moves. It's a sad loss for the Fairvalley Community."

Trees bare, dead leaves, a crust of snow. Laura remembers a vivid sky and sunlight in Andrew's hair. That's why she always sees him falling against a landscape aglow with color.

"Edith sold the farm for a bundle. Used to get her goat the way Andrew ploughed the profits back into the land but it's paid off for her.

"And the next thing we knew, the church was booked. Edith is no beauty but she sure got herself another man fast enough. Maybe it's the money, ha, ha.

"She asked me right off to be Matron of Honor but I made excuses. Andrew scarcely cold in his grave. I think they should have waited. The community would have felt better about it. Not that there's talk or anything.

"They sure seem stuck on each other and I guess that's all that matters. I didn't think Edith would get over Andrew so soon but things have sure worked out for her, haven't they?"

"You're going to stay in every night until you confess," Mr. Damion says. "For the rest of the term if necessary. And just because today's Friday, there's no need to hurry. Your scribbling is illegible. Erase it and start over."

Laura drops the chalk and swings to face him. "I lied. I lied. I did call Edith a —" She lets the word explode into the room — "*bitch!*"

If Edith is doomed why doesn't she look sad? She doesn't look sad because things sure worked out for her.

Usually, Laura doesn't respond to Betty's letters for weeks, or months. Now she gets writing paper and a pen. She sits at the kitchen table and forces herself to call up a stark November day: bare trees, darkly stencilled limbs, a crust of snow, a red jacket. An eye. A rifle scope. A man falling.

"As you say Edith is no beauty. She certainly doesn't have the kind of face you'd expect a man to kill for. It must have been the money." Crumples the paper. Picks up another. And another.

She recalls the illustration in the Grade Five Reader, a pen and ink drawing of the Village Gossip on the hilltop, dress billowing, plump arms lifted, hands flinging feathers into the wind. Recalls the sketch of curlicue feathers spiralling across the page.

Laura holds that picture in her mind as she jots down ideas, rearranges, crosses out. It's just a matter of time, before she finds the right words, words that will carry weight and yet be light. Light as feathers. "Dear Betty," Laura begins and smiles as she imagines her words — Laura's feathers — floating all over Fairvalley Community.

7
Ann Walsh
AH, SWEET STEWART

TWENTY years in a Grade Three classroom has not made me particularly amenable to taking orders from a bird, not even from a mutant budgie who has just applied for membership in Mensa. "Stewart" — her self-christened name was Athena, but 'Stewart' was the first word I ever heard her say and to me she will always be 'Stewart' no matter how often she insists on being referred to as a Greek goddess — Stewart-Athena had, after a year and a half of sharing my home, become a noisy, obnoxious, opinionated bully.

My stewardship of her had begun innocently enough. I had allowed Mrs. Amos, the sweet if slightly deaf tenant of the apartment downstairs, to persuade me to adopt the budgie. I had been extremely reluctant at first, never having thought of myself as suited to pet ownership, but when I realized that the bird's repetition of the name "Stewart Bitz" was actually an avarian epithet directed at her owner (an uncomplimentary reference to Mrs. Amos's intelligence followed by a noun that is correctly applied only to female canines,) I allowed my curiosity to overcome my reluctance and brought the bird home — to my great regret. For Stewart not only could talk intelligently, but did so loudly and often. After only a few days the novelty of being the keeper of this twentieth-century miracle (caused, the bird insisted, by the placement of her parental cage too close to a video display terminal) had worn decidedly thin.

I have to admit that the bird did have some useful attributes. She enjoyed grading papers, and she did it competently. Once or twice a parent questioned me about the tiny holes in the upper corners of a child's notebook, the result of Stewart's page turning, but my marking load decreased substantially. And the bird had been invaluable early in the school year when, faced with the worst class I had ever had to deal with, I had taken her, cage and all, to school. She had free reign (or flight) of the classroom once she had indignantly shown the janitor that she was, indeed, well trained.

"Honestly, Jane," she had complained to me. "This is a bit much. How would *you* like to have to perform such a personal function in front of a perfect stranger?"

The janitor admired my skill at bird training, told the sulking bird that she was a "pretty boy," and Stewart-Athena became the best snitch I have ever had in a classroom. From her command post on my desk she surveyed the room, making patrols of suspected spit-ball throwers, marching across desks to read notes yet unpassed, squawking loudly when some infraction needed my immediate attention. I could leave my class unattended, yet have a full report within seconds of my return, even to verbatim quotes. These reports of Stewart's, given in a voice inaudible to the class as she perched on my shoulder, were as detailed and complete as any general ever received from a spy behind enemy lines. And the bird loved doing it, delighting in watching the punishment being meted out to the culprits, chiding me harshly when she felt I had been too lenient.

Within a month Stewart and I had so terrified the class that she was able to spend her days at home in the apartment again, paying only the occasional return visit to the school. I ignored the half-heard rumors of witchcraft that spread among the students, and didn't complain when a few parents removed their offspring from my class. On the whole, teaching had never been easier, and my status in the staffroom had risen dramatically.

However, life at home with Stewart-Athena was anything but easy. I had never married, by choice, no matter what the bird insinuated, and yet this collection of green and yellow feathers was causing me more anguish than a dozen husbands.

I think the bird's nagging began when she noticed my affinity for several strong drinks after work. There is nothing at all unusual about that. Any teacher will tell you that there are some days when only the comfort of a drink or two will prevent you from phoning your principal and resigning. Yet Stewart, not caring for the taste of any alcoholic beverage herself (after sampling an assortment of everything in my liquor cabinet), begrudged me that simple pleasure.

"The cost, Jane, the cost. With your monthly outlay for booze we could save enough for a downpayment on a house in a few years. Not to mention what it is doing to your brain. Just the other night CBC did a program on alcohol and its effects on the body and . . ."

I tuned her out. It wasn't the death of a few brain cells with every drink that bothered me; it was the wake the other cells kept throwing for them the next morning that was difficult to live with.

And this house-of-our-own notion. The bird wanted freedom, trees, privacy. She had an idyllic vision of herself perched on a grape arbor, daintily picking off the choicest insects, executing graceful loops around a blossom-laden tree before landing picturesquely on a rose bush. Not only had Stewart become carnivorous since her arrival (my fault, I gave her caviar that first night), but she was now asking for *live* meat. At the rate she was going through the bugs that came in my bedroom window, always open slightly so she wouldn't have that incarcerated feeling, I had visions of myself soon having to bring home live baby mice, a delicacy usually reserved for snakes, not budgies.

I do *not* want a house. Apartment life suits me. And who did the bird think was going to have to fertilize and spray those rosebushes, trim the grapevines, and rake the leaves? I was firm. No house. Stewart was quiet for a week or so, quiet, and almost pleasant. I found myself thinking that there were some advantages to living with this bird. Not only was she invaluable in the classroom, but she evicted an intruder from the apartment one night by suggesting, in her deepest voice and most colorfully explicit vocabulary, that he remove himself at once as she had a gun leveled at parts of his anatomy he probably wished to retain intact. For a while it wasn't too bad having Stewart-Athena around. I had almost forgotten about her persistent complaints about my drinking, my weight, and the insufficient quantity and quality of the reading material I brought home for her.

Then she began insisting that we take a trip to Greece. The bird must have been exposed to too much educational TV when she was a chick and developed some inane notion about her parentage — although Leda and the Budgie doesn't have quite the same ring to it as Leda and the Swan. She also read voraciously, and much of her reading was from ponderous volumes of Greek mythology that she badgered me into bringing home from the library. Not only had she chosen the name Athena after a favorite goddess, but she would quote at great length from those volumes, and had become almost unhealthily obsessed with the subject. I should have realized that, sooner or later, the notion of going to Greece would occur to her. So I wasn't really too surprised when she began to insist that she needed to visit her spiritual home, find her mythical roots, see the Parthenon, light pensively on the ruined temple of her namesake goddess, and allow her soul to find itself in the cradle of culture.

Ignoring my stony silence on the matter, Stewart soon had the trip organized, even to the size and style of the personalized traveling case I was to have made for her. I foolishly brought her a handful of travel brochures on Greece, and within hours they had been read and re-read until the upper corners were braille-like with beak holes. My refusal to give up my old dial telephone for a push-button speaker model was, I am sure, the only thing that saved me from arriving home one day to find that the tickets had been bought and the arrangements for the trip finalized — all on my credit card, of course.

I let the bird read the brochures and dream about visiting Greece, but I remained firm. I already had my summer planned, the same vacation I had taken each year for fifteen years. Stewart had accompanied me last summer to the rustic cabin by the quiet lake, and had not been impressed. She claimed lack of intellectual stimulation; I strongly suspect that it was the presence of larger and possibly predatory birds that made her reluctant to return. So I had made alternate arrangements for her. I planned on leaving her in the tender care of old Mrs. Amos and the large white cat that now lived with her. Not that I anticipated anything nasty happening to the bird, but if fate and a cat took matters out of my hands, I could return to my pre-Stewart existence and un-badgered lifestyle.

Although this arrangement had not been mentioned in Stewart's presence, I am sure she listened outside Mrs. Amos' window the day I finalized matters. The bird had, months ago, become a peeping Tom — or a peeping budgerigar — who was quite capable of listening to even *my* private conversations. My neighbors were amused by her presence on their window ledges at breakfast, and tolerant of her haughtly rejection of stale toast. They would not have been nearly as tolerant nor amused had they heard the bird's reports of their activities, for breakfast was not the only time of day that Stewart snooped. In fact, there was one couple whose eyes I could no longer meet if we chanced to pass in the hallway — and I had thought them such nice young people, too.

Stewart had no intention of spending the summer with Mrs. Amos and her cat, confined to a cage and denied access to the remote control which allowed her to watch all the educational programming she wished. Stewart wanted to go to Greece. After I refused for the final time to even consider the trip, showing the bird my savings account book and coaching her once again through the arithmetic of every teacher's summer — two months with no salary — she stopped talking. I began once again to explain, the bird's computational skills being much below her verbal abilities, but she ignored me, returning to her seldom used cage and sitting in silence with her head tucked under one wing for the rest of the evening. I blessed my depleted savings account for the unusual peace and celebrated by having an extra Scotch. The bird didn't even notice.

The next morning there was a half-carat diamond ring beside the coffee perk.

"Stewart!" I shouted, then, remembering that she would answer only to her goddess name, lowered my voice, steadied it, and called sweetly, "Athena, would you come here for a moment, please?"

She swept haughtily down from the top of the cupboard and landed beside my coffee mug. "You really should reduce your intake of caffeine, Jane. I've told you several times what medical research warns about caffeine and the nervous system — especially an aging nervous system."

I didn't rise to the taunt. "Where did this ring come from?" I demanded, years of schoolroom management making my voice as haughty as her. "Exactly where did you acquire this?"

Stewart turned her head away, lifted a wing, and pretended to preen. "I stole it," she said. Feather muffled though her voice was, I had no difficulty at all understanding her. I had expected no other answer.

"From whom?" I demanded, my voice stentorian.

"No one we know, Jane. A couple from the apartment two blocks over. I've been — ah — keeping an eye on them for a while as they are going through a rather ugly, but extremely psychologically interesting, divorce. If only you'd invest in that word processor, then these studies of mine on the diversities and complexities of human mating behavior could be recorded. I'm sure that *Psychology Today* would be interested in . . ."

"Don't change the subject," I snapped. "Take this ring back. Now."

"Oh, but I can't do that, Jane. They've closed the window. Besides, she took it off last night and threw it at him. By now she's probably convinced herself that she managed to throw it out the window, and is already filling out the insurance claim."

"I don't care whether or not it's insured. Take it back."

Among the bird's other un-avarian characteristics is an ability to be extremely, almost hypnotically, persuasive. Within a week the fruits of Stewart's "psychological studies" had netted us three more rings, one large ruby pin, and several dozen gold chains, and I had initiated conversations with a fascinating but rather unsavory character who frequented the bar where I had spent so many "Happy Hours" before the bird entered my life. Besides, I had always fancied Greek food, and the negotiations with my new friend had resulted in an increase in my savings account that would more than cover not only a trip to Greece, but a leisurely Mediterranean cruise as well.

However, Stewart-Athena was greedy. We didn't need any more — uh — merchandise, the trip had been booked and paid for, and I was getting a bit nervous about making another healthy deposit at the bank, beginning to wonder just how many rich uncles can reasonably die before someone gets suspicious. But Stewart was not only greedy, she was spiteful. She had never forgiven Mrs. Amos, her first owner, for those months that she had been caged, humiliated, and misunderstood by being treated exactly like any other budgie. My personal suspicion is that she resented the name Mrs. Amos had bestowed on her ("Greenie") and the old woman's continual references to her, Athena-Stewart, in the masculine gender, as much as anything else the poor woman had done. But for whatever vengeful or simply nasty reason of her own, the bird was determined to add Mrs. Amos's twenty-four inch strand of pearls to our holiday finances.

A large pearl necklace with a gold clasp isn't very heavy when worn around a human neck, but to a bird who has to be weighed on postal scales, it poses a formidable job of weightlifting. Stewart went into training. She had me purchase an imitation necklace, approximately the same size and weight as Mrs. Amos' heirloom pearls, and, using her beak to flip it over her neck, would fly around and around the livingroom for hours on end. The beads dangled perilously close to the floor when Stewart began her training flights, but within a week she was able, assisted by almost inaudible grunts, to lift them to window height with ease. Then we began adding tiny brass washers, one at a time, compensating for the weight of the gold clasp. With each addition the bird would again fly slowly and painfully around, barely clearing the carpet at first, but rising higher and higher each day.

When she could lift the necklace and six washers ceiling high in silence, she began doing the Twenty Minute Workout twice a day, complaining bitterly that the exercises were not designed for birds. She coerced me into attempting the program with her once, but it didn't take me the full twenty minutes to discover that the exercises weren't designed for middle-aged humans, either.

After almost two months of intensive training, Stewart was ready. She could fly across the room, pick up the necklace and eight washers, flip it around her neck, and be out of the window in seconds. And one hot June night, just a week before the end of school and our departure for the Greek isles, the Fates were ready, too.

Mrs. Amos appeared unexpectedly at my door. "Oh, Jane, may I come in? My air conditioner isn't working, and they can't send anyone until the morning. I've got all my windows open, but it isn't helping and it's *so* hot! May I sit with you a bit until everything cools down tonight?" She didn't wait for an answer, but settled herself down in front of the air conditioning unit, audibly adjusting her false teeth and scattering an assortment of colored yarns and crochet hooks around her.

Stewart left her cage, circled slowly around Mrs. Amos, then dipped her wings at me before heading for the bedroom where the window was, as always, open far enough for her to get in and out at will. The game was afoot — well, aflight.

At ten o'clock that evening when Mrs. Amos finally allowed herself to be ushered out, her visit having stretched into several long hours, Stewart still had not returned. I hurried to the bedroom. No twenty-four inch strand of pearls. No bird. I smiled smugly. "I'll wager she couldn't lift the necklace, even with all that training, and she's out there sulking, ashamed to come home," I thought. "Well, perhaps now that avarian super-ego of hers will shrink, and bless all her ancient gods I won't have to listen to any more work-out music!"

Smiling to myself, carefully planning my first sarcastic words when the chagrined bird did return, I heard the doorbell give several frantic peals and went to answer it.

Mrs. Amos stood in the hallway, pale and shaking, a large white cat tangling itself possessively around her ankles. "Heart attack!" I thought as her lips moved soundlessly and she gulped for air. "Or stroke." But before I could make my dash for the phone to summon medical aid, words began to tumble from her, and I realized that it was not illness that had brought her back to my door.

"Oh, Jane, I'm *so* sorry. I never should have left the windows open, and you know cats, they can't help themselves."

She thrust her hands out at me and I saw, nestled on a clean linen napkin, an anatomically impossible arrangement of beak, claws, and green and yellow feathers. Budgie feathers. Dead budgie feathers.

"I'm so very upset, Jane. He must have tangled his little feet in my pearl necklace on the dresser — it was lying on the floor — and then the cat ..."

I gingerly took the napkin and its contents, seriously considering whether I should celebrate my liberation from the bird, or conduct a proper Irish wake for her. Either way I suspected that large quantities of Scotch would be involved. "Maybe it's not ..." I began hopefully, suddenly overcome by a wave of melancholy as I thought of my savings account.

"Oh, but I know it's Greenie, dear. It has to be him because he wasn't quite ... I mean, when I got there he was still, uh, you know. And he said, clear as a bell and so loudly that I could understand him even without my hearing aid, he said that name he used to say at me all the time when he lived with me. "Stewart Bitz," he said. "Stewart, Stewart Bitz.""

I looked down at the mess in my hand and wondered what on earth to do with it. "Yes," I said, almost regretfully. "Yes, she was."

8
Wade Bell
TRACIE'S REVENGE

SHE was pinch-mouthed, somewhat paranoic and — or, at least, as she'd been so often told — completely inconsiderate of anyone's feelings except, at times, those of her son, aged three.

She stood at the sink in jeans and a yellow T-shirt looking through the small kitchen window at a line of white birch trees. Because she could not see beyond them, the birches were in her eyes the start of a forest that went on northwards into the unknown probably forever. The trees and the warm dish water always combined to make her daydream. She thought of her husband at the sawmill and hoped an accident there would take his life so that she would inherit his insurance money and the pickup truck. If that happened, she would as instantly as in that moment's reverie transport herself to the city where she would live in a pleasant apartment overlooking a park and at her own cautious speed select a well-off husband from among those who would court her. She had no imagined image of what this man would look like. She did not consider that a man's looks had any relevance to her dream of security and comfort for her and her child.

The telephone rang and she reached for a towel to dry her hands, then stopped. The phone continued to ring. It would be no one she wanted to talk to. She plunged her hands back into the water telling herself that getting the dishes done was more important than hearing herself be commanded in a gruff voice on the other end of the line to be sure to tell her husband that this or that would be repossessed if he didn't make a payment first thing next morning. Certainly no one would call to be nice. And if someone did, if there were someone who might, she would cut that person off, not wanting to hear niceness any more than threats and intimidation.

When the ringing stopped, she became aware of the soft banging of Rambo hitting his head against the wooden frame of the back screen door. Gene had nicknamed the boy Rambo just because of that habit. She knew she should take the child to a doctor to see about his head banging as well as his unnatural refusal to cry that Gene was so proud of and his inability to utter more than a dozen one or two syllable words. In the city she would take him to the doctor first thing.

If the phone call were from someone collecting a debt, it would mean Gene wasn't at work because they always went there first to look for him and phoned him at home as a last resort. He wouldn't be in the bar or any other place in town where they could find him. He'd be driving around the country roads with a bottle of rye and his rifle.

The soft banging went persistently on. She poured the dirty water from the yellow plastic basin, dried her hands, and, though she didn't like music or the warped excitement of announcers' voices, turned on the small radio that sat on the sill in front of the screen in the window above the sink. The only singer she liked was Hank Williams and they almost never played Hank Williams. Hank Williams was the one good memory she had of her father, who had sung his songs at dances when she was a child, before Social Services came and took her away.

Pretty soon the banging would stop and Rambo would fall asleep on the step in the sun.

She dried the frying pan and, thinking of her son, was glad she'd had her tubes tied. She wasn't stupid. She knew where she was going and taking one person with her was just right. The man who would find her in the city would probably have children of his own. He would leave them with their mother. He wouldn't mind Rambo. No one could mind Rambo. He was so good. He wouldn't wake up when she opened the screen door and quietly slipped out. When he did wake he'd find her sitting beside him. He'd look at her with Gene's big brown eyes and she'd look at him with her big blue ones. It wouldn't matter if they didn't smile. They both knew how phony smiles were and how they hid a person's real thoughts, which were always aggressive and intended to do you harm. She and Rambo didn't have to smile. They knew how the other felt. They trusted each other.

The phone rang again as she was putting away a pot. Maybe it was Gene. If it was, she'd tell him when he got home and asked that she'd been in the yard hanging out clothes. Except that she hadn't washed clothes today. She'd tell him she was in the garden, though if he looked he'd see it hadn't been weeded or watered. She'd think of something before he arrived.

She finished the dishes, turned off the radio and went outside. Rambo was where she knew he'd be, flat on his stomach on the middle of the three steps. She sat on the top step, leaned back against the wooden door frame, pushed her long blond hair away from her forehead and closed her eyes. The sun was hot; she wouldn't be able to stand it for long. Soon she'd be as sleepy as Rambo and then he'd wake up and she'd want to lie down on the couch. If she did, he wouldn't let her sleep. He'd keep tugging at her until she got up. If she lay there dead, she thought, he'd find a way to revive her and get her to her feet and walk around. She'd never seen anybody as persistent as Rambo, not even his father who also always tried to get his way but whom she'd taught to leave her alone when she told him to.

The cat walked out of the birch trees and across the lawn. He sniffed at Rambo's feet as he climbed the steps. When he reached Tracie, she picked him up and threw him back on the grass. She didn't want him licking her. You never knew what he'd been eating out there. Without complaint he disappeared around the corner of the house.

She thought about Gene, about how he always said he'd never go back to the city, how he couldn't go back to the city. It meant he wouldn't come after her. He'd been born in the city, lived all his twenty-four years in the city except for the three he'd been here. He said if he went back he'd be dead in a month, if not sooner. There were certain people he wouldn't be able to stay away from, he said. Dangerous people. When she got there she'd have nothing to do with people like that. She knew how to pick out the bad ones. They'd never get her with their drugs and gambling the way they got Gene. She wasn't stupid. She hated the way Gene looked at her sometimes like she was the enemy, the way he'd stare at her as if she'd pulled a deal on him or like he'd pulled a deal on her and was waiting to attack just a split second before she attacked him.

Sometimes when she glanced at the white trunks of the birches and wasn't thinking she had the impression that they were snow, that it was winter and everything was white. Now, for the moment that she was able before she had to lower her eyes because of the sun, she looked at their green, shivering tops and imagined, as she often did, black war planes appearing just above them, coming out of nowhere, maybe from a secret runway not so far away inside the trees. The planes with their horrible roar wouldn't drop hundreds of bombs but only one, one meant just for her.

Gene wouldn't want the child. Anyway, Rambo was more hers than his. What had Gene done except plant the seed? Rambo came from her body. Rambo was her.

She must have been dreaming of the cat because when Rambo woke her, tugging at her T-shirt, she yelled and pushed him down the step where he landed on his back, then rolled onto his stomach. She was angry at the cat first and then at the sun because she was sure her face would be red, even if she'd only drifted off for a few minutes, and when her face got red it got sore and she hated that. As she watched Rambo get to his feet it occurred to her it was lucky Gene hadn't gotten around to putting in the sidewalk because if Rambo had landed on cement he might have died. She stood up and rubbed the back of her neck because it was sore from the way she'd been sleeping.

"Juice," she said.

"Juice," Rambo replied.

As she peered into the bathroom mirror for signs of the sun's damage, Tracie considered that except for the lines around her mouth — lines she'd had since she was twelve years old — she pretty well looked her age. Gene said she was too thin but that was the way she wanted to be. Fat women got nowhere in this life, she said to herself. She'd said that to Gene one time and he'd growled, "Where do you think you want to get?" She'd never said it again, though she thought it all the time. She knew what Gene meant when he said she should be fatter. He just wanted her breasts to be bigger, her thighs to be meatier so there'd be more to grab onto. In the city her man wouldn't think of changing her.

She was sitting at the kitchen table looking at the TV schedule when there was a knock at the back door. The knock frightened her:

it was too strong to be Rambo.

She didn't move. Her finger stayed on the line that said what the Cosby show was going to be about.

"Yo," somebody said, a man. If she leaned across the table she'd be able to see who it was.

"Hello," he said.

She leaned across the table. He was old, probably in his thirties or forties.

"Where's Gene?" the man said. He was tall and thick set, in jeans and a black T-shirt. He had long hair and a moustache. He wasn't the police and he wasn't a repo man. His eyes were the kind she knew all about. He wasn't the type to care at all about jobs or the law.

Her first thought once she got over the surprise of the man appearing out of nowhere was for the four thousand dollars Gene had stashed in jam tins in the basement. Her second thought was for Rambo.

"Gene?" the man asked, smiling in a funny way as if talking to someone who had a hard time understanding.

When she didn't answer he said, "I want to see Gene."

"You can't," she said.

"And why can't I?"

"He's not here."

"The disappearing Gene," the man said. "Gene's nowhere."

"He's at work."

"He's not at work."

"He's at work," she repeated.

"I know he's not," the man said. She couldn't see past the man to find out where Rambo might be.

The man said, "I just want to see him for a minute."

"He's not here."

She wondered why he was waiting on the step. If he wanted to he could open the door and walk right in. It occurred to her that if she sat down so that he couldn't see her he'd do just that.

"You sure?" He had that look again.

"Yes." Then she thought of something. "His truck isn't here. He can't be here if his truck isn't here."

The man paused for a second. "Right," he said. He opened the door.

She rushed passed him as he walked in. He made no movement to stop her. The screen door slammed.

Rambo was sitting in the pile of sand Gene had ordered to make concrete for the sidewalk. The cat was lying on the grass. Both of them looked at her.

She went back inside, thinking of the jam tins.

The man was sitting where she'd been sitting. A set of false teeth lay on the TV schedule, the paper underneath them growing wet and dark from saliva. "Take my advice," the man said, gumming his words so that the c came out as a whistled s. "Keep your teeth as long as you can. Don't let anybody talk you into having them out. They hurt like hell."

Without the teeth his jowls sagged and his moustache seemed to have swallowed his mouth. She looked away from his face as she sat down. Her eyes landed on the teeth and seemed to stick there, mesmerized.

"You won't need false teeth for awhile," he said, and she looked up to see him studying her. She immediately knew what he was thinking. She always knew as soon as they did when men started thinking about that.

"Not for a long time," he went on, leaning back in his chair. "What are you, twenty-four, twenty-five?"

"Twenty-one." She got up and walked to the screen door, then returned to the table and sat down, thinking about the jam tins but forcing herself not to picture exactly where they were because you never knew about a man like that, how much of her mind he might be able to read.

It never occurred to her to tell him to leave. Her first impression of him was that he was one of those men who you couldn't tell to do anything.

She tried to keep her eyes away from the teeth.

"Where is he?" the man said. He sounded like an old man.

"I don't know," she said. She was listening for Rambo at the door.

"Think," the man said. He leaned forward and slid his hand across the table.

She watched it come towards her. "At the hotel, in the bar."

"He wasn't at the bar. Or the pool hall. Or in the coffee shops."

At that moment the phone rang again. The man sprang to answer it, grabbing his teeth and shoving them in his mouth.

"Yo," he said.

He listened for a second then said, "Randy."

He listened for a moment more. "I've just come to visit you, old bud." Then after a pause, "Don't be that way. Where are you?"

He said, "I know you're around. Just tell me where around."

Then he said, "Fuck you, too, buddy!" and hung up.

He continued standing. He asked her where Gene would go if he wasn't in the town.

"Driving around," she told him.

"He'd have telephoned from town," the man said. "So now he'd leave and go driving around. That right?"

She nodded.

"Where?" With his teeth in his voice was powerful. She had to answer. It kept her from picturing the jam tins.

"On the country roads."

"Which ones?"

She told him about a road half a mile away that dead-ended in a ravine. The ravine was wooded and had a trickle of water running through it.

"Does he have a gun?"

A devil sprang up inside her. "He'll be shooting rabbits," she said. "If he's really mad, he might kill a deer. He likes to shoot."

"What kind of truck does he drive?"

The devil danced inside her. "A green Ford half-ton. Ten years old."

"Licence plate?"

She told him.

He nodded his head as if not wanting to say anything more because talking might make him forget the number.

When he left, walking — he must have parked his car somewhere down the road so that Gene, if he'd been home, wouldn't have heard the sound of a vehicle in the driveway — she picked up Rambo from the sand, brushed his clothes and took him in the house. The cat came in with them. She sat at the kitchen table with Rambo on her lap until he wriggled away and went to sit on the living room floor.

Sometimes when she had to think she made a cup of tea and drinking it seemed to help. This time, however, the thoughts came quickly. She didn't need tea.

She didn't think for long. The devil inside her had told her: this was the opportunity; now was the time.

It wouldn't be stealing. She could never steal. Stealing was stupid because it got you in trouble and she wasn't stupid.

It was her inheritance.

She got a plastic grocery bag from under the sink. She went down to the ill-lit, unfinished cellar and found the jam tins. She took the lids off the tins, removed the bills, and stuffed them in the grocery bag. Back upstairs, she fed Rambo and the cat and made herself a peanut butter sandwich and drank a glass of milk.

There was nothing in the house she wanted to take with her. Never in her life had there been anything she possessed that had value for her.

Then she remembered Gene's movies that were due back at the video store today and went and got them from where they sat next to the TV. Rambo sat silently rocking, his palms pushing hard against the floor.

There was an evening bus to Edmonton. She put Rambo in the stroller. She would push him as far as she could on the gravel, then he'd have to walk the rest of the two miles to town. She'd leave the stroller by the side of the road. In the city she'd buy another one. She had plenty of money now.

She wouldn't take a suitcase, just a jacket for herself and one for the child. She'd buy clothes for them both when they got to the city.

She put the cat outside and watched him run to the birch trees.

She and Rambo set out to catch the bus, the bag of money and the jackets and the videos stuffed in a large straw tote. The stroller pushed awkwardly on the gravel. The afternoon sun was very strong. She wished she had sunglasses. When she got to the city she'd buy sunglasses just to wear to walk in the park. She'd never worn sunglasses before. She'd always hated sunglasses. Sunglasses hid your eyes. You couldn't trust people with sunglasses. She wondered what was coming over her, wanting a pair.

She stared away from the sun and into the trees. She imagined the man looking for Gene in the wooded ravine. After a while she lifted her son from the stroller and set him down beside her. She knew the walk would be difficult for him but she also knew he wouldn't complain. She thought about his not complaining. Then she looked down at him and said, as if it might make a difference to him, as if it might somehow help release him from his silence, "You're not Rambo anymore. From now on, you're Paul again."

As they slowly walked she listened for the sound of the gunshot that she knew at any moment would come from far away inside the trees. It wouldn't matter which of them got killed. Either way, Gene wouldn't be around anymore. But she hoped it would be Gene. If it was, there would be the insurance money and the truck. She began to wonder how the insurance company would find her in the city, then decided not to worry about it. People like that always knew how to find you when they wanted to.

9
Gail Helgason
WILD STOCK

ON A good day I'm in the office by eight. I'm supposed to dream up two ideas for editorials by nine, and be prepared to defend them before the rest of the editorial board of Edmonton's largest daily. So you can understand why I do not welcome the distracting news this morning that Bernie Lapicki may be on the loose again.

My job is really less difficult than it sounds. I got the hang of it after a few weeks. I understood the absolute need to squirrel away information on some clearly-defined issues, like redevelopment of the rail yards. Plus some recent facts and figures, the phone number of a reliable expert on health care economics at the university — you know the kind of thing I mean. I am also learning how to change the paper's policy on key issues, how to build my case so rationally and reasonably that even the publisher won't realize what's happened until it's too late, and it's all out there in print. The thought of the subtle power I wield makes me smile.

Still, I'll be the first to admit that this type of journalism requires concentration to do well. So the news about Bernie Lapicki is doubly distressing on a Friday. My busiest day, damn it, with editorials for the Saturday, Sunday, and Monday holes to fill.

Bernie Lapicki. The Lapickis lived two blocks away from the house where I grew up in Swan Creek, Manitoba. Bernie was three years younger than me. He had a strawberry birthmark on one side of his face, thick amber hair, and such a long thin neck that we called him The Giraffe. He lived alone with his father, Wasyl, the janitor at the public school. No one seemed to know where Bernie's mother was. When I asked my mother, she'd just shake her head and say I should be nice to Bernie because he didn't have a mother.

Sometimes Bernie would come over on Saturday mornings, when I'd be reading on the porch or helping my father wash the car. Once in a while he'd offer to help, but usually he'd just sit on the steps, whistling and digging in his mouth with a toothpick.

One time he came over when I was working on an essay for my social studies class, cribbing like crazy from Will Durant's *Story of Civilization*. He asked me what I was writing about, and I started telling him all about Babur, the founder of the Mogul dynasty, and how he could kill five enemies in five minutes. Bernie seemed really interested, and asked if he could read my paper when I was finished.

But when Bernie left that day, my mother noticed that the money she'd put out for the milkman was gone. After that, I more or less knew that he wasn't welcome in our house.

"A person has to draw the line somewhere," my mother told me.

By the time Bernie reached his teens, he stopped coming over for good. There were stories that he was involved with a rough gang from another town. And there was the night we went tobogganing.

Phil has scrawled "See me" on a yellow sticky pad and attached it to a copy of a story about the Lapicki sentencing seven years ago. The clipping shows a grainy picture of Maureen Hicks. High forehead, hair brushed back in a ponytail. Gunned down at sixteen, in a service station in southern Alberta.

Phil must have pulled the story from the microfiche this morning. Typical. In at five to start compiling the international pages, and still makes the time to wrest out this story, to refresh my memory. As if it needed refreshing.

We lived together for two years, Phil and I, after I'd finally gotten off "beat" reporting and had a chance for a more normal life. We got together after discovering our mutual passion for birdwatching. Our favorite thing was to drive down to Banff on Friday nights in the spring, and then get up at four the next morning to hike into the swamps below Johnston Canyon, where we actually made the first sighting of willow flycatchers one year.

Phil sometimes reminds me of a shorebird himself. He's tall and thin, and has a nervous twitch that appears on the right side of his mouth when he's worried about something, which is often.

Sometimes I tease him about resembling a common merganser, blending into the reeds from habit even where there are no reeds to act as camouflage.

Me, I've always been the one to show my plumage. I tint my hair auburn, and wrap myself in golds and purples and reds, and I even once considered buying cinnamon-tinted contact lenses to bring out the depths in my eyes. I pride myself on not having worn beige since high school. If I were a bird, Phil says, I would be a golden eagle. I know he says this to please me.

When we were living together, Phil couldn't stand the way I'd eat my breakfast standing up, like a grebe, and how I could never wait for him to end his sentences. I loathed his meticulous ways. Once, when we were out for a walk, I tried to get him to cross a street before the walk light came on.

"For Pete's sake, there's not a car in sight," I hissed. Then I grabbed him and pulled him right across the intersection, half ripping the sleeve of his favorite jacket.

When we split up, I think we were both equally relieved. But Phil and I still have dinner once a week, on Fridays. For Christmas he gave me a beautiful ruby-red hummingbird feeder and an Audubon bird call that actually attracts all kinds of wild birds. You just twist the stem around to vary the tone and pitch.

We still watch out for each other, I think. Like birds singing a warning.

The phone rings and it's Phil, calling from the newsroom. "You got my note?" he asks. I lean back in my chair and put my legs on the metal desk. "Yeah. So what?"

As I speak, I reach for the file where I stash emergency ideas for editorials. I'd planned to try to convince the board today to back a hands-off policy on a wildlife sanctuary on the city's outskirts where a utility company wants to dig.

But now I feel too distracted. Something more straightforward would be better today. I sift through the clippings, and then I notice that a parents' group wants $55,000 to help fund a city-wide task force on youth violence in the schools. Easy prey. I've found my issue-of-the-day.

"How do you know he's out, anyway?" I ask.

Phil says there's been notification over the wire, from the court reporter at the *Winnipeg Free Press*, Fred Gariepy. I remember Fred now from the trial, a pale-faced man with hooded eyes and a tweed cap, who'd been covering Bernie's case since the juvenile courts.

"That son-of-a-bitch should get life," he'd told me, as we watched Bernie Lapicki brought in for sentencing. Naturally the judge went for manslaughter, with a plea for clemency because Bernie had been under twenty-one at the time of the slaying.

Phil urges me to call Gariepy. For all we know, Lapicki may have been out for months. Or he could be at a halfway house.

"Why don't we drive up to Jasper for the weekend?" Phil asks.

Phil has never liked my insistence on living alone, in my little ravine house. He worried about it in my days as a police reporter, which is one of the reasons I let him move in with me for a time. Even today he insists that I sleep with a knife under my pillow, or at least keep one in my briefcase. He actually made me check out burglar alarms, although I nixed that idea as soon as I priced a few. Now Phil lives by himself five houses down the block, and sometimes he still behaves like an elderly aunt.

"Can't possibly get away," I say. I wince and notice a paper cut on my index finger. Bright red blood oozes out.

"Can't even make dinner tonight, I'm afraid."

I explain about the panel I'm on tomorrow. I'm to represent the paper in a discussion on sentencing reform, at the annual meeting of Alberta trial lawyers. The topic is: "The Role of the Media in Justice." They probably asked me to appear after my series of signed pieces on sentencing reform last year.

"Well, be careful, and check with Gariepy," Phil urges.

"Not to worry," I say. "Besides, I have Maverick."

I was thirteen years old, and on my way to my best friend's birthday party. Walking by the school, I saw Bernie Lapicki's figure in the bushes by the steep toboggan run that Mr. McClennan built of packed snow. I knew Bernie had not been invited.

It was February, and Janine McClennan's parents had arranged an evening toboggan party. Janine had sun-colored hair and what my dad called "a disposition to match." I couldn't wait to present her with my birthday gift, a pictorial book about Eleanor of Aquitaine.

After the outing, we were all invited to go back to the McClennan's for cake. I could already taste Mrs. McClennan's angel food cake, smothered with strawberries and maple-flavored seven-minute icing. Inside, the cake would be stuffed with quarters, carefully wrapped in wax paper.

Ivor Small, the mayor's son, stood at the top of the hill, wearing purple ear muffs that reminded me of my mother's bathroom slippers. I noticed that Katie Solman, the minister's daughter, had been invited, even though she was still in elementary school.

We decided that Janine should have the first run down the hill. She jumped on the toboggan and plunged down, out of sight. The snow was hard-packed and the toboggan made a slithering sound, like two pieces of silk rubbing together.

We listened for Janine to shout from the bottom of the hill. Nothing. Then we heard a soft whimpering sound, and Mr. McClennan tore down the hill faster than I'd ever seen a grown-up move.

Seconds later, Mr. McClennan yelled up at Ivor to call an ambulance. Afterward, there was an investigation, and the RCMP found that someone had tied wire between two trees across the bottom of the run. I overheard my parents say it was lucky Janine wasn't decapitated.

Janine withdrew from me after the accident. She didn't want to go for long walks around the marsh anymore, or go skating in winter. She just wanted to stay indoors, doing boring and safe things like practicing comb-outs. We stopped being close friends.

My dad, who taught biology at the high school, suggested that I write an article for the school paper about the evils of vandalism. I wrote a compelling essay, and I won a prize in a competition sponsored by the Knights of Columbus. I didn't mention to anyone that I had seen Bernie Lapicki near the place where the wire was strung.

I'm not in the best mood at the editorial meeting. David Pearson, the city-hall-reporter-turned-editorial writer, comes up with an ill-formulated argument for more inner-city social housing. I take it upon myself to point out the fuzziness of his logic.

"The latest statistics show that ninety-seven per cent of Canadians living in poverty have color TV," I protest. "And seventy per cent of all Canadian kids have been to Disneyland."

Frowning, David mutters something about poverty being relative. The board isn't buying.

Then I attack the funding request by the parents' group.

"If violence in the schools really is a problem, then surely it's up to the parents' group to take the initiative in fund-raising?" I ask.

I do feel like an eagle sometimes, arguing for the status quo most of the time, attacking whatever moves below. The board has a well-deserved reputation for conservatism, but there's a good reason for it, I think. Unlike the staff cafeteria, the editorial board of Alberta's largest newspaper is not the place for easy answers.

No one opposes me. Great. I'll spend some time on research and have a passable editorial ready by five o'clock. Maybe even have time to do some work for tomorrow's seminar.

As I walk back to my cubicle, Ardis, the new editorial writer, stops me. She's fresh from *The Ottawa Citizen* and says she's having a hard adjusting to Alberta politics. Privately, I think she should spend more time brushing up on the province's history and less in the media club.

"How do you roll off all that stuff — all those statistics — just like that?" she asks.

"I just do my homework," I say, and brush on by.

I was twenty-three years old, new to Edmonton, new to Alberta. Fresh out of Carleton University journalism school, I had the luck to land a reporting job at one of the big Southam papers. Pay so good the paper could thumb its nose at the newspaper guild, not like those Thompson rags, and name cards ordered for me the day I arrived. At the bush-league papers you actually have to pay for them yourself. Sure, it was only the police beat, but you had to start somewhere, didn't you?

And then it happened. I was taking a shortcut through the bus depot on my lunch hour when I saw Bernie Lapicki standing behind the cafeteria counter. He was ten years older, and his hair was black, not amber, but I would have known that giraffe neck anywhere, even if I couldn't clearly see his birthmark from where I stood.

A warrant has been out for Bernie's arrest for weeks, ever since the shooting of a sixteen-year-old service station attendant in southern Alberta.

I knew I had my story.

It's eleven before I call Gariepy. Lunch hour in Winnipeg. The news-room receptionist says he'll be in court that afternoon but she'll try to get him to call back before he leaves.

I beaver away at the youth violence piece and eat an egg salad sandwich at my desk. I write: "In this period of unprecedented pres-sure for public funds, city council must simply learn to say 'no'."

Before I got Maverick, my Doberman pinscher, I used to work out at the Y during my lunch hours, when I wasn't on a heavy dead-line. Now I exercise when I get home. Maverick and I go for ten-kilo-metre runs at least three times a week. I hold his leash correctly in my right hand and pat his wedge-shaped head as he tries to keep up with me. He's my freedom ticket, and I know it.

Once I wrote a well-received piece on the absurdity of the idea that economic power has freed women. What baloney, when we can't even walk alone without fear in public parks.

My index finger is still bleeding. I go into the washroom and wash the blood off my hand.

By four, just as I'm polishing my editorial, Fred Gariepy calls back.

"He got out, all right," Fred says. "Skipped Kingston three days ago. But he's been picked up. The RCMP got him on a routine check by Brandon. Stupid bugger stole a car."

By five o'clock, the editorial page editor has approved the youth editorial, and I'm on my way. The phone rings just as I'm gathering up the files I need for the panel discussion.

"You sure you should go home?" Phil asks.

"It's okay," I reply. "Bernie's been picked up in Manitoba."

"Okay," he says, in that cautious way of his. "If you're sure."

"Honestly, Phil," I say. "Even if he hadn't been picked up, the chances of anything happening are about one in ten thousand. What's with all the paranoia??"

I don't tell Phil, but something in his voice gets to me. I open my briefcase and slip the knife he gave me into my skirt pocket. Then I head for home, enjoying, as always, the view of the North Saskatchewan River and its tree-lined banks. The sky is the color of milk.

The thought of the evening ahead energizes me. A quick change of clothing, a run along the river in Hawrelak Park, a hot shower, micro-waved cannelloni in marinara sauce for dinner, à la Barbara Kafka, some reading and note-taking for my speech tomorrow, and then some relaxation. Maybe I'll catch some of "The Firing Line" episodes I've taped, or finish reading the last chapter of *Swim with the Sharks without Being Eaten Alive*.

I love this house, I think, as I flick on the automatic garage-door opener and wheel into the one-car garage. It's a storey and a half house that the real estate agent called a "starter" — probably because it has only one bathroom. Would that deficiency be enough to categorize it as substandard in the book of some bleeding heart, I wonder?

The first year I lived here, I sunk one third of my savings into improvements. I wanted to blow a bundle more, but my accountant said that really wouldn't be a rational thing to do, what with house prices going down. So I made do with sanding the hardwood floors, retrofitting the windows, and buying cream and china-blue carpets from Ikea. Now the house is nearly the way I want it. The right kind of house for a professional who doesn't want to get too distracted.

Normally Maverick greets me at the door. I walk into the living room, still carrying my briefcase, and I notice that I've left a water glass on the oak mantle. I hope it won't leave a mark.

And then I feel his eyes on the back of my skull.

"Afternoon, Carma," the voice says, coming closer.

I turn and see that same giraffe neck, the same bruised, birth-marked face, only now Bernie Lapicki's complexion is white as rice paper and there are strands of gray in his amber hair.

"Hello, Bernie," I say. I try to speak slowly, to act controlled, the way I do when one of the other editorial writers has enraged me with a knee-jerk opinion, and I want to disarm him by being all sweet reasonableness.

"What are you doing here?" I ask.

Bernie looks relaxed and calm, almost professorial, in khaki pants and a green turtleneck, except for the brown work gloves he's wearing, and the handgun he points at me.

"Just calling in on an old friend," he says. He stops in front of the pile of *Economists* and picks up the top one, with Margaret

Thatcher on the cover. Then he leans against the cream Italian leather sofa.

I hear a whimper from upstairs.

"Your dog's not going to help you," Bernie says. "Took three bullets."

Now the house is absolutely quiet. From somewhere down in the ravine I hear the distinctive honk of a pheasant.

"You were the one who taught me to appreciate history," Bernie says, still looking at the cover of the *Economist*. "Babur, Ivan the Terrible, right up to Billy the Kid and the Iron Lady. Inspiring for a little small-town boy."

I smell my own sweat, mixed with my Shalimar perfume and a disturbing odor I can't identify. That's when I notice the blood seeping through the tips of Bernie's right-hand glove.

He hasn't caught my look. He's still staring at the magazine cover. Then he looks up.

"Now I want to see if I can match Babur's record, Carma," Bernie says. "Only five people in five days is good enough for me. You, the judge, the defence lawyer, the jury chairman, and that snotty little reporter from Winnipeg. All the fucking people who put me in Kingston."

I hear Maverick whimpering again. There's no other sound. Then Bernie speaks again.

"First thing, I need something for my hand. You got a first aid kit?"

Bernie holds up his bleeding hand.

"In the bathroom," I say.

"Okay, let's get it," Bernie says. "I'm going to be right behind you, so don't try anything."

I nod. We walk slowly to the bathroom, on the other side of the hall on the main floor. I open the door and take the first aid kit down from the cabinet above the sink.

This is the moment that so often comes disguised as calm, like the moment when Janine plunged down the toboggan slope, or when the editorial board pauses before coming down hard on one side of an issue, and you know if you don't say something then it will be too late.

"Give me your hand," I say. I turn on the cold water tap. The old linoleum squeaks underfoot.

Bernie gives me his right hand, training the gun on me with his left. I tug the glove off and see mangled red flesh. Both Bernie's middle and index finger have been chewed off just above the knuckle.

"Some dog, eh?" I say.

Bernie doesn't say anything.

"This needs antiseptic," I explain. "Spread your hand down here, flat as you can."

Bernie spreads his hand on the wide rim of the old-fashioned sink. I notice the gleam of the porcelain and the dirt under his thumbnail. I open the tube of antiseptic and breathe in the pungent scent. Not far away, someone is mowing grass.

I draw the knife out of my skirt pocket and bring it down with all my strength on Bernie's ring finger. His flesh feels like the tough stalk of asparagus, until I reach the bone.

Bernie screams in pain and surprise. He drops the gun.

I figure I have about four or five seconds. That's how much I need to get out the door.

I don't go back to the house for hours. When I do, there are still a couple of police cars in the driveway. The paper's police reporter, Dan Takchuk, breaks away from a conversation with one of the officers.

"You know they found him in the ravine, eh, Carma?" he says. "I'll need a quote."

I smile as sweetly as I can and say: "No comment," although I know I'll have to call him later. Let him sweat it a little.

After the police leave, Phil and I go to the vet's. Maverick's in shock, the vet tells me, but the bullets missed his vital organs.

"Some tough dog," he says.

Phil and I share a pizza at our favorite old spot on 109th Street. It is Phil who has taught me that Greeks make the best pizza. But tonight the pizza tastes like a thick, damp soda cracker. I hold my coffee cup with both hands, trying to absorb as much warmth as I can. I am still so angry I'm shaking.

"Thanks for insisting that I take those precautions," I say to Phil. "I mean, the knife and all."

Phil shrugs.

"That man they picked up in Brandon resembled Lapicki all

right," Phil explains. "How were you supposed to know it was a case of mistaken identity?"

After we finish the pizza, Phil drops me off at the paper. I go to my computer terminal and punch in the code to retrieve Monday's editorials. I see that Dave Pearson has an editorial on poverty among seniors all ready to go.

Thankfully, I notice that Pearson's editorial is the same length as my editorial on youth violence. I replace mine with Pearson's in the Monday line-up, then proof the thing once more.

Now I highlight my editorial and press the "delete" button on my keyboard. Where do deleted items actually go, I wonder? Can they really just disappear forever?

10
Bill Dodds
CRIME OF PASSION

THINGS go wrong on elderly freighters, too, you know. It just doesn't make the newscasts like a liner disaster would. I guess I shouldn't have been as surprised as I was.

It was an old ship, one of those mistakes in marketing even the smartest shipwrights make. You must remember that model — the one where they tried to cut costs by making the astrogation and reactor computers into one pseudo-intelligent fixture? Just our luck this one was still in service. When the reactor started overheating and guidance shut down completely, we couldn't even find out what was wrong. The ship didn't feel like telling us. Said it wasn't feeling well.

There wasn't much to do. We couldn't stay in space with the reactor off, and we couldn't leave it on running hot. We couldn't make a fast run to a service port, either, with guidance out. So we looked for a planetfall — *any* planet — and broadcast a call for help.

I counted nine passengers. Two crew. Cargo made up entirely of a vat of live *blugh* worms bound for some fancy restaurant. All of us thinking really friendly thoughts to the nitwit who designed the stupid can so we couldn't find out what to fix.

I was going to be late for work. They let me out of the Station on compassionate leave when the Egg Festival started — early — at home. My partner would be stuck with some rookie and my captain would be thinking unkind thoughts about *me*, while I sat on some stupid rock.

That's right. I'm a cop. Supposed to be on vacation.

The bulkheads, reactor-side, were fluorescing faintly when we finally persuaded the ship to land us somewhere. I was not sure it didn't pick that particular planet out of malice.

Thick atmosphere, vague distinction between land and liquid, slow rotation, all sorts of unappetizing wildlife. Your typical primordial-ooze joint, for us to squat on until the reliable-but-glacier-slow rescue team got to us.

The couple from Felch announced that, since they were on their honeymoon, they didn't care where they were as long as they were together. It was clear they were very much in love — whole parts were already missing from both of them. To each his own.

I moved away from them as far as I could in the crowded common room. That put me beside a Dorvil who was hanging in the corner, just in time to hear its voice tube declare it would find a tree on landing and use the time in meditation.

Nobody talks to Dorvils much. There's too much danger they will decide you're being impertinent, and . . . take measures. Small, but deadly. Anything can — so the stories go — be taken as rude.

I moved away in what I hoped was a neutral and polite manner.

"Excuse me," said something on the deck.

"Stand by for landing," said the pilot. Scramble, scramble.

Then we were down.

The pilot was a nervous little ursinoid who was obviously taking the whole unscheduled stop personally. As soon as exterior sensors confirmed it was safe he virtually ordered us out so he could putter around inside and be alone.

The thing in the tank spoke up. It was a life insurance agent. It managed to make its mechanical voice ingratiating and slickly friendly. It would stay in the ship, if the pilot didn't mind. Its tank wasn't portable.

That was just as well. Pushy so-and-so had already tried to sell me a policy on my maternal aunt and two neighbors. It's not that I believe the rumors those agents honor their actuarial tables by direct intervention when policies lapse. I just don't like life insurance salesmen.

Evidently I was not alone in seeking escape. The adolescent T'Kungo smashed off through the undergrowth — to get some exercise, she said — and the couple from Felch went for a walk. I stood in the little clearing made by our landing and took stock.

"You're doing it again," came a voice.

"I beg your pardon?"

"Standing on me. Look ... eeugh, there ... we haven't met. I'm ... ah ... a shoe salesman. Names 007. What's yours?"

I'd wondered who the ninth passenger on the manifest was. And where. Those patches of intelligent moss were habitually inconspicuous. I introduced myself.

It turned out 007 played cards quite well. Expensively well. We settled down to pass the time around the corner from the lock.

At sundown the pilot set turns for keeping watch. The saurian ship's mechanic loudly declared he had a girlfriend waiting at the next scheduled landing and he was going to *fix* the stupid ship. He went back inside, lashing his tail. The rest of us took turns making disparaging remarks about the planet. Then the Dorvil found its tree and spun a cocoon, making one pointed remark about how rude it was to disturb nocturnal meditation. We all went to our cabins with polite speed.

At dawn we found the corpse of the mechanic by the open cargo lock.

The pilot hastily called us together again. There was some debate about disturbing the Dorvil, but since it was hanging only a short distance away, we decided on a posture of careful ambiguity on the issue of inviting it.

There was the mechanic, to one side of the clearing, on his face, with large parts of his exposed neck and arms eaten away.

The pilot wanted to know why nobody had heard anything. So did I.

Each watch had reported on time. Each watch had heard the mechanic working noisily and cursing himself and the universe in general for the delay. The last watch was the Pilgrim who was traveling to the Cult planet of Ollollu.

"I was seeing or hearing nothing until just before the coming of light," he said very slowly and judiciously. "Nothing, that is, but esteemed mechanic arriving." I was offering many prayers he might find peace. When silence was coming, I thought — I was thinking — he found it, and rest."

Well, he was right about that. Patient questioning brought out there had been no sounds of struggle or alarm. I pointed out we could tell that from the surprised look on the mechanic's face, and the absence of wounds sustained from the front.

We searched the area and doubled the guard. The two from Felch went off for another walk. One returned noticeably shorter.

At dinner — ship's stores again, of course — the T'Kungo opined she wasn't sad something had gotten the mechanic. Noisy, rude fellow. The Pilgrim took this as an invitation and led the armored youth off to lecture her on respect. I sat down with my back to the ship and got out my cards.

Weapons had been issued to those willing and able to carry them. The moss, naturally, declined. He had enough strength in his tendrils to hold a winning hand but not a gun, he said. Besides, he told me when we were alone, he did not expect violence that night.

"Why not?" I asked. "There's something out there that kills, quickly and without warning. Why not again tonight?"

He won another hand, took some time gathering the cards.

"Incompatibility, my dear Inspector. Check the ship's detailed printout of our scans. Our friend the mechanic was in bad taste when he was on the ship — but here, he was impossible taste. Nothing born here could eat him."

I cradled my blaster nervously. It no longer felt like a comfortable but dull night stakeout.

"Then it was one of us."

"Yup. Your turn. And I'll tell you something else. Y'know the Pilgrim?"

I barely noticed him rake in another pot.

"Well, the ol' Pilgrim is no such. It's forbidden in the Cult to pray after sundown."

"We must inform the Pilot at once!"

"Let it wait. I'd like a restful night, if you don't mind."

I thought 007 knew a great deal more than he was telling.

"Yes," he said, "I do."

Nothing happened that night, except the moss took about a week's salary off my claws.

When it was clear that we were all there at breakfast — except for the taller Felchian, who had fewer ears — the Pilot looked relieved. I almost regretted telling him and the others what the moss had revealed and records confirmed.

When he heard he sat down in the lock doorway with a bump.

"But ... but he ... but if ... but then ..."

"Exactly. Pilot, gentlebeings, I have no authority in this matter, but I must ask you to co-operate in what informal measures I take to discover the culprit in what I believe must have been foul play."

"There are planets where elimination of a foul being isn't foul play," the young T'Kungo said sullenly.

"Like T'Kung?" asked the Pilot with fear.

"And Felch," said the Pilgrim. "I have been thinking."

"Gentlebeings, that may be, but it is not relevant. Murder is lawful between consenting adults or duly authorized agency and legally liable citizen. None of that applies. One of us has broken the law."

"More or less," said the T'Kungo.

"Indeed," said 007.

I spoke with the Pilot in the control room, where he had hidden to be alone after our breakfast meeting.

"Pilot, do you have any theories?"

"Oh, dear me, no. Nothing like this has ever happened on one of my ships before, and I've been in space since ... well, since I was a cub. But ... surely you have suspects, Inspector? Some lead?"

"There is — no, Pilot, nothing I am sure of. But there is one concern you and I have, which I am sure of."

The Pilot leaned on his control panel and waited with huge eyes.

"We've got to get out of here. We can't wait for the rescue crew. Not with a murderer among us. Not when we don't know who ... It could be you. Or me. At least one of us is not what we seem."

"That's ... true," he got out after a moment.

"The murderer will have drawn the same conclusions. I assume you are the only other being capable of diagnosing and repairing the damage, or malfunction, or whatever. You are in danger."

He nodded. We left the control room together. I did not intend to let the murderer get at the Pilot without tipping his hand.

Sunset came. I ate sitting beside him. The moss and I found him easy pickings at cards. When we were ready to retire, we set our best guard — a mercenary robot-soldier who came cheap — at the lock. Some chance remark by 007 made me pause at the lock. When I turned back, the Pilot had entered and the lock's outer door was closed.

I was already off holiday status in my mind, and so panicked at once. Nevertheless, it took suspiciously long to get the door open. We could find no sign of tampering, when we examined the lock later. But now I ran and 007 undulated into the ship.

We found, as we passed the passenger cabins, no sign of anyone awake. And we did not find the Pilot either, until 007 came upon his corpse by the cargo hold.

Victim showed no sign of surprise or struggle. Cause of death, very heavy blow to the back of the head. Likely weapon: heavy wrench found by body. No signs of any imprinting on wrench, except from mechanic.

The passengers all claimed to have been asleep in their rooms. No one had heard anything suspicious. I risked life and limb for sake of thoroughness, and went out to look for the Dorvil.

The Dorvil was hanging from a different tree. And awake. No, it replied without anger, nothing seen or heard.

I called them all out into the clearing, and illuminated it with full power from the ship's lights.

"Gentlebeings, there is a murderer among us, who has now struck twice. I have reasons for believing the murderer does not want us to leave this planet. I request your co-operation. I would like to interview each of you privately, while the others remain here in the clearing, guarding each other. I am assuming there is at least one of you who is *not* the murderer." Let them think about that!

I took the soldier robot with me because I wanted a quick victory. I studied programming in the Academy; if the robot was involved, I could find out, and if not, I could use the Police Override to gain an ally.

Nothing on his memory spools. I closed down his "for hire" option and sent him back to watch the rest.

I casually interrogated the life insurance salesman in his tank, which, as far as I knew, had not left the common room. Then I checked what he told me against the ship's library resources. The capabilities of his species did not include dry-land excursions or swinging wrenches.

Too bad.

So I called in the two from Felch. I didn't bother with any formal interrogation, just slapped truth rays on their necks as they came in, and let them babble. No need to bend one's mind out of shape trying to get past ethnic differences, when you're looking for a liar anyway.

And Felch breeds some really odd minds. So the newlyweds just sat and babbled happily about the glories of erotic dismemberment. Occasionally, I tossed them a question.

Why didn't the T'Kungo like them? (Not that she liked anybody.)

They became quite excited about how, in the blackout in the common room on our second day out, one of them had mistaken the T'Kungo's tail for an appendage of the other.

Oho. T'Kungo are touchy, especially when young.

Could they account for their whereabouts during either murder?

Oh, indeed, both could vouch for the other. And it had all been very . . . exciting.

Why couldn't I get more out of them on location or how they felt about the two victims? Their inhibitions? Mine? Or . . .?

They were on the list, then. Killing for kicks. Working as a team to manage surprise and concealment.

I sent them back out.

And called in the T'Kungo.

The T'Kungo are not noted in law-enforcement circles for being pleasant interviewees. This one was no exception.

They are bigoted. This one wasted no time in telling me she knew the murderer must be either the couple from Felch or the Dorvil. Why? Because they had all three of them wilfully offended her. Creatures like that were capable of anything.

She also felt the murderer should be apprehended in order to give him an award, because the T'Kungo didn't like the Pilot or the mechanic either.

Did she have any reason for wishing our voyage interrupted? Why did I want to know? I apologized. One apologizes a lot with this species. I pointed out the murderer didn't seem to take kindly to efforts to get us under way. She claimed surprise. Hadn't heard, she said.

I got rid of her, sat back and scratched my carapace. That time, again? Oh, well.

The T'Kungo bustled back in with the air of a being who had just accomplished someone else's task by dint of humanitarianism and brilliance. Come and look at the life insurance salesman's area of the common room, she ordered.

I did.

From the cargo hold, past the tank, were faint tracks in the floor. Something had wriggled or crept there. A lot. The tracks were very dim indeed, and wet.

I asked the T'Kungo what she thought. I was going to hear anyway.

She allowed as how I was the detective, but the incriminating nature of this decisive clue should speak for itself. Doubtless some sort of conspiracy.

I started to tell her I was virtually certain there could be no interspecies conspiracy afoot. The passenger manifests made it clear none of the races aboard had seen each other for quite a time. But a wave of dizziness broke off my explanation.

Molt time again. Set off, no doubt, by working when I was supposed to be on vacation. I called the survivors together and issued instructions: Everybody stays in the common room tonight. It had its own lavatories, food dispensers. No leaving, for any reason. They were cosmopolitan enough to realize I was in no mood to argue when I explained my condition and tottered off to my cabin.

I certainly didn't have the heart to protest when 007 picked up the cards and followed me. Molting is not really a time to be alone.

We sweated (figuratively, in his case) the night out together.

"So how's the shoe business?" I managed to ask at one point.

"The what?" he thought back absently. He was still winning, even though he had, chivalrously, declined to play for money, given my condition.

I said it again.

"But what ... oh. Why, um, fine. Fine."

Some time — fever clouds my sense of hours — later I opined he didn't seem like the salesman type. He said he took that as a compliment. Never did like salesmen, I think he said.

I thought, the next morning, he had told me something else,

about undercover work and memory, but I think now that was a dream. Well past the middle of the night I tottered to the common room, made certain everybody was dormant (or faking), and went back to try to get some sleep. In the morning I'd have to talk to the insurance salesman and the Dorvil.

I must have succeeded in sleeping, though in the morning my nerves felt like finely stretched wires. Molting was over, anyway.

And I didn't have to talk to the Dorvil. It was found dead in the lavatory.

This time I looked for those funny tracks. They were there. New, though, or old? Dry, but left by something damp. No way to tell how old.

"Gentlebeings, I must have your fullest co-operation, which I am sure will be forthcoming, even if only out of self-interest. I mean — 'graveyard humor' — I don't want to be able to make an arrest when there's only two of us left, me and the murderer. Ah, hah."

"Or three," said the T'Kungo.

"Or only one," said 007. "How do we know you're a policeman? At least one of us is not what we seem."

So I went through the presentation of credentials to him while the others were reporting what they had seen and heard the night before. The Dorvil had retired last. Before doing so, it had made its customary prayer for day's end: "Supreme Being, bless all its conjugate-mates, forgive it its larval retentiveness, speed and safety to this journey . . ."

One of the Felch said the Dorvil had not seemed to be anywhere near the lavatories.

All the survivors said no one had stirred after the Dorvil became silent. There were only the usual sounds of the ship running on standby mode. No, none could say for sure there had been no sound of stealthy movement.

I told them all to stay where they were, and went back to my cabin. I settled onto the unpadded perch and tried to think. My legs felt like stale noodles, my antennae like used pipe-cleaners. The only person left who didn't seem worried was 007. Why? He had no evident means of self-defence.

The T'Kungo didn't like the Dorvil. Or anybody. But was she

smart enough to cover over her race's habitual means of slaying, which involves pulling all the big bits off and stamping on the remains?

For that matter, did they teach T'Kungo or Felchians to cover their tracks and actions this well? Maybe the whole thing was an exercise in actuarial tidying. But the salesman was not mobile. For somebody confined to his tank he seemed to have an affinity for making tracks.

"That's right," offered 007, "you're running out of suspects."

"I didn't say anything."

The moss said nothing more. Nobody likes a smart aleck, especially when they're a vegetable.

I gathered what was left of us in the common room. The Felch were unhappy with my latest strategy: Lock everybody in their self-contained staterooms, separately, and wait the days left for a rescue team to get here. The shorter one, who had only three arms now, shrieked incoherently about the unbearable anguish of lovers parted, added several, um, prayers? about wanting to go home, go home *now*, and ran off.

The taller Felch, the moss, and I separated to search for it. I was alone when I found it by the cargo hold hatch, quite unerotically and thoroughly dead. The others were nowhere in sight when a zzap*blam*-zzap took me back to the common room at a scuttle.

"What was *that*?" I threw into the common room ahead of me. Then I stopped, held by a scene that was obviously charged with meaning, but not for me.

There was a tentacle-thick hole in the door to the bridge, still smoking at the edges, obviously the result of a ray blast from the aft corridor. The surviving Felch was cowering in the opposite corner. The moss was sitting serenely, for what that was worth, beside the insurance salesman's tank.

Which had another equally fresh hole right through it.

I admit it was a mistake to tell the Felch what I had found aft. I suppose I was still a little muddled by the molting. Already in shock, the Felch went off the deep end — for a normal creature — and continued shrieking, now hacking off small bits of itself and hurling them about the common room.

The only decent thing to do was to stun it with my police issue ray thrower. I put the snoring creature in one of the common room's waste receptacles and sat on it.

There was a little gray creature at the bottom of the tank. He had a neat hole through him, too, and so was in no state to supply the answers I had to have.

"I think you and I had better talk," I suggested to 007, and made sure he noticed the gun.

"I don't have to tell you anything," 007 said calmly. "You're the policeman, *you* solve it. We all have our jobs to do."

Odd. Private murderers are usually only too ready to help — either hoping to mislead, or angling for better treatment if caught. Was this some kind of really sloppy assassination plot? Politics, fanatical causes — I've seen many a sensible creature dummy up when completing a suicide mission.

"Close," he said, "but not close enough. And not the answer you want, anyway. I could —"

What he *could* be, or do, in this crazy situation, I didn't want to hear. So I ripped him off the floor, wadded him up, and stuffed him into a wine bottle from the table. All I needed was a little time. Corked, he'd keep.

I went up to the bridge.

A place where murder's been done is never cozy. Neither is an alien planet. On duty or off, you couldn't pay me to face both together alone. But a creature's gotta do what he's gotta do.

The hole through the door didn't stop there. A matching hole pierced the instrument panel, right beside the homing beacon transmitter that was supposed to bring the rescue team to our little playground. Well, I thought, that's lucky, anyway.

"Computer?" It ought to be still working. 007 said he'd used it, and had no reason to lie about *that*. "Computer?"

"Yeth?" Great — the audio was going.

"Emergency computations, starting now. Priority law enforcement override 096 —"

"No."

"What?"

Nothing more. That should have been a clue, but, like I said, I wasn't thinking too clearly. So I did it manually from the hard-copy ship's log, and right away got, as they say in the Nest, enlighten-ment which casts shadows.

My friend 007 was operating on a commercial clearance as a shoe salesman, all right, but it was a clearance five standard years out of date. A desk stint at work turned out to be useful after all. He couldn't be what he said he was. Gotcha, I thought.

Neither was the insurance salesman genuine. He was supposed to be green, with little fins, according to his passport.

So? Shiploads of guilt, sure, but no explanation. Deep shadows indeed.

As I wandered around the ship, sick with . . . well, to be honest, sick with a weird mixture of fear and professional embarrassment, I found another ray thrower at the end of the aft corridor by the cargo hold. Covered with slime. Then I really did feel embarrassed. What do they teach you first in detective training?

Had to move delicately, though. First I went and uncorked 007. Confirm the least deadly hypothesis first. The bottle had not been empty. As he struggled to sort himself out, I tried to relax. If I was right, 007 was no danger to me.

"Very poor bouquet," I began, "but in all, a pretentious little moss. And somebody's spy, right?"

"'Sright. Do no harm to let you in onna mission now . . . annif you blab, we got ways."

"Like miniature ray-thrower components sewn into the roots, eh? But why? And what about the others?"

"Why? Don't you know what that . . . monster . . . did? Can't you guess who he was?"

No, I told him, I didn't. It's a big universe, with too many mon-sters in it to keep track of. That's why there are bureaucrats.

The story came out, rambling, full of invective, but complete in the end. The victim of 007 was indeed a life insurance agent, given a hasty cover identity by his company. My friend claimed to be an agent of "MI5" — Moss Intelligence. I don't know what the "5" is for. Sent to close his case once and for all on the express orders of the home government.

The Prime Minister and Royal Family on 007's home planet, all carefully insured, had outlived their usual expectancy, and been "tidied up" for statistics' sake by our friend in the tank.

I was oddly pleased. Out of my jurisdiction. Politics. When the weed-killer starts flying, plain cops just get out of the way. But what about the others?

"Hoped you realized. Assumed you could hear what I hear. Slightly telepathic, you know? Surface thoughts, so on . . . somebody's still there. Still wants to kill us."

Well, that was no surprise. And no worry any more.

"You know, don't you," I asked, speaking very loudly and carefully, "the rescue team will be along in a few days, no matter what happens. And they will see what *has* happened. And the freighter run will be completed, completed even if we're all dead?"

He started to contradict me, picked up one of those surface thoughts, and loudly agreed. Then we waited. In a moment or two there was a loud click, and a blurry voice announced it wanted to make a complete confession, and it threw itself on the mercy of the agents of justice, and lots more about the furies of new loved threatened with parting.

Eventually, we had to turn the ship off so it, and we, could have a rest.

Cherchez la femme, they always say. Sure, I should have twigged to it right away, when the ship wouldn't let us know the nature of the malfunction. These pseudo-intelligent models go bonkers when they malfunction, and this one must have missed an inspection check or so. When the microchips were down, it conceived a blazing passion for the only creatures on hand that were not its masters.

Which were not unaware.

Which were slithering around in the hold, ready to be released.

Which the ship knew were on their way to unloading and eternal parting, thanks to some faceless but cruel fast-food chef.

Which the ship was ready to kill for — just to stay with them.

Like I say, I should have got it sooner. But then, I was on holiday.

The ship, of course, could be fixed, and then wouldn't even regret its deeds. 007 would be off to zap somebody else, on orders. And I would get back to work.

There was only one thing that bothered me. A crime I knew had been committed, but could do nothing about.

That dirty telepathic plant had cheated me out of all my loose cash.

11

Silver Donald Cameron

A FIEND IN THE FORTRESS

(A RADIO PLAY)

CAST:

ZWICKER	MRS. MACLEOD
MRS. CROUSE	OZZIE
MORGAN	RUDGE

SOUND   A dozen people walking casually over pavingstones in the Fortress of Louisbourg.

Dr. Robert Morgan   (*Conversationally*) Oh, I enjoy it, Dr. Crouse, I really do — I mean, getting all dressed up in eighteenth-century costume and leading a candlelight tour is just a lot of fun. That's what the Fortress of Louisbourg really is, you know; it's a huge toy for people like me.

Crouse   Extraordinary place. Imagine reconstructing an entire walled city from the French Empire away down here in Cape Breton. How much did you say it had cost the federal government, this toy of yours?

Morgan   (*Almost laughing*) About twenty-five million. I *love* the feeling of it at night, incidentally it's terribly eerie, isn't it, with this whole city silent all around you and only a candle here and there? Watch out!

SOUND   A splash of water on the pavement.

Crouse   Good Heavens, what was that?

Morgan   Someone emptying a chamberpot. (*Louder, to the whole tour group*) Watch out, now, don't step in that. Someone's emptied a chamberpot. (*To Crouse*) It's only water, but why spoil the illusion, eh?

Crouse   An exceedingly elaborate work of theatre. Mother? All right?

Mrs. Crouse   Yes, Edwin, I'm doing fine.

Crouse   Well, don't over-exert yourself, now; we can go whenever you feel fatigued.

Mrs. Crouse   No, no, I'm enjoying this very much. Don't fuss! How many people do you have acting out these roles, Dr. Morgan?

Morgan   I'm not sure exactly, but it's around a hundred and sixty.

Mrs. Crouse   That many! And how many of those would be former coal miners?

Morgan   Oh, I doubt that any of them are, Mrs. Crouse. When the reconstruction began, quite a few miners came to work on it, but they were really involved in the excavating and construction part of it. There aren't even many of them left on that side now; most of them have learned new trades and gone off to work at them elsewhere, as stone masons, or carpenters, or whatever.

Mrs. Crouse   But the Fortress must still be quite an important industry?

Morgan   Oh, it certainly is — ah, excuse me, we're at our next stop. (*To the tour group*) Just come through this little door, now, and gather inside the building. This way, this way — right, everyone in? Good.

This is the Magazin de Rodrigue, a kind of large warehouse owned by the merchant Michel Rodrigue. As I've said before, you must remember that Louisbourg was not like New France at all: here we had an economy based on fishing and international trade, not on agriculture and fur. Many of the fishermen worked for entrepreneurs who were also merchants, and Michel Rodrigue was one of these. He was deeply involved in the triangular trade route between Louisbourg, the West Indies, and France itself; he also owned a number of *chaloupes*, fishing boats, which he manned with hired *pêcheurs*, fishermen who might spend the fishing season in Cape Breton and the winters at home in France.

Here we see a representation of an event that occurred in this building in 1741. You see the fishermen, mending Rodrigue's sails. The foreman, Joannis Detcheverry, has occasion to go somewhere else, and he leaves them at work. Here he goes — make way for him, please, thank you — and that's the last time anyone sees Detcheverry alive.

SOUND   A bloodcurdling scream, bubbling into silence. Gasps and sounds of alarm from the tourists.

A Man's Voice   (*Laughing*) Now *that's* what I call realistic!
A Woman's Voice   That *is* part of the tour isn't it, Dr. Morgan?
Morgan   (*Uncertainly lecturing on*) — Er, yes — yes, of course. The foreman's body was found in the morning with its throat cut from ear to ear. The murder was never solved.
Mrs. Crouse   (*Whisper*) How many were in this party at the start, Edwin?
Crouse   Thirteen, Mother.
Mrs. Crouse   I wonder about that scream, dear.
Crouse   Well, there are only twelve of us now.

MUSIC   The Zwicker Theme. Fade to:

Mrs. Crouse   (*Back in the motel*) Edwin, I just knew it! Even if a corpse falls out of our motel closet, you said, I won't investigate. This is Professor Crouse's vacation with his mother, and I'm not going to change my identity under any circumstances whatever. And now see what happens: our third day away from home and we have a fine, gory corpse, and you're about to become Arnold Zwicker. Really, Edwin, it's too much. Why can't you just let the police handle this?
Crouse/Zwicker   (*With amusement*) Two good reasons, Mother.
Mrs. Crouse   Which are?
Zwicker   One, Dr. Morgan is calling Halifax to ask his friend, the celebrated detective, Arnold Zwicker, to help deal with this unpleasantness quickly and quietly, so it won't hurt the Fortress at the height of the tourist season. Two, the sooner it's solved, the sooner

Dr. Crouse and his mother can get on with their vacation. We won't be allowed to leave for days, you know, while the Mounties go blundering about looking for the obvious.

Mrs. Crouse Where did you get your arrogance? How can you be so sure the Mounties won't solve it?

Zwicker This murderer is a man of imagination. Now the Mounties have many admirable qualities, and piles of money and manpower, but one thing they don't have in the whole force put together is enough imagination to make up one single junior advertising copywriter.

SOUND   Phone rings.

Zwicker That's Diana, I imagine. (*In Crouse's voice*) Hello? Hello? Yes, this is Dr. Crouse. (*In Zwicker's voice*) *Bon jour, ma belle.* Well, Mrs. Crouse was just saying much the same thing. Where Edwin goes, can death be far behind?

Mrs. Crouse (*In background*) — Well, *really*!

Zwicker (*Continuing*) — Yes, Morgan said he'd be calling. Just tell him Zwicker has dropped everything and will be in Louisbourg faster than he thinks possible.

(*Pause*) Oh, a delightful holiday. Something for everyone, even poor forgotten Zwicker. Sad for one American tourist, though. Mmm? His name was George MacLeod, a retired businessman from Beverley, Massachussets, travelling with his wife. First time they'd ever been to Nova Scotia.

(*Pauses briefly*) Well, that's a puzzle, isn't it? If one assumes he wasn't killed entirely at random, why *was* he killed, a total stranger? Of course, maybe he wasn't quite a total stranger — or maybe someone followed him here from the States.

(*Pause*) The Horsemen won't like it, they never do, but if Bob Morgan tells them Zwicker is here at his request and that of the museum staff, they'll make room. (*Pause*) Good, and I'll call you in a day or two, maybe sooner. *Bon, mon morceau de peau bien aimé.* Be well.

Mrs. Crouse Why *was* he killed, do you think?

Zwicker Mrs. Crouse, you're doing it yourself. One shouldn't even speculate until at least some scattered facts have announced themselves.

Mrs. Crouse And where do you expect to find those facts?

Zwicker   The widow of the late George MacLeod has a few, I expect.

MUSIC   Bright, tense — The cat is on the prowl.

Mrs. MacLeod   (*A Massachusetts accent*) I don't think he had many enemies or many friends, Mistah Zwickah. We led a very quiet, private life. Of course he was over fifty when I married him, and he never did say very much about his early life.

Zwicker   No? But he must have told you *something*, surely?

Mrs. MacLeod   I know he was born in Nova Scotia, it says so on his passport. He'd been in Beverley at least twenty years when I met him, though he had friendships going back that far. He must have been no more than thirty or so when he came to Beverley. He was in the American Army during the last war, so I guess he was a citizen then. You have to be a citizen to be in the army, don't you?

Zwicker   You don't *have* to, but generally you are.

Mrs. Crouse   Whatever he did in the army, it had to do with producing guns. That's how he got into the weapons business aftah the wah.

Zwicker   (*Perking up*) He was in the weapons business, was he?

Mrs. Crouse   Yes, they did most of theah business with the government. They made small ahms, I believe.

Zwicker   That bears thinking about. Was he married before?

Mrs. MacLeod   If he was, I nevah knew it. He didn't trust people easily, but I think he got lonely as he got oldah.

Zwicker   What do you think he was hiding?

Mrs. MacLeod   Ah don't know if he *was* hiding anything. He might have been. (*Her voice quavers*) He — he wasn't a happy man. He used to say that these last twenty yeahs — since we were married — gave him the — the only happiness he evah had . . .

Zwicker   Mrs. MacLeod, I really am sorry to be putting you through all this.

Mrs. MacLeod   That's all right, that's youah job. But it was so sudden, I still can't believe that — that he's gone.

Zwicker   Of course.

Mrs. MacLeod   (*With sudden force*) Ah had a funny feeling evah since we got to Cape Breton Ahland! He was *different* heah.

Zwicker   Different?

Mrs. MacLeod   He was worried, he was irritable. Ah thought perhaps he came from heah in the first place, but he just snapped when Ah asked him. He said *No! Ah was nevah heah in my life!* But he seemed to know his way around, and when we'd see things Ah didn't know, he seemed to know them already, half the tahm.

Zwicker   What sort of thing?

Mrs. MacLeod   Oh, Ah don't know — he didn't seem surprahsed that the Bra doah Lakes were salt watah, or that they mined coal and made steel heah for yeahs and yeahs. He knew abaht how fah it was from Sydney to Louisbourg without looking at a map. We just came on the spur of the moment. But it all seemed to be *familiah* to him.

Zwicker   What about people? Did he meet anyone here that seemed familiar? Or threatening?

Mrs. MacLeod   Now theah's a funny thing. That happened twice. One man we met in the tavern right here in Louisbourg made George very nervous.

Zwicker   What sort of a man?

Mrs. MacLeod   Well, *Ah* didn't see what was fraghtening abaht him, Ah must admit. He was just a shoht, stocky man in a workshirt and olive pants and workboots.

Zwicker   How old?

Mrs. MacLeod   Oh, possibly fifty-five or sixty. He was going gray, and balding a little. Theah was no place to sit, and he was alone at a table, so we asked if we mahgt join him. We introduced ouahselves, and he said, George MacLeod? There was a George MacLeod in — Ah don't know, one of the towns neah-by — yeahs and yeahs ago, you wouldn't be that fellow? George said No, he had nevah been to Cape Breton Ahland befoah. But the othah fellah kept aftah him abaht it, and George became quite abrupt with him — Ah thought he was anxious, foah some reason.

Zwicker   And then you left?

Mrs. MacLeod   No, the othah man just changed, very quickly, and he was *absolutely* chahming aftah that.

Zwicker   You said there were two occasions?

Mrs. MacLeod   In Sydney, at the motel, when we were checking in, a man came by and said, Hello, George, and George said Hello and introduced me, and then the other fellow went away again. George was very unfriendly towards him.

Zwicker   Who was he?

Mrs. MacLeod   His name was Ranger or Granger, something like that. George just said he was someone he'd known in business. He didn't seem to know him very well, but Ah think Ah saw him befoah, in Boston, and Ah do believe he was at a restaurant in Montreal.

Zwicker   On this trip?

Mrs. MacLeod   Yes. Ah thought he maght have been following us. George told me Ah was being silly, but he didn't seem very certain ...

MUSIC   Deep thought is going on.

Zwicker   (*Sorting it out loud*) How well do you know the museum workers, Bob?

Morgan   Well, I know most of them — but you see the problem, Arnold, there are probably a dozen men working here who are between fifty-five and sixty, grizzled and balding and dressed like that.

Zwicker   Can you get me a list, and some biographical stuff on them? And photographs, if possible: Mrs. MacLeod might be able to identify that fellow in the tavern.

Morgan   I'll get what there is.

Zwicker   Let's go through it again. MacLeod's throat was cut right outside the Magazin de Rodrigue. Everyone known to be in the Fortress had a pass, and all but two of them have solid alibis. Of those two, one was a college girl who weighs about 100 pounds; she's not a very promising candidate. The other fellow turned up at the Park gate and signed out five minutes after the murder — he's possible, but not very likely. So the odds are it was someone who wasn't known to be in the Park.

Morgan   It wouldn't be hard to get in or out without being seen, so long as you kept away from the roads.

Zwicker   Yes, but remember it was foggy that night; there ought to have been some kind of a trail in the dew, but the Mounties didn't find one. No footprints along the shore, nothing like that.

Morgan   I thought you didn't have much use for the Mounties.

Zwicker   Well, they're good at *that* kind of thing. They should be, with the resources they've got.

Morgan   Of course he could have come by boat. He must have been pretty fit and energetic.

Zwicker   The Mounties are trying to find out now if anyone saw a boat in the general area. But don't hold your breath. A foggy night, a quiet boat — a rowboat or a canoe, or something like that — hardly a chance in a million he'd be seen.

Morgan   What about motive?

Zwicker   Not so far, anyway. But look, suppose we *do* look at motive. It's not much better than method. Either he was killed by someone local — in which case we haven't the faintest notion what the motive might be, because we know so little about MacLeod himself and his possible background around here — or he was killed by or for someone who knew him through his life and work in Massachusetts. That seems much more likely, but we'll have to do a massive research job to find out just who that someone might be.

Morgan   What about this Ranger or Granger?

Zwicker   My sources in Boston say there's a James Granger based in that area who works for an apparently legitimate consulting firm, but he's rumored to be an intelligence agent of some kind. His firm *has* done some work for MacLeod's company. The Mounties can do more with that kind of thing than I can; they're going to let me know what they find out.

Morgan   What will we do next, Arnold?

Zwicker   In the morning, I want you to show your pictures to Mrs. MacLeod; and I'm going to prowl around the harbor a little . . .

MUSIC   Up, Establish, Fade out behind.

Zwicker   (*Outdoors, Introducing himself*) Lovely morning!

Ozzie MacDonald   One of d' best.

Zwicker   Lovely spot you've got here. Last house along the shore before the Fortress, are you?

Ozzie   Yes, b'y, right out at d' end of t'ings. And a grand view of d' harbor.

Zwicker   You have a little punt yourself, I see.

Ozzie   Ah, just a little t'ing for jiggin' about d' harbor.

Zwicker   You wouldn't consider loaning it to me for an hour or so, would you?

Ozzie   I s'pose. Where were you wantin' to go?

Zwicker   Over to the Fortress and back. I want to see how long it takes.

Ozzie   Ah!

Zwicker   I'm investigating that murder the other night. If the killer came over by boat . . .
Ozzie   Right, right — you need t' know how long it would take him.
Zwicker   That's it . . . (*Fade to:*)

MUSIC   Stalking music. Establish, then fade to:

Inspector Rudge   (*In motel room*) Well, Zwicker, I have to thank you. This time you *were* some help to us.
Zwicker   How pleasant.
Rudge   Granger's our man. The Americans will probably refuse to have him extradited, mind you, but at least we can close the file. This MacLeod character was no retired tourist; he'd been in Montreal setting up a deal to sell a new laser-sighted automatic rifle to — well, to a country that shouldn't have it.
Zwicker   I noticed he had the unlisted number of a Cuban diplomat in his briefcase.
Rudge   (*Somewhat disconcerted*) You knew that, did you?
Zwicker   Yes, but I concluded there was probably less in that than met the eye.
Rudge   Well, Granger stopped him, anyway.
Zwicker   And you can't touch Granger.
Rudge   Well, I don't know that for a fact, Zwicker, but you can guess the odds as well as I can'. And, by the way, all this is naturally confidential.
Zwicker   (*Ironically*) "Naturally." They must love us in Washington: we let them stage hunting trips at their pleasure, and we're *very* discreet.
Rudge   Look, we appreciate your help, Zwicker. But the case is *closed*.

SOUND   Knock on the door.

Zwicker   Come in!
Morgan   (*Entering*) Oh, hello, Inspector. I'm not intruding?
Zwicker   Not at all, Bob.
Morgan   I showed those pictures to Mrs. MacLeod, and she found three that might have been that man in the tavern.
Rudge   You don't need to worry about that any more, Dr. Morgan. It's all over: we've got our man.

Morgan　Who, Granger?

Rudge　Confidentially, yes. Zwicker will tell you about it. I'm off,
Zwicker.　Thanks again.

Zwicker　You don't mind if I poke around a bit more, do you,
Inspector? Discreetly, of course.

Rudge　It's entirely up to yourself. But there's nothing more to find.
Goodbye, Doctor.

Morgan　Goodbye, Inspector.

Zwicker　Thanks for coming by.

Rudge　My pleasure, I assure you.

SOUND　Door opens and closes.

Morgan　You're not satisfied, Arnold?

Zwicker　Not really. Granger may very well have been assigned to
kill MacLeod, but that doesn't prove he actually did it.

Morgan　What makes you doubt it?

Zwicker　The method again. Look at it: Granger checks in here at
5:15 — that's not sure, but someone very like him did check in at
that time, and we know he was in Sydney earlier in the day. By 10:00
that night he's contrived a way to get out to the Fortress, do
MacLeod in, get back, and nobody the wiser. That's superhuman
efficiency, even for a Yankee. Then he hangs around overnight, and
coolly boards a plane for Boston. Why do it at the Fortress, with all
those people around? Why stick around — why not catch the late
flight for Montreal, rent a car, and be back inside the States that
same night?

Morgan　But those things could be explained. Why arouse suspicion by a sudden departure, for instance?

Zwicker　Any one of them could be explained, but in total I don't
know. Besides that, I've got something suggestive here.

Morgan　It looks like a button from a pair of coveralls.

Zwicker　That's what it looks like to me, too. I found it in a heap of
ashes. Now why would a man burn a set of coveralls?

Morgan　Because they were worn out.

Zwicker　Possibly. But people don't usually *burn* clothing, and a
man who uses coveralls usually needs wiping cloths and that sort of
thing. But someone wanted to *destroy* these coveralls.

Morgan　Where did you find the ashes?

Zwicker   In Ozzie MacDonald's yard. You know Ozzie, the fellow whose punt I borrowed —
Morgan   Yes, yes.
Zwicker   I wonder if he was the man they met in the tavern. I want to try a little experiment, Bob, and I need your help. Now here's what I have in mind ... (*Fade to:*)

MUSIC   More intense, more insistent (Crossfade to:)
SOUND   Two people walking on paving stones.

Morgan   He's working on The Cassagnolles house, down at the end of the quay. I'll point him out to you —
Mrs. MacLeod   And Ah'm supposed to shout out, *That's him! That's the man!* or something like that — and that's all?
Morgan   The next move is up to him, you see?
Mrs. MacLeod   Ah suppose so.
Morgan   This was rather a low-life part of Louisbourg in the old days — little taverns catering to the fishermen and the sailors and what-not. The end of the quay here was known at the Place du Port, the Fish Market, that's what the English called it — ah, now here's the Cassagnolles house. The workmen are just finishing the timbered structure, you see, and the gaps will be filled with stones and rubble, that kind of building is called *charpent* — (*In a low voice*) That's him up there in the green doeskin shirt, wait till we get a bit closer now. (*Normal tones, guiding his touring companion*) You know, it's almost surprising, with all this reproduction going on, to realize that some parts of the city are actually original — these paving stones, for instance were never really disturbed, and the French walked on them 200 years ago and more —
Mrs. MacLeod   (*Screeches*) That's him! That's the man I meant! That's him! Stop him! Dr. Morgan, that really is the man!
Morgan   Man? What man? Ozzie, come back here! What's got into you? (*Fade down Morgan's last words and fade in running footsteps. We've moved to Ozzie's position*).
Ozzie   Oh no! Oh no, you don't! *Ahhh — oooff!*

SOUND   He has run headlong into Zwicker.

Zwicker   Stop a minute, Ozzie, I think we need another chat.

MUSIC   Strong, bright, triumphant. Fade to:

Zwicker   Did you ever know a man named Granger?
Ozzie   Granger?
Morgan   You can't protect him, Ozzie, you'd best tell the truth.
Ozzie   I'll tell you de trut', but not wit' his wife here.
Zwicker   Mrs. MacLeod, perhaps it would be best if you —
Mrs. MacLeod   No, I want to know —
Ozzie   Ma'am, I got nutten against ye, I ain't saying a word wit' ye here.
Morgan   Arnold, perhaps I should take her —
Zwicker   Yes, I think so. I'll see you later, Mrs. MacLeod.

SOUND   A door opens and closes.

Ozzie   How did you get onto me, anyway?
Zwicker   Process of elimination. The murderer began to look like a middle-aged working man who had a good knowledge of the Fortress and easy access to a boat. You fit. Then I found this burned button in your yard — you had blood on your coveralls, that's why you burned them, right?
Ozzie   T'at's right.
Zwicker   So I went down to talk to you three or four times about the murder. I borrowed your boat to check the timing. You must have known I had figured out a good deal about it. I was deliberately trying to spook you. I guess I did.

SOUND   Door opens and closes.

Morgan   Did what?
Zwicker   Spooked him into running away like that.
Ozzie   Well, you may depend I was spooked, all right.
Morgan   What I want to know is why a fellow like you would kill a complete stranger.
Ozzie   T'at's a long story, Dr. Morgan. He wasn't no stranger though. (*Pause*) I hope she don't have to know it all.
Zwicker   Why don't you tell us, Ozzie?
Ozzie   She's a nice woman, you know; I don't t'ink dere's any reason to say what kind of a bastard she was married to, right to her face.

Zwicker   What kind of a bastard was he?

Ozzie   (*Bitterly*) He was a savage beast, t'at feller! All dose bastards was.

Zwicker   What men were those?

Ozzie   Company p'lice. T'at's a long time ago, now.

Zwicker   What happened?

Ozzie   Back in d' Twenties, d' company here was BESCO.

Morgan   British Empire Steel and Coal.

Ozzie   Right, b'y. Now you want to talk about some mangy, rotten company, BESCO was it. Starve d' miners, starve d' steelworkers — in dem days, d' steelworkers worked 11 hours on d' day shift an 13 on d' night shift, and shift change, every two weeks, dey'd work 24 hours straight t'rough. No overtime, b'y, and when things got slack they'd cut the wages by half quick's you'd blink an eye. Nothin' you could do, the unions wasn't strong like today.

Zwicker   I've heard a bit about it.

Ozzie   Oh, dey were bad times. Me old dad worked in d' mines, and I've seen the day he'd come home with $8.00 in his pay packet, an' when he'd paid for his coal, an d' company house, an d' grub at d' company store, he'd wind up owing d' company money! An den ye'd go on strike, why dey t'ought nothin' of sendin in the army, troopers on horseback, machine guns an' barbed wire. But d' worst of dem was d' company p'lice. You want to see a blackhearted son of a bitch dat'd slit his grandmudder's t'roat for a candy bar, d' BESCO bull is your man.

Zwicker   And George MacLeod was one of them.

Ozzie   Yes, b'y.

Morgan   But that was fifty years ago.

Ozzie   Dare's t'ings you don't forget. I ain't sorry for slittin' his t'roat, b'y, not me. Twas fifty year overdue, that's all.

Zwicker   What did he do?

Ozzie   (*With low intensity, not really speaking so much to Zwicker as to God*) We was just after goin' to Mass, there was dozens of people in d' street. I was eight year old. Me mom was wit' me, and me da, and me brudder. Me mom was in d' family way, too. Dere was a strike on: d' mines had been shut down for weeks. Beautiful Sunday afternoon, d' finest kind of a day. Me da was tellin' jokes, an' me mom looked like a girl, she was that happy. Den all of a sudden dey went to screamin' and shoutin' down d' street, and people run- nin' everywhere — and I couldn't see what was d' matter, bein' small an' everyt'ing — and den I got knocked down on d' road wit' all the pushin' and shovin', and I looked up an I seen d' horses. Oh man, I dreams about dem horses by times and I wakes up screamin. Big black horses wit' deir eyes rollin' an' deir heads plug- ging, and deir hoofs stabbin' an' dancin' on d' roadway — Jasus, b'y! An' d' p'lice in deir uniforms wit d' long clubs, swinging at everyone dey could reach. An one horse was comin' right for me, goin' to trample me down, an' me mom t'rew herself down on top o' me. D'horse started to swerve, and d' rider pulled him over and I could see his face — to me dyin day I'll remember t'at face, red an' snarlin and d' eyes rollin' like d' horses, like a wild animal — an under d' chin a white scar in d' shape of a seven. He swung d' club and hit me mom a crack on d' head dat sounded like he'd hit a pumpkin, an' she just went all soft on top o' me, an' me da jumped at him, an' he screamed, I'll kill ye, George MacLeod, I'll kill ye! But d' p'liceman just hit him a crack in d' face that knocked him down and away he went wit' his horse and his club — murder, b'y, it was plain murder.

Morgan (*Incredulous, shaken*) The same George MacLeod?

Ozzie (*With power*) Yes, b'y! D' self-same bastard!

Zwicker How did you know?

Ozzie D' coal marks in his skin, and d' scar like a seven.

Zwicker Ahhh!

Ozzie We never seen him again after dat day. Me da was hurt pret- ty bad, but he got better. But me mudder died t'ree days later, and so did d' baby, dat would have been me only sister. An' George MacLeod, nobody ever seen him in Cape Breton ever again.

Zwicker Until last week, at the tavern.

Ozzie Right, b'y. Him and his wife, dere, dey come into d' tavern an found it full, so dey asked if dey could sit wit' me. Well, I said, sure; I'm Ozzie MacDonald, and he said, I'm George MacLeod. An' right away I heard me old da screamin, *I'll kill ye, George MacLeod, I'll kill ye!* But o' course, dere's no end o' George MacLeods in d' world I'm sure, it didn't mean not'in.

Morgan But then you saw the scar.

Ozzie Not right away I didn't. But I did see d' coal scars, you know, d' marks a miner gets into every little cut in his skin where d' coal dust just gets in dere and stays, like a tattoo. So I started askin where did he come from, and what did he do for a livin, t'ings like that, was he ever in Cape Breton before, did he ever go down a coal mine? Well, he said no. Well I knew he was lyin', see?

Morgan   But that wouldn't prove he was the same George MacLeod.

Ozzie   No, but dat's where d' scar comes in, see? I got him to look at d' ceiling, and sure enough, dere was d' scar in d' shape of a seven, right under his chin. It was faint, but it was dere.

Zwicker   So then you convinced them to go on the candlelight tour, and rowed across and cut his throat.

Ozzie   He shouldn't a screamed. I was a commando during d' war, ye know, I know how to do it silent. But he give a squirm when I wasn't expectin' it. Look here, Mr. Zwicker, if I coulda got away wit' it, I would. I knew when I did it I might get caught, though, and I was bound to do it anyways. I don't have no regrets whatsoever. You can take me to d' Mounties, I don't mind.

Zwicker   (*Slowly*) I don't know what that would accomplish.

Morgan   You're not suggesting that — what *are* you suggesting?

Zwicker   Well, Ozzie here isn't going to go and kill anybody else, and the Mounties are already satisfied with Granger — who isn't going to suffer any consequences, all the same. So who needs to send Ozzie to prison?

Morgan   (*As the idea comes clear to him*) I see!

Zwicker   The only person whose interests are served by convicting Ozzie is me — I could make Inspector Rudge look like a great booby, which he is. But I'm happy enough to forego that little pleasure.

Morgan   What about Mrs. MacLeod?

Zwicker   A trivial difficulty . . . (*Fade to:*)

MUSIC   Something perky and mischievous. Fade to:

Mrs. MacLeod   Mista Zwickah! They've arrested that man Granger!

Zwicker   So I hear. They have quite a good case against him, I gather.

Mrs. MacLeod   They won't tell me anything more. The Mounted Police say it has to do with national security.

Zwicker   It does, Mrs. MacLeod, it does. They've sworn me to secrecy too.

Mrs. MacLeod   But what about that man from the Fortress?

Zwicker   Ozzie MacDonald? I guess he was afraid he'd been an accidental accomplice. I gather he kept on drinking that night and he met Granger. Granger pumped him for information, and they got to talking about how you could murder someone during a candlelight tour. Ozzie told him exactly how it could be done — so you can imagine his shock next day when he found out it had *been* done just that way.

Mrs. MacLeod   And when Ah pointed him out —

Zwicker   — he thought somehow he was going to be held responsible.

Mrs. MacLeod   What a coincidence!

Zwicker   (*Gravely*) There have been quite a number of coincidences in this case . . . (*Fade to:*)

MUSIC   More mischievous music. Fade to:

Zwicker/Crouse   So you see how it ends, Mother. Ozzie MacDonald is innocent, James Granger is guilty, Inspector Rudge is triumphant, and Arnold Zwicker has failed.

Mrs. Crouse   Poor dear.

Zwicker/Crouse   And Edwin Crouse is relieved. He and his mother can get on with their vacation.

Mrs. Crouse   Well, that's something.

Zwicker/Crouse   And somebody, away up there in the sky, is vastly amused.

MUSIC   The Zwicker Theme.

12
Stan Rogal
DRESS REHEARSAL

THE room is square and windowless. White prevails: white ceramic floor, white plastic walls, white ceiling. Only the presence of fluorescent lighting allows for a faint blue glow to emanate from the otherwise pale and antiseptic setting.

A single door blemishes one white wall and opposite this, off-center, near the back corner of the room, a rectangular table is situated surrounded by ten figures, four on each side and one at either end. The conversation appears casual. There are no papers or pens to suggest a business meeting. Elbows rest on the pale arborite, hands support chins, stroke beards, or simply stir the air. An odd head occasionally turns and glances about the room. There is no semblance of order, no items which might indicate leadership, neither itinerary, nor special seat, nor gavel. Except for the table, ten chairs, and ten figures, the room is bare. To disturb the silence, the murmur of a fan and ten voices — calm, dim, textureless — voices as might be heard in any waiting room, mingling with the air, clinging to the ceiling, unable to generate enough substance to form a shadow.

When the door splinters, so the calm glass of the room shatters. Words, half-words, melt down the corners of mouths. Blood pumps, igniting cheeks and foreheads. Pores steam open. Flesh dissolves. Muscles, tendons tingle and jump spasmodically. Every head twists towards the door. All eyes report the entry of four men who place themselves strategically between the table and the open door. Revolvers rise, fix at eye-level; gloved fingers squeeze. Figures at the table collapse as breath escapes through tiny holes drilled in throats. Others attempt to flee but only succeed in allowing bullets to penetrate: temples, spines, chests, bellies. One figure covers his face with his arms. A bullet shatters his forearm, bone fragments explode into his cheeks and eyes. The next shot pierces his heart. Two others manage to overturn the table and use it as a shield, a battering ram, to attack, but bullets cut through and bluntly strike or else carve the soft wood into a barrage of deadly spears and arrows, felling the two in mid-charge, dropping them like inadequate bison. Another figure, wounded, takes advantage of the diversion, the slight attention paid to the charging table, to stumble towards the group huddled by the door, to raise his arms above his head, to remain standing long enough to plunge the sharpened end of a split wooden chair leg into the surprised chest of one assassin before the butt of a rifle efficiently crushes his skull and ends his death-dealing.

Of the four who entered, three are left to stand together and silently survey the bloody scene. One checks his watch, scribbles something in a notepad. A second gazes down at his dead comrade, grunts, then returns his attention to the group. The three face each other, shake their heads, slap shoulders and exit.

The room is square and windowless. White prevails: white ceramic floor, white plastic walls, white ceiling. Only the presence of fluorescent lighting allows for a faint blue glow to emanate from the otherwise pale and antiseptic setting.

A single door blemishes one white wall and opposite this, off-center, near the back corner of the room, a rectangular table is situated surrounded by ten figures, four on each side and one at either end. The conversation appears casual. There are no papers or pens to suggest a business meeting. Elbows rest on the pale arborite, hands support chins, stroke beards, or simply stir the air. An odd head occasionally turns and glances about the room. There is no semblance of order, no items which might indicate leadership, neither itinerary, nor special seat, nor gavel. Except for the table, ten chairs, and ten figures, the room is bare. To disturb the silence, the murmur of a fan and ten voices — calm, dim, textureless — voices as might be heard in any waiting room, mingling with the air, clinging to the ceiling, unable to generate enough substance to form a shadow.

When the door splinters, so the calm glass of the room shatters. Words, half-words, melt down the corners of mouths. Blood pumps, igniting cheeks and foreheads. Pores steam open. Flesh dissolves. Muscles, tendons tingle and jump spasmodically. Every head twists towards the door. All eyes report the entry of four men who place themselves strategically between the table and the open door. Revolvers rise, fix at eye-level; gloved fingers squeeze. Figures at the table collapse as breath escapes through tiny holes drilled in throats. Others are blown backward against the wall, their rib-cages torn apart. Streaks of red trace their descent on the white-plastic walls, their bodies blood-sliding to the floor. One mammoth figure refuses to fall under the hail of bullets, lunging at the attackers like a wounded mastodon, chest raging crimson, shoulder length blonde hair and beard drenched and dripping red. His arms form tusks aimed at the throat of one crouched gunman, the fingers pointed, the nails hard and sharp as carved ivory, his entire body and movement centering upon one action — impalement. Revolvers continue to fire into the now-dead beast, this giant who blindly rolls like a tidal wave towards a beach, the momentum of his massive frame still threatening to crush, drown, or suffocate the crouched marksman. They aim at his legs, whittle him down until he drops under the weight of his own body. Power-spent, he tumbles and rolls forward, a gentle wash, barely touching the foot of the gunman who has not budged except to fire into this ton of maddened flesh, now motionless, save for the blood — the blood foaming, bubbling from numberless holes, oozing thick as satin and covering him in a mantle of scarlet.

The four stand erect. Unmoving. No one speaks, merely scan the room, check watches, scribble a few marks in a notepad, then exit.

The room is square and windowless. White prevails: white ceramic floor, white plastic walls, white ceiling. Only the presence of fluorescent lighting allows for a faint blue glow to emanate from the otherwise pale and antiseptic setting.

A single door blemishes one wall and it hangs open, the wood split and shattered, as if forced by heavy boots. Four men enter the room. They wear white smocks and carry various pieces of equipment: pens, clipboards, camera, assorted measuring devices. The man who operates the camera snaps open the leather case and raises the lens to eye-level. He sets to work photographing the area, beginning with general shots of figures positioned nearest the table. Next, he divides the area visually into four sections, pans right to left, concentrating on details regarding figure posture and placement. He then enters each quadrant in turn, crouches over individual figures, isolates the various sections of the bodies, focussing separately on facial expressions, twists of necks, bends in arms, hands and fingers, curvature of torsos, crooks in legs and feet. Moving slowly, methodically through the grid, the camera's attention shifts, finally, to one fallen figure who had managed to separate from the others. The camera hovers over, circling like a fat vulture, curiously clicking back view, side view, front, then swoops backward in order to secure a perspective capable of illustrating the distance between the prostrate figure and the table.

As the camera busily clicks, a second man handles a measuring tape and calculates distances — table to chairs, chairs to figures, table to figures, figure to figure — soberly recording them on a lined form. At one point, he pauses, regards the massive figure pinned flat to the floor, looks back to the table, then to the figure, shakes his head, makes a mental calculation, scribbles a brief note and continues measuring.

A third man meticulously examines each body for bullet holes, totalling their number and recording them on a blue form. In his right hand he clutches the clip board and pen. In his left hand he holds a stiff, 1 1/2″ paint brush. He uses the brush to temporarily clear the impact areas of blood and debris, thus tending to eliminate the possibility of recording two holes resting side by side as a single wound or mistaking a wound formed by a wood splinter as a wound formed by a bullet. Having determined this, he flips the handle of the brush between his index and middle finger, transfers the clipboard from his right to his left hand, carefully avoids the contact of paper to blood, rests the board on his left knee and writes. The fourth man shadows the third, his part to mark the locations of the holes schematically onto a large yellow sheet of paper already containing the drawn outlines of ten figures. When these two men eventually reach the prodigal tenth figure, their efficient routine slumps. The tiny brush flutters like a confused butterfly above the body, unsure of its landing place. Pens are immobile; paper remains unblemished. The two men shrug and a half-hearted attempt is made to brush away some of the now-coagulating blood. The action is quickly abandoned though, and a notation is made by the third man which is, at best, a feeble approximation of the actual number of holes. The fourth man merely takes his pen and strokes a large 'X' through the outline.

Gathering near the door, each of the four men verifies the completeness of the others. The man with the camera points to the tenth drawn outline, points to the figure on the floor, then laughs as the third and fourth men pocket their pens and dismiss personal responsibility with an explanation of hands — upraised, waving, their fingers firing blame in every direction except upon themselves. They check their watches, then more laughter as the group turns, slaps shoulders, and exits.

The room is square and windowless. White prevails: white ceramic floor, white plastic walls, white ceiling. Only the presence of fluorescent lighting allows for a faint blue glow to emanate from the otherwise pale and antiseptic setting.

A single door blemishes one white wall and opposite this, off-center, near the back corner of the room, a rectangular table is situated surrounded by ten figures, four on each side and one at either end. The conversation appears casual. There are no papers or pens to suggest a business meeting. Elbows rest on the pale arborite, hands support chins, stroke beards or simply stir the air. An odd head occasionally turns and glances about the room. There is no semblance of order, no items which might indicate leadership, neither itinerary, nor special seat, no gavel. Except for the table, ten chairs, and ten figures, the room is bare. To disturb the silence, the murmur of a fan and ten voices — calm, dim, textureless — voices as might be heard in any waiting room, mingling with the air, clinging to the ceiling, unable to generate enough substance to form a shadow.

When the door splinters, so the calm glass of the room shatters. Words, half-words, melt down the corners of mouths. Blood pumps, igniting cheeks and foreheads. Pores steam open. Flesh dissolves. Muscles, tendons tingle and jump spasmodically. Every head twists towards the door. All eyes report the entry of four men who place themselves strategically between the table and the open door. Revolvers rise, fix at eye-level; gloved fingers squeeze. Figures at the table collapse as breath escapes through tiny holes drilled in throats.

Some attempt to rise but are snuffed half-way, their bodies blown backward, tipping out of their chairs. Others remain seated, slump awkwardly, a few sliding onto the floor. Two figures manage a step. One is hit and drops in a heap. The second falls to his knees, crawls a few feet, stretches his arms skyward in a sort of prayer and is snuffed out.

The four gunmen merge at the door, each checking his watch. A note is made on a small pad. A smile almost forms on the lips of one man but erases when a groan is heard from across the room. "Damn!" A revolver slips from its holster, aligns the sound and fires twice. There is a second of silence. "Damn it all!" The four again check their watches. A correction is made on the notepad. The men exit.

The room is square and windowless. White prevails: white ceramic floor, white plastic walls, white ceiling. Only the presence of fluorescent lighting allows for a faint blue glow to emanate from the otherwise pale and antiseptic setting.

A single door blemishes one wall and it hangs open, the wood split and shattered, as if forced by heavy boots. Four men enter pushing a large wheeled bin. One fellow halts immediately beside the massive figure lying spread-eagle nearest the door. He places his hands on his hips, mutters something indiscernible, and joins the others beside the bin. "We'll save that one for last." They mumble agreement and begin emptying the bin of its contents: plastic sheets, nylon ropes, tape, mops, wash cloths, disinfectant, and buckets of hot, sudsy water. From their white, uniformed pockets they produce gloves, rubberize their hands, and start separating the stilled figures. Systematically, they stretch the forms horizontally on the floor into a sort of prostrate attention, spines laid straight, arms pressed tight along the sides. Strands of looped nylon cord are utilized to strap the hands across stomachs and to tie the ankles together. Once strapped, each body is rolled onto a plastic sheet then bundled, bound in tape, and piled three abreast, one layer atop another, inside the bin. After disposing of nine bundles in this fashion, the four men turn their attention to the one remaining figure. At first, there is some discussion that the last plastic sheet is too small to contain the giant, but they discover that by having two men stretch the plastic while a third presses down on the body and the fourth quickly tapes, the body could effectively be wrapped and bound. Not so simple was the matter of lifting the body off the floor, onto their shoulders, above their heads and into the bin. Requiring a few false starts, some rearranging of positions, the body slipping heavily to the floor twice and almost three or four times, they finally manage to heave the bulky thing onto the pile. With much heavy breathing and mopping of brows, the four congratulate themselves and continue with the rest of the clean-up. Particles of wood, flesh, and bone are swept up and deposited in a bucket. Blood is wiped, scrubbed, sponged, and squeezed into a second plastic container. Once again spotless, the entire area is disinfected and everything loaded back onto the bin or carried by hand outside the door. Next, the room is put back in order, the furniture removed and replaced with one rectangular table set off-center, near the back corner and ten chairs, four on each side and one at either end of the table. The four men take one final glance at the room, check notepad, watches, nod approval, slap shoulders, and exit.

The room is square and windowless. White prevails: white ceramic floor, white plastic walls, white ceiling. Only the presence of fluorescent lighting allows for a faint blue glow to emanate from the otherwise pale and antiseptic setting.

A single door blemishes one white wall and opposite this, off-center, near the back corner of the room, a rectangular table is situated surrounded by ten figures, four on each side and one at either end. The conversation appears casual. There are no papers or pens to suggest a business meeting. Elbows rest on the pale arborite, hands support chins, stroke beards or simply stir the air. An odd head occasionally turns and glances about the room. There is no semblance of order, no items which might indicate leadership, neither itinerary, nor special seat, nor gavel. Except for the table, ten chairs, and ten figures, the room is bare. To disturb the silence, the murmur of a fan and ten voices — calm, dim, textureless — voices as might be heard in any waiting room, mingling with the air, clinging to the ceiling, unable to generate enough substance to form a shadow.

When the door splinters, so the calm glass of the room shatters. Words, half-words, melt down the corners of mouths. Blood pumps, igniting cheeks and foreheads. Pores steam open. Flesh dissolves. Muscles, tendons tingle and jump spasmodically. Every head twists towards the door. All eyes report the entry of four men who place themselves strategically between the table and the open door. Revolvers rise, fix at eye-level; gloved fingers squeeze. Figures at the table collapse as breath escapes through tiny holes drilled in throats. Some attempt to rise but are snuffed half-way. A few dive, try to disappear beneath the table but the gunfire is too rapid, the gunmen too precise — death nabs the fugitives fleeing, crouching and drags them to the floor. In quick succession the figures are bagged and it is only their stillness which causes the firing to stop, the revolvers to retire to their holsters. The four gunmen back towards the door, check watches, scribble a note onto a pad, face each other, face the room, then grin, slap shoulders, and exit. There is no longer any movement in the room and the only sound is the murmur of a fan and the applause of feet padding down the hallway.

MYSTERIES

13
Carol Shields
INVITATIONS

ON MONDAY she looked in her mailbox, although she had no reason to expect a letter so soon. But there it was, a small, square card. She held it in her two hands, testing its weight.

It was an invitation to an exhibition of drawings at a private gallery. The name of the artist was only faintly familiar to her, and she couldn't decide if she'd ever seen his work or not. She tried to imagine what kind of drawings she was being invited to view — would they be primitive or abstract or what was sometimes called "magic realism"? She summoned these categories to mind and then decided it didn't matter. What mattered was that she had been invited.

The invitation pleased her, though she wasn't such a fool as to think she'd been specifically singled out because of her aesthetic sensitivity or because of her knowledge of modern graphics or even because of the pleasure of her company. The address on the card had been typed; her name, in fact, was misspelled, the last two letters transposed. Somewhere, no doubt, she'd turned up on a mailing list — that was all.

She would wear a certain printed velvet skirt she had and with it a black turtleneck sweater. No one would expect her to buy a drawing or even to comment on the exhibition. It was necessary only to accept a glass of wine and a cube of orange cheese and stand for a minute or two in front of each drawing, nodding comprehendingly and perhaps murmuring something properly neutral into the air such as "nicely detailed" or "wonderful sense of space." There was a good chance no one would even speak to her, but it would be better than spending Saturday evening in her new apartment, sitting in an armchair with a book and feeling loneliness drink her drop by drop.

The previous tenant had left behind a single item, which was a paperback copy of Jane Austen's *Mansfield Park*, a book that, oddly enough, she had always intended to read. She couldn't help feeling there had been something deliberate — and something imperative, too — about this abandoned book, as though it had been specifically intended for her and that she was being enjoined to take it seriously. But how much better it would be to be going out; how much easier it would be to say, should anyone ask, that on Saturday evening she would be attending an opening of an interesting new exhibition.

On Tuesday she was again taken by surprise, for in her mailbox there was another invitation, this time for a cocktail party given by a distant friend of a friend, someone she'd never met but whose name she dimly remembered having heard. It was a disappointment that the party was being held on the same night as the gallery opening and that, furthermore, it was at the same hour. For a minute she entertained the possibility of attending both functions, galloping breathlessly from one to the other. But no, it was not feasible; the two parties were at opposite ends of the city. It was a great pity, she felt, since invitations are few and far between when one moves to a new address. She would have to make a choice.

Of course she would choose the cocktail party. The gallery opening, now that she stopped to think about it, was no more than a commercial venture, an enticement to buyers and patrons. It would be fraudulent of her to attend when she'd no intention of buying a picture, and besides, she was drawn to cocktail parties. She was attracted, in fact, to parties of all kinds, seeing them as an opportunity to possess, for a few hours at least, a life that was denser, more concentrated and more vigorous than the usual spun-out wastes of time that had to be scratched endlessly for substance. She could still wear her certain velvet skirt, but with a pretty red satin blouse she'd recently acquired.

On Wednesday, strangely, she received a third invitation — and it, too, was for Saturday evening. This time the invitation was handwritten, a rather charming note which she read through quickly three times. She was being invited to a small buffet supper. There would be only a dozen or so guests, it was explained. The author of a new biography would be there, and so would the subject of the biography who was, by chance, also a biographer. A particular bald-ing computer scientist would be in attendance along with his wife, who was celebrated for her anti-nuclear stance and for her involve-ment in Navajo rugs. There would be a professor of history and also a professor of histology, as well as a person renowned for his love of Black Forest cakes and cheese pastries. There would be a famous character actor whose face was familiar, if not his name, and also the hairdresser who'd invented the Gidget cut and raised razor cuts to their present *haute* status.

Of course she could not say no. How much more congenial to go to a supper party than to peer at violent works of art and mutter, "Interesting, interesting," and how much more rewarding than standing about with a drink and a salty canapé and trying to make conversation with a room full of strangers. Her green silk dress would be suitable, if not precisely perfect, and she could gamble safely enough on the fact that no one would have seen it before.

Thursday's mail brought still another invitation, also unfortu-nately for Saturday evening. She smiled, remembering how her mother used to say, "It never rains but it pours." The invitation, which was for a formal dinner party, was printed on fine paper, and there was a handwritten note at the bottom. "We do hope you can make it," the note said. "Of course we know you by reputation and we've been looking forward to meeting you for years."

It had been some time since she'd attended a formal dinner party, and she was flattered to be sent an invitation with a hand-written note at the bottom. It pleased her to imagine a large, vaulted dining room and parade of courses elegantly served, each with a dif-ferent wine. The gleam of light through cut glass would sparkle on polished linen and on the faces of the luminaries gathered around the table. Her green silk, with perhaps the double strand of pearls, would be festive enough, but at the same time subdued and formal.

She wasn't entirely surprised to look into her mailbox on Fri-day and see that she'd been sent yet another invitation. The paper was a heavy, creamy stock and came enclosed in a thick double envelope. There was to be a reception — a *gala* it was called — at the top of a large downtown hotel on Saturday evening. The guest of honor, she read, was to be herself.

She felt a lurch of happiness. Such an honor! But a moment

later her euphoria gave way to panic, and when she sat down to collect herself, she discovered she was trembling not with excitement but with fear.

On Saturday she surveyed the five invitations which were arranged in a circle on her coffee table. These missives, so richly welcoming, persuading and honoring, had pleased her at first, then puzzled her. Something or someone was conspiring to consume a portion of her life, of herself, in fact — entering her apartment and taking possession of her Saturday evening just as a thief might enter and carry off her stereo equipment or her lovely double rope of pearls or a deep slice of her dorsal flesh.

She decided to stay home instead with a cup of coffee and her adventitiously acquired copy of *Mansfield Park*. Already it was dark, and she switched on the small reading lamp by her chair. The shade of the lamp was made of a pale, ivory-yellow material, and the light that shone through it had the warm quality of very old gold.

It happened that people passing her window on their way to various parties and public gatherings that night were moved to see her, a woman sitting calmly in an arc of lamplight, turning over — one by one — the soft pages of a thick book. Clearly she was lost in what she was reading, for she never once glanced up. Her look of solitary containment and the oblique angle with which the light struck the left side of her face made her seem piercingly lovely. One of her hands, curved like a comma, lay on her lap; the other, slowly, thoughtfully, turned over the pages.

Those who passed by and saw her were seized by a twist of pain, which was really a kind of nostalgia for their childhood and for a simplified time when they, too, had been bonded to the books they read and to certain golden rooms which they remembered as being complete and as perfect as stage settings. They felt resentment, too, at the cold rain and the buffeting wind and the price of taxis and the hostility of their hosts. They felt embarrassed by their own small, proffered utterances and by the expanded social rubric they had come to inhabit.

As they moved to and fro in large, brightly-lit rooms, so high up in glittering towers that they felt they were clinging to the sides of cliffs, their feet began to ache and exhaustion overcame them. Soon it was past midnight, no longer the same day, but the next and the next. New widths of time clamored to be filled, though something it seemed, some image of possibility, begged to be remembered.

Outside, the wind blew and blew. The sky slipped sideways, turning first yellow, then a mournful, treasonous purple, as though time itself was drowning in a waterfall of shame.

14
David Helwig
RED BARN, INTERIOR

CARL leaned back against the wall as he watched them bringing out the painting. His legs were aching and he couldn't find a comfortable position. It was a terrible thing to grow so old that it was no longer possible to stand and watch something without pain and awkwardness.

He looked at the painting as they put it on the easel. Of all the Sachs paintings, this one was closest to him. The figure had never really left his mind since the first day.

"The next lot is number 34," the little gray auctioneer said. "The Red Barn, Interior, by the Canadian symbolist, Reuben Sachs."

The light on the outside of the barn, the bright painful sunlight on the freshly painted red walls, the whole texture of daylight on the back of the barn swallow that perched on the edge of the door, the grass stems rising beside the open doors that disappeared out of the sides of the painting with a distortion of perspective that was more real than any right perspective could be.

"What am I bid to start? One thousand dollars, do I hear one thousand dollars?"

Remmnant turned towards Carl, looked at him for a couple of seconds and then winked. Carl turned away.

"I have fourteen hundred, ladies and gentlemen, now fifteen."

Carl tried to see who was doing most of the bidding. Fat old Bernard Webber would likely buy the painting. He bought nearly all the Sachs paintings, but he wouldn't buy them privately from Remmnant. Somehow he was never sure of the value of anything unless he'd bought it at an auction and knew that someone else wanted it almost as badly as he did. He paid more that way, but it gave him a certain satisfaction.

"Nineteen hundred and fifty dollars, a very fine painting, do I hear two thousand?"

The dark interior, dark, yet with the almost outdoor light that a barn had with the light coming in through holes in the walls, so that there was a strange light on the back of the steer that stood and looked out of the painting. And on the clothes of the man.

"Twenty four hundred dollars, ladies and gentlemen, is that your final bid? Twenty four hundred, once, twice, sold. The next lot, number 35, a landscape by the English artist Thomas Parr, dated 1837."

Remmnant crossed to where Carl was standing.

"Webber again," Remmnant said.

Carl just nodded.

"Listen," Remmnant said, "that fairy from the Art Gallery has been at me again to get me to talk to you about Reuben Sachs. He's got Webber all excited about the idea of a book on him, but he can't do anything unless he can talk to you. He figures maybe you'd set it up for him to talk to the sister."

They were taking the painting down now. Carl stared, fascinated, at the figure of the man in overalls, hanging upside down from the barn beams, dead, but with his eyes open. The figure was astonishing, frightening, the most powerful in any of the Sachs paintings.

"How about it?" Remmnant said. "Will you talk to him?"

Carl shook his head and walked away. He was tired and angry and he wanted to get out on the street again and see the sunlight, especially the sunlight as it shone on the old bricks of some of the buildings near his home.

He went down the steps of the auction gallery as fast as he could and started walking west towards his place. As he walked, he thought again about the inverted figure in the painting, especially the way the trousers hung. He remembered once watching Reuben painting a pair of trousers that he'd thrown on the floor of the small barn where he worked. Carl tried to recall the details of that painting, the color and shape, but it wouldn't come back.

He walked across Bay Street without waiting for the light to change and heard someone honking and braking, but he didn't look. He was too old to care how he'd missed dying, as long as he'd missed it.

When he got home, he thought, he might do some nudes. Remmnant was always happy to get some. Carl had a small reputation for his drawings, especially his nudes, but he was better known as the man who had known Reuben Sachs, who was the intermediary between Nellie Sachs and the public, the man who now and then could talk Nellie into parting with one of Reuben's paintings and putting it on show or even selling it.

All this because of the hours he'd spent in that small barn, watching Reuben paint. From 1914 till Reuben's death in 1919.

Carl walked quickly and already he was nearly at Spadina, where he was able to find, here and there, the kind of old brick walls that he'd wanted to see when he was in the auction gallery. A few blocks more, and he'd be at the factory where he'd worked as a night watchman for twenty years, and where the walls were so dark and worn and lovely that Carl would sometimes stand for hours and watch the changes of the light as it shone on them.

At the time when he worked in the factory, he had lived far from here, in a small house near Cherry Beach, but when he'd decided to leave, decided to let his wife have the calm and peaceful home she'd always wanted, he'd made his way to the familiar district of the old factory and found himself an apartment there with a big sunporch that he used for a studio.

He wondered if his wife was still alive, still neatly present in that little frame house. When Carl left, she probably brought out doilies to put on the arms of the chairs, the way the chairs had been in her mother's house in the town where they'd both grown up.

Carl wondered if the young man who wanted to write a book about Reuben might try to see Nellie Sachs on his own. If Carl refused to talk to him, he might. Carl decided that the next day he should get the money from Remmnant and drive up to see Nellie.

He reached the old factory and stood on the street looking at the front of it. A man came out of the door and shouted to him. It was Jim Meyer, foreman back in the days when Carl had been the night watchman here, now a part owner of the factory and half retired, he came and went as he pleased, observing, complaining, making himself happy. He wasn't looking well these days, and Carl noticed as he got into the car that he moved slowly, as if he could only just control his muscles. Everyone was getting old now.

Carl looked away from Meyer's car and back at the walls of the factory. The afternoon sun was shining across the walls at an angle; here and there fell patches of shade from the Manitoba maple that had grown wild in the bit of yard beside the factory door. The texture of the wall, the direction of the light, and the pattern of light and shade were so intense that Carl thought that a blind man could feel them with his fingers. He walked over to the wall, closed his eyes, and put his hand on the surface, trying to feel the slant of the light, the pattern of light and shade. Sometimes he thought he could catch it.

He opened his eyes, looked at the wall again, then walked away and went towards home. He hoped that the children in the apartment upstairs didn't have the television set on. He wanted it to be quiet.

When he walked in the front door of the house, he stood still and listened. No television. He was pleased and walked down the hall and opened the door, hoping that Mary would be there and not too busy to pose for him.

As he opened the door, she spoke to him from the big armchair where she was sitting and reading a book.

"Did the painting get a good price?" she said.

"Twenty-four hundred."

"That's very good."

"Not bad."

"Do you want some tea?"

"Come into the studio. I want to do some drawings."

"I'll put the kettle on first."

Carl walked into the studio and began to get himself ready. As he walked around the room, surrounded by light and seeing the green of the grass and weeds and the trees in the yard outside the windows, he began to relax, and as he began to relax he started to feel how tired he was. He hated going to the auctions, but he always felt that he must be there.

He got out paper and charcoal and moved a table close to him so that he could have a place for the tea that Mary was making. He went towards the door of the kitchen.

"Bring in a whole pot of tea, Mary," he said. "I'm a little tired."

"Maybe you shouldn't work right now," she said.

"I want to."

He went and sat down and waited for her to come. While he was waiting he thought again about the day he'd watched Reuben paint a picture of a pair of his old trousers, and now when he thought about it, he remembered that he had thrown them on the floor at first but then had picked them up and hung them upside down over the end of a workbench.

Mary came in with a pot of tea on a tray with two white cups, plain white china cups from Woolworth's that had always struck Carl as very beautiful as they sat on the tray with the dark brown tea pot. There was a row of white cups in one of the Sachs paintings.

Mary poured two cups of tea and put one of the cups and the tray on Carl's table. She took her own cup to the other side of the room and set it down on the trestle table while she took off her clothes. She undid the buttons of her blouse, put it on the table, then reached her two hands around behind her, undid the brassiere and slipped it off. Her big breasts with their pink nipples hung in front of her as she turned to one side to unfasten her skirt.

"Wait," Carl said. "Can you stand just like that?"

"If it doesn't take too long."

Carl quickly took a mouthful of the hot tea, almost burning his tongue with it, and then picked up a stick of charcoal and began to draw. He had drawn Mary hundreds of times, but with luck he could find, even yet, a movement, a pose, that made it as exciting as the first time.

Mary was strong and patient, and she made a good model. He was excited now about the shape of her body, the way her arm pressed against her breast, the crease at the side where she had turned. He used the skirt spreading out from her as a kind of base for the drawing, a way of letting the body disappear away from the focus of the breasts. He worked quickly, happily.

First thing in the morning, he must definitely get the money from Remmnant and drive up to see Nellie, just in case the man did decide to find her on his own.

When Carl finished the first drawing, he stopped for a minute to let Mary have some tea and to have some himself and then had her pose again, still wearing the skirt, this time sitting down on the long bench in front of the trestle table.

He finished the second drawing and began a third, posing her so that her body was strangely distorted, looked shorter and heavier than it was. Carl had drunk three cups of tea by this time, but he was aware that he was still very tired, and after he finished the third drawing, he put down the charcoal and rubbed his fingers clean on his trousers.

In the old days, Carl would have taken Mary to bed and made love to her, but today he was beyond that. He worried sometimes that she would leave him for a younger man, but she seldom seemed restless. Carl wondered why.

He stood up. He was a little dizzy and not very steady on his feet as he moved across the room.

"I think I'll go to bed," he said. "I want to drive up to see Nellie Sachs in the morning."

Mary came across to him and put her arms around him to walk with him towards the bedroom. Carl climbed onto the bed with his clothes still on, and Mary lay beside him, holding him against her big soft breasts. As he moved towards sleep, he was thinking of Reuben Sachs and trying to remember a painting of black-eyed susans.

He seemed to dream a lot during the night, but most of his dreaming was confused, chaotic, events disappearing and reappearing. Then there was a dream in which he was looking at the painting of the red barn again, but this time the figure of the man was the figure of Reuben, and he was not dead but hanging inverted, alive, telling Carl that he was preparing himself to paint. Carl wanted to get away, and he was aware of trying to bring Mary into the dream to help him, yet he was aware at the same time that the dream was taking place in the past and that Mary was not yet born.

When he woke from that dream it was morning, and Carl found that during the night Mary had undressed him and moved him under the covers. She had already left the bed, and he could hear her in the kitchen preparing food and singing. He should always wake to hear someone singing, he thought. When he began to climb out of bed, he felt a little sick, but he sat still on the edge of the mattress for a moment and then felt better. At first he couldn't remember what duty it was that this day held in wait for him, but he remembered the trip, and for a moment, the two presences, the Sachs house and the barn were in his mind, linked, but quite separate as they always were, for the few feet of grass between them was a greater separation than years of time and worlds of change. The house and Nellie, the barn and Reuben; from the moment that he remembered he was going there, they were present in his mind, sounds and smells and feelings, the time that once was.

He put on his clothes, the same ones as the day before, for he was superstitious sometimes and knew that there were days when he shouldn't change his clothes. He walked out of the bedroom and into the studio to look at the drawings he had done the day before; two of them, he thought, were very good. He sprayed them so that the charcoal would not smear and rolled them to take to Remmnant when he went for the money. Remmnant would frame them and sell them within a few weeks.

Carl put down the drawings and walked into the kitchen where he saw Mary in an old blue flannel robe that she always wore in the mornings. Something, probably the sight of her right after the pictures, touched Carl and made him feel suddenly affectionate. He reached out his hand, put it on the back of her neck and squeezed gently. She looked towards him for a second but soon went back to measuring out the coffee.

"I'm going to drive up and see Nellie Sachs today," Carl said.

"To take her the money?"

"Yes. I'll stop and get it from Remmnant on the way."

She nodded without speaking. A moment later she looked up.

"Do you think you'll be bringing back any more paintings?"

"I don't know. I might."

"You still look tired," Mary said. "Why don't you wait and go on the weekend?"

"No. I have to go today. There's somebody who wants to write a book about Reuben and might go and see her."

"That man at the Gallery?"

"Yes."

"Have you ever talked to him?"

"No. I'm not going to."

"You think he might go up to talk to Nellie?"

"He might."

Mary began to serve out the breakfast, soft-boiled eggs, toast, and coffee. Carl wanted to think, not eat, but he knew that if he was going to be driving, he'd better have something in his stomach. It took about an hour and a quarter to get to Nellie's place, even if the traffic getting out of the city was reasonable.

Nellie had given him breakfast once when he had been there. A cup of tea and a piece of toast with ancient-tasting marmalade. Nellie never went out, and when she wanted to get food, she'd send the neighbor's boy down to the grocery store with a note. She had rather old-fashioned ideas about what was available at grocery stores and never bought anything that wasn't there years before when she'd been in the habit of going out to do her shopping.

"Would you like me to drive up with you?" Mary said.

"No. Nellie doesn't like meeting strangers."

"I could stay in the car."

"I'm not so old that I can't manage to drive the car that far."

"I know, but I've always been curious about her and that town. I'd like to see where you grew up."

"It's the same as all the other country towns."

"I suppose."

She was silent for a moment.

"How long is it now since Reuben Sachs died?" she said.

"Fifty-one years. I was fifteen."

He thought how the years immediately after Reuben's death were different from those before it, more real or less real, depending how you used the word. Carl had lived his life once again among ordinary boys and girls. He'd played hockey and lacrosse, hunted and fished, taken a job, and after working for a few years had married a local girl. And then suddenly, after his marriage, he'd needed to leave, and he'd taken his wife to Toronto and equally suddenly and much to her surprise, told her that he was an artist. She'd never seen him draw or heard him mention drawing. Now in the middle of her first pregnancy, he'd demanded that she strip herself naked and pose for him. They had fought long and hard over that, and once or twice, tense and grudging, she had posed for him, but she was so tense that he could not draw properly, his arm was stiff and awkward, and he had given it up. But he had drawn and painted, begun to exhibit. A few years later he had taken the job as a night watchman because it would give him some free time during day-light when he could work.

Mary offered him some more coffee, but he refused and stood up, ready to go. She walked across to meet him at the door and kissed him on the cheek. He touched her on the side of the head with his fingers, went to the studio to collect the drawings and walked out through the dark hallway. He could hear the television set upstairs.

Carl walked out of the house and around the block to the laneway where he left the car in a neighbor's garage. It was an old car, but he never drove it very far or very fast, and it was good enough for a trip up to Nellie's.

Carl took out the car and drove slowly through the streets leading to Remmnant's gallery. It was hard to find a parking place in the streets nearby, and Carl had to park a block and a half away and walk from there. When he walked into the gallery with the drawings rolled up under his arms, the secretary at a desk halfway back smiled at him. He saw Remmnant near the back of the gallery holding the elbow of a middle-aged woman and talking very intensely to her. Carl walked over the soft rug and towards the back of the gallery where the framing room and Remmnant's office were situated. He went into Remmnant's office, and while he was waiting, opened the drawings and looked at them. The first of them was the best, the breasts heavy and fleshy, and the pose suggesting that the figure was on the point of movement.

In a few moments Remmnant came walking quickly into the office.

"How about that twenty-four hundred for the barn eh? We got to get some more out of the old girl."

"I'm going to see her today," Carl said.

"Can you get any paintings?"

"I'll see."

He held out the drawings to Remmnant who took them and quickly flipped through them.

"Beautiful," he said. "Great stuff. To tell you the truth, I like these a hell of a lot better than that morbid stuff of Sachs. But the newspaper guys can't find such smart things to say about them. They are what they are. Boobs are boobs eh? We'll get these framed and sell them, anyway."

"I want to take Nellie the money," Carl said.

"Sure. I'll just get Myra to make out the cheque."

He walked out of the office. Carl followed him, for the little room was beginning to make him sweat and make his head spin. The young secretary took out a cheque book and made out a cheque in Carl's name. He took the cheque, folded it and put it in his wallet.

"What kind of split do you make with the old girl?" Remmnant said.

"None. I give it all to her. I don't need the money."

"Hell, you should be taking a commission," Remmnant said. "You earn it."

Carl started towards the door.

"Good luck," Remmnant said. "Next time I see you, I hope you have a painting to show me."

"I think I will," Carl said, and suddenly he felt that was true. He walked out of the gallery and back to his car.

Driving slowly and systematically, Carl made his way north through the city and out to the highway that led northwest to the town he'd left forty years before, where Nellie had stayed.

Once or twice on the way, Carl pulled off the road and took out the little sketch pad and pencil that he kept in the glove compartment and made a quick sketch of a building, or the shape of a set of fields and fences that intrigued him. There were many sketches in the book now, and Carl noted that he'd soon need to buy a new one.

When he arrived at the edge of town, the summer sun was so bright that he couldn't lift his eyes away from the road, and even the black asphalt seemed to reflect the brightness at him. He drove down the main street where there were a few women out shopping and then turned left and down a quieter, even more familiar street that led him to Nellie's house.

The house hadn't been painted for thirty or forty years, and the blinds and curtains were drawn, but the lawn was kept trimmed by one of the neighbors, and in the back corner of the yard, near the spot where years before Carl crossed over from his parents yard into the Sachs', there was a big bunch of black-eyed susans growing wild. Carl walked around to the back of the house and knocked loudly on the door. He waited for a few minutes and then put his mouth against the keyhole.

"It's Carl, Nellie."

He heard her coming towards the door and stepped back so that she could peek round the corner and get a good look at him.

"Come in Carl," she said. He followed her into the house, and the smell of the place, of a place closed but kept clean, vaguely feminine, as if there were rose leaves somewhere far off in the upstairs rooms, made this visit continuous with all the others, as if there had been no break in between.

Nellie walked down the hall ahead of him, a big boned woman becoming gradually smaller, thinner, more bent with the passage of years.

"Reuben's out in the barn," she said. "Working night and day. He's got himself a little cot out there ... but I suppose I've told you that."

"How are you Nellie?" Carl said.

"Fair, Carl. Just fair."

She was sitting in an old chair and had picked up a piece of red glass, a small cream pitcher, from the table beside her. It said "A Souvenir of Buffalo, 1898." She was turning it around in her big fingers. The whole room was full of old glass and china knick knacks, all of them dusted and kept in their same place always. At each visit Carl saw them in their places, poised in the strange light of the room behind the drawn blinds.

"Does anyone else ever come to see you Nellie?"

"I see Jessie Knoebler from time to time, but she's the only one."

"Has anyone ever come to ask you about Reuben?"

"No. Why should they?"

"About his paintings."

"I don't bother my head about them," Nellie said.

"If someone came to talk to you about them, I think it would be best not to see him."

"I don't usually see people unless I know them well. I've just lost the touch of meeting new people."

"Yes. I suppose that can happen."

They sat quiet for a moment. Nellie put down the red pitcher and began to straighten a mat on the table beside her chair.

"I've brought some money for you," Carl said. "From one of the paintings."

"I don't need any money, Carl."

"I'll put it in the bank for you. In case you're ever in need of it."

"You've done that before, haven't you? Put money in the bank?"

"Yes, there's quite a lot there."

"In my name? Or Reuben's?"

"In your name Nellie."

She stood up.

"Would you like a cup of tea?"

"Yes, I think I would."

"I'll put on the kettle."

She went out of the room. At first Carl was going to follow her, but he stayed in his chair. From the street outside he heard the noise of two teenage boys shouting at each other, and the sound made the silence of the house more complete, more oppressive. Carl looked at the little red pitcher and wondered who had brought it here. Nellie's mother likely, having gone to Niagara Falls and Buffalo for a holiday, bringing back the little gaudy souvenir to prove that she had been away, that she had really left town.

The silence of the house made Carl think of the different silence in the barn, a male silence, Reuben's silence, a silence of dying. Carl remembered the fire in the corner of the yard, and Nellie coming from the house behind him, her clothes rumpled, for she and Carl had been lying on a couch, kissing, holding one another, touching, when suddenly Carl had moved and seen through the window the pile of canvases burning.

All his life since, Carl had wondered what it was that made it happen. What was the final pain? Was it Carl and Nellie?

Reuben had known somehow without appearing to have known. It had seemed to Carl that Reuben wouldn't care about it, that it had nothing to do with him really.

Nellie came into the room with a plate of biscuits, an English kind that Carl hadn't seen for years. He took one and ate it. For a moment he wished that he'd let Mary come with him to protect him from the flood of memories. It was the same each time he came, but each time they seemed to get stronger, as if the past were coming closer and closer, pursuing him, on his heels, about to throw a great dark bag over his head and proclaim an end to all but itself. A few events, a few years of time: he was their prisoner.

Nellie brought him his tea.

"Thank you Nellie."

"I'm always pleased to make tea for an old friend."

"Yes. I know."

They drank their tea in silence except for the soft sounds of their drinking. Carl ate a biscuit, and the sound of his chewing seemed to echo through his head. He wished this to be over now so that he could go out to the barn and make his visit there.

Finally the tea was gone. Carl put down his cup .

"Thank you Nellie," he said. "I think I'll go out to the barn now."

"Of course Carl," she said, but she didn't look at him.

Carl walked to the back door, took the key from its nail and went out. As he walked across the few feet of lawn, past the lilacs to the barn door, he held the key tight in his hand, as if it were a talisman to get him safely in. It was like this every time. Even when he was a boy and had started to look in the door on his way to school, he'd been afraid, at first, of the man inside, who stood, so concentrated on his work.

It was usually morning, at first. Carl would go out the back door of his own home, always the back door, for he wasn't allowed to go out the front past the parlor. He'd eat his breakfast at the kitchen table, smelling the yeasty odor of bread and buns set to rise which would be put in the oven after he'd left for school and perhaps eaten for lunch if there weren't some older and staler available. It always annoyed Carl to be given a stale crust for lunch when he could smell the fresh bread that had been put away in the cupboard, but his mother was convinced that young boys were provided by God for the virtuous disposal of stale bread and buns, and until the stale bread and buns were eaten, Carl would not see the fresh.

One morning, entirely by accident, Carl had gone out the back door, planned a shortcut to school, and on his way through a backyard had found the barn and Reuben Sachs. He had noticed that the door of the little barn was open, and he could see the figure of a man inside. Curious but half afraid, Carl walked close to the door and looked in.

The man inside was short and stocky with fat little fingers, and in those fingers he held a paint brush. That was how it had begun. Carl remembered it all again as he unlocked the door of the barn and stopped inside.

The barn was the same as ever. Nellie had told Carl to lock it the day after the funeral, and no one but Carl had been in it since.

It was only a few weeks after the door had been locked that Nellie began to refer to Reuben as alive and working in the barn. That bothered people in town, and there was talk of sending her away. People said that neither she nor Reuben had been right since their mother died five years before, leaving them alone together. It was easy to find a dozen remarks or actions of Nellie's, even the fact of Reuben's paintings, his death, that could justify suspicion and fear. But Nellie's old aunt, the only relative she had left, had defended her and insisted that she was harmless, and the town learned to forget her. She became a kind of ghost, present, but never seen. The children called her place The Haunted House, but no one was troubled by her strangeness. They became almost fond of it.

Carl sat down on the little stool in front of the easel and breathed in. Still the same smell as on all the days when he watched Reuben work. Five years. Reuben never talked much, but Carl had known that he liked him there. Once or twice he had used Carl's shoes or his legs in paintings, but he never drew or painted his face. Carl always wondered why but never dared to ask.

Carl stood up from the little stool and reached over to the cupboard beside him and took out brushes, oil, pallete, and a box of paints. He spread them on the white table and walked to the corner of the barn to get a canvas, one of the dozens of old fashioned stretchers that Reuben had prepared but never used. He set the canvas on the easel and took a deep breath again, letting the smell of the barn and the paints carry him back.

It was only in the last year of their time that Reuben had encouraged Carl to draw things, but once he started Carl had become excited by the power of his pencil to make a thing on paper, and instead of watching Reuben paint, he would often sit in the corner of the barn and sketch what he could see through the door or what he saw hanging on the walls, his pencil moving faster and faster as the excitement of it gripped him. Reuben would seem to work faster too, his strange, almost misshapen face glowing with the energy of his work.

Minutes, hours, days, weeks, months. The two of them in that barn. Carl would sometimes stay away from school so that he and Reuben could work together in the barn, and for a while his parents talked of forbidding him to go there. Carl had promised never to miss school again and had avoided the question that way, but there was always a look on his mother's face as he went out the door that suggested how little she approved of his pastime. Carl never cared. It sometimes seemed that he wanted nothing but to be there with Reuben, unspeaking, everything silent except the tiny sounds of their work.

Carl could no longer remember how it was or when it was that he started to become interested in Nellie. She was three years older than he was, and gradually he had come to notice that she was a woman with a woman's shape and gait. He remembered the picture.

One day he had left Reuben at work and gone into the house to draw a picture of Nellie as she sat in her chair. When it was done, Nellie had been pleased with it and had taken it to the barn to show her brother. Reuben had stood for a long time holding it in his thick fingers, then had said abruptly that it was no good and tore it in half. Nellie had turned on him, bitterly, saying it was better than anything he had painted, that Carl had more talent than he did. Reuben didn't speak, only went on with his painting. It was the one with the white cups in it, Carl remembered that clearly, and Reuben had worked away, stolidly, deliberately, ignoring what Nellie said to him until finally she turned and walked out of the barn, and Carl followed her, like a puppy that is confused but follows its mistress because it can think of nothing else to do.

It was in the week after that day that Reuben painted the red barn picture. Carl had praised it highly, absurdly, trying to make up to Reuben for what Nellie had said, but Reuben ignored his praise.

And it was in the week after that that Carl had caught a glimpse of fire from the window of the house and jumped up to run from the house knowing that the fire was made of Reuben's paintings and coming out of the back door he realized that there was nothing left of them, nothing of his work but hot ashes.

Then they had gone to the barn, he and Nellie, knowing what they must find. Wondered how they had failed to hear the shot. No one, as it turned out, had heard it.

The barn, the body, the hot ashes: once again Carl reached the end of the series of memories. For the others were unimportant, the funeral, the other events. They weren't real.

Now that he had reached the end of his memories, Carl looked around him. It was starting to get dark outside, and he had to strain his eyes to see the painting on the easel. The sunflowers, the wild sunflowers. He stared in astonishment at the way in which the flowers seemed to be becoming faces, yet weren't. It was hard to see it in this light, but the feeling was right. It was just what he remembered. It was Reuben's painting.

Sometimes Carl had wondered about them. Once or twice it had seemed to him that he could no longer remember Reuben's paintings, that he might have imagined them all, imagined the whole five years, but as he looked at this one now he was sure. Sure.

He sat down on the stool and closed his eyes. Later he'd go into the house to see Nellie, but first he must rest. He wished Mary was beside him. It seemed to him that he was more tired than he'd ever been in his life.

15
Helen Pereira
THE CORONATION

THE boatman hoists the gangplank behind me as I leap aboard. He nods, tips his cap in greeting, tugs and secures the rope.

Clang! Made it. The ferry.

What am I doing here? Why am I rushing to attend a party on Ward's Island? "Celebration," Iris called it when inviting me. Celebrating what? Whom? Islanders and artists — and Iris is both — are bad with information, details. It's neither a launching nor an opening if it is at her cottage.

My attendance seemed a *fait accompli*. I can't remember her actual call or the invitation. A blank.

Why am I bothering to go to this dumb party? Vanity? The young people?

All social events make me edgy, especially those on islands. Being captive. Miss a boat and you're a prisoner. Devil's Island, Ellis Island.

The top deck. Brisk breeze. Mist. Windy gray evening. No sunny summer crossing, this.

I like Iris, but not her sister Rose. Nor do I like their bratty sister Lily. And I do not like their crazy mother, for naming her daughters after flowers. Why? A frustrated gardener? *Nursery.*

A teen-age couple at the end of my bench neck. Hands grope savagely under ponchos. I walk to the rail, lean over. The boat's wake. Froth, sinister dark currents.

Wake. We call pre-funeral gatherings wakes. Surface gaiety, like froth? Hiding pull to darkness? I turn away, lean my back against the rail, stare.

Passengers. The usual. Urban escapees carry blankets, six packs; Island shoppers tote groceries, kids; animal lovers bring dogs to run and spoil the beaches.

Thump! Always that crunch with Island landings. Is bad eye-
sight compulsory for ferry boat captains, so they misjudge distance,
space, and land forcefully? Skill from some special ferry captain's
school? Crash course? We lurch, stumble, clutch belongings. I tight-
en my arms around the litre of French red in the brown paper bag.

One thing to look forward to, get me through the celebration.
Everybody serves white these days. Chilled. So cold. Red wine is
comfort, warmth. Blood. Communion.

Down to the lower deck. Passengers crowd against metal lattice
gates. They push, shove, jostle as though their lives depend on it.
The boatman smiles at their desperation. I pause on the iron stairs,
know he will wait as long as possible to open that gate. I clutch the
rail with my free hand, marvel that no one has fallen and fractured a
skull on the iron staircase during these violent landings. (A long time
ago, when my son was about fourteen, he fell against the rail and
knocked out a front tooth. After a two thousand dollar orthodontia
job.)

Passengers funnel out, rush up the gangplank, cross the dock.
Mount bicycles; walk towards home, beaches. Dogs on leashes pull
owners. I follow, and stroll along the Bayfront path towards Iris'
weatherbeaten cottage. Like most Islanders, she is always on the
move. Ward's to Algonquin, back to Ward's, Bayfront to Second
Street, etcetera. I turn at Second Street and walk to number 29.

Bicycles lean against gray insulbrick; there is a strong smell of
cat; green hyacinths pierce mud at the side of the wall. The front
steps have been removed, awaiting some never-to-be-completed ren-
ovation. I walk around to the back.

Party sounds. Laughter, music, shouts. "Wanta beer?" The side
door is pale purple and on it Iris has painted (cute, cute) a deeper
purple iris. I let myself in without knocking, the Island way.

Iris stands before a wooden block table cutting wedges of cheese
and putting them on a tray. She turns, smiles, leans towards the living room door, yells, "She's here!" She smiles, rushes to hug and kiss
me, butcher knife waving in the air.

"Hi. You look great, Iris." She wears her uniform: plaid shirt and
jeans, long brown hair in a single braid. She radiates health, vitality.

I set my bottle of Kressmans near assorted bottles beside cheese
and bread trays.

"Glad you came," she says, "come and meet the others." She still brandishes the knife. Iris is always awkward, endearingly clumsy.

"Neat house," I say, my arm around her waist. We enter the livingroom. Rose holds court in a roomful of strangers. In the center. I know from experience that the drink she gulps is gin-and-tonic. She's pretty enough, but lacks Iris' talent. She compensates for this by making hard-drinking her trademark. She waves one arm at me, winds the other around a slight, dark, curly-haired young man. He grins, waves in recognition and heads for me.

Who is he? He grabs both my hands tightly in his, kisses my cheek.

"I've been waiting for you," he says. He kisses my mouth. A real I-want-you kiss. I respond, then resist. This guy is a stranger, mistaken. I pull away. He grabs my hands tighter.

"You don't know me, right? But I know you. You're Elinor. I've been waiting for you . . ."

Rose interrupts. Relief. She drags an older fair man across the room. "This is his friend." No names. I nod at the newcomer, but can't offer my hand because the dark kid still has it. "They live next door. Our new neighbors." She hiccoughs, swivels round and dumps these guys on me. The fair man winks, says "Excuse me," leaves in pursuit of Rose.

I'm stuck with the dark one. Still gazing at me lustfully. A long time since a man looked at me like that. I'm not flattered. It's so *inappropriate*. The kid has a problem. He slides an arm around my waist, faces me, clasps my other hand.

"Let's dance."

"No."

"You'll have to, sooner or later. Might as well face it. Nothing to fear."

Who says! He is one of those weirdos, a clinger. The more I resist, the more he'll pester me. I'll go along with him for now, then sneak away early. Some party. Damn Iris.

A fiddler appears, turns off the record player, resins his bow, tucks fiddle under chin, and plays. Real country music. He's very good, as good a fiddler as my friend Pete. Mr. Fiddleman, we called Pete. Remembering him usually makes me sad, but I'm caught up in the music. My body moves, my shoes lead me effortlessly through complicated steps which I dance with the dark young man. Like *The Red Shoes*, that old movie. Yeah. The ballerina whose shoes run away with her. I *know* these dances! My Ottawa Valley ancestry. The Irish.

It's difficult, now, not to be attracted to dark Mr. No-Name. We dance so well together. He holds me close, closer; kisses me again. I enjoy this. Time to mention the husband and grandchildren.

"I know you're married," he says, "and I'm crazy about older women. I know all there is to know about you."

"But I don't know anything about you. What do you do, for instance?" This conversation. Like a beginning courtship.

"I'm an undertaker." He smiles. "It's wonderful work. I love it."

I shiver, try to pull away. He holds me tighter.

He looks at me, amused. "What's wrong? Such a beautiful profession, working with the dead. I'm crazy about the dead. So lovely. Their bodies."

I am cold, shiver again. I've allowed myself to be kissed, fondled, and embraced by a stranger who handles corpses. I even enjoyed dancing with him.

Deja vu. A medical student I know had an anatomy professor who introduced his first year students to cadavers by holding a tea dance in his anatomy lab. "Desensitization," he'd called it. After the initial shock, the medic told me it had been a barrel of fun. Something like that. Yes.

"Actually I've misled you, bragged a bit. I'm only an undertaker's assistant," my dancing partner confesses. "I work for my friend." He points to the blond guy pursuing Rose.

I cringe at his touch, want to escape, but he fascinates me. Morbidly. I need a drink. Red wine. Warm.

"I'll get you some wine. Red." He smiles into my eyes, slides his hand along my hip as he leaves.

Frantic, I look for Iris. Can't see her. Hear her in the kitchen, talking. I won't follow him. I search for a familiar face among guests leaning on walls, sprawled on floor cushions. None. Iris has really cleaned the place up. Windows so sparkling I can look right through and see the cottage next door. Home of the undertakers. I turn away. I don't want to look at their house.

The only furniture in the room is at the end. Near the front door which doesn't open. It seems to be some sort of altar on a raised platform. Has Iris or Rose joined some crazy cult? My friend Jessie had a daughter who did that. Became a pagan and swiped Jessie's livingroom drapes "for our altar."

Iris returns bearing a tray of Ritz crackers. I take one. I do not want to eat it. The dark guy returns and puts the glass of red in my other hand. I giggle. Here I am facing an altar with a wafer in one hand and wine in the other.

I lift my glass. "Here's to women's ordination." Iris and the guy laugh, we clink glasses, drink.

"By the way, Iris, what's with the altar?"

"We got it for the coronation."

"*Cremation*," the man says.

Weird. Jokes aside, I am drawn to this altar, and especially to a large, covered copper platter on the center which shines orange against the dark wood. I love copper, polished copper, especially this platter. The way it lights up the gray room. I move closer to inspect it, and see some kind of gold crest on top.

"Iris, when did you get this gorgeous platter?"

"We got it for the coronation."

"*Cremation!*"

I touch the cover. "Don't open it," Iris says.

The guy moves close to me, whispers, "Go ahead, look."

I pause, gulp more wine. It warms me, encourages me. So does the kid's arm around my waist. I'm captured, so curious about the platter's contents that I trust a morbid stranger instead of a friend.

There are little handles on either side of the lid. I touch them, turn to see if Iris is watching. She is. *"I said don't open it, Elinor!"*

He nudges me. "Go ahead."

I lift the lid, set it aside on the altar. I'm excited. The contents must be very important to evoke such strong differing reactions from two people. Something wonderful? Jewels?

I lean over and look. Ashes. Gray. In a gritty mound.

"Yech! Iris, where did this stuff come from?"

"From the coronation."

"*Cremation!* I ought to know, it's my profession."

I want to replace the cover quickly, hide the grisly mess. My hands tremble. What if I knock the platter over, spill ashes? I steel myself, carefully cover the platter.

Iris wrings her hands. "Oh Elinor, I'm so sorry! I tried to stop you. I didn't want you to know!"

The dark youth pats my back. "Atta girl."

I break away, run out of the livingroom, force my way out the back door, away from Iris, Rose, strange undertakers, the fiddler. I stumble along the Bayfront path. Light through fog. It's the last ferry.

I'll make it. I speed up, breathless, run.

The boatman watches. The dark man follows.

16
Linda Manning
WOLF

CLARA flops her feet onto the rough flooring of the cabin and sighs. Her head has turned on but she still can't write. Nothing since she arrived three days ago. She pours herself another glass of wine, lights another cigarette. Her domestic umbilical cord refuses to let go and she slides back to the children, Brian, her parents, guilt. It's only for the first week, then the kids go to camp. Her life is back there in a neat domestic bundle.

Being alone is not what Clara expected. The darkness which from childhood has terrified her is warm, almost protective. Her domestic pain dissipates, drifts around with the cigarette smoke, disappears out the half open door. She pulls on her faded caftan and follows.

Clara can't remember the last time she walked alone in the moonlight. Ragged bushes unobtrusive during the day stretch long gnarled shadow fingers down the approaching slope. As she trudges upward, the smell of wet driftwood mixes with lake water and sand.

Her muscles complain by the time she reaches the brow; she stops to catch her breath. A brilliantly lit moonscape reveals rows of hills arching around the curve of the black lake. The ghosts of glaciers and a primeval scent turn her uneasily back towards the cluster of trees that holds her cabin. It has disappeared into a camouflage of leafy branches.

"It's not as though I'm lost," she thinks, turning back. "I know where I am."

The sand on the downward slope sifts between her toes. Years fall away. She picks up the hem of her caftan and, for a few reckless moments, outstrips time and gravity in great airborne leaps. She's running down towards the bridge to meet her mother coming home from work. She has on a clean sun dress that billows out as she leaps higher and higher. The charade ends as she trips on a branch, falls unceremoniously back to reality. Sand coats her face, her toe smarts with pain. She is on all fours and rolls to a sitting position, spitting sand, shaking it from her.

"Fool," she mutters, hunching herself forward and up. "You might have broken your leg."

The bottom of the hill envelopes her in a pocket of darkness. A distant shriek is followed by a swish of wings. Somewhere beyond the barren sand hills something howls. A dog perhaps.

She considers going back but the next hill is too inviting. "One more won't make any difference ... it's not as though anyone will miss me."

The steepness of the next hill tests her untoned muscles. She hunches forward, neanderthal style, determined to reach the top. In spite of this, a strange buoyancy elates her and she hums a long forgotten childhood tune — "a-away you rolling river" — until a faint intrusion of sound halts her in mid-phrase. For a moment the silence breathes only silence, then a loosened pebble rolls downward sifting the sand behind it. The hairs on the back of her neck lift slightly. Common sense tells her to go back.

Ahead, on the brow, long bunches of grass masquerade as shadows. The outlines of rock formations loom black yet reassuring against the sparkling sky. "I should come up here and write, tomorrow before it's too hot."

Without warning, a series of shouts invades the silence. Fear explodes in Clara's head, drains down through her neck and arms. The voices repeat, multiply and echo back, male voices that demand respect, obedience. Syllables strike against the next hill, bounce back to assault her.

"Hello-o-o there ..."

A whole gang of them, she's sure of it. How could she be so stupid.

"Hey ... you!"

A child's voice. It can't be. She should get the hell out of here, make a run for it. A small shadow approaches from behind some distant rocks.

It *is* a child. Someone could be lost or hurt Clara thinks. "Over here." She waves her arm, runs towards the voice.

An awkwardness halts them both. The child is seven or eight, shabbily dressed in a faded too-long dress and apron, her hair in straggly wisps about her face. She clutches the sides of her long skirt, stares up at Clara.

"My father says you'd better come with us. The wolf is out." Her urgency is almost humorous.

"The wolf?"

The child is gypsyish, out of time somehow. "How did you know I was here?"

"My brother's on lookout." She motions. "Behind those rocks. He saw you in the moonlight." She pulls at Clara's caftan. "Hurry."

A grown man and two half-grown boys approach, all with rifles. They wear loose homespun shirts, baggy pants. High boots from another era.

"You'll have to come back with us until morning, Miss," a male voice breaks in. "The wolf's out."

"My cabin's right back there," Clara says, feigning confidence. "I'll be fine. I'm just out for a walk."

Three sets of male eyes mock her.

"You wouldn't stand a chance. Come on." The statement has the finality of an ultimatum.

The three younger ones lead the way while the man moves in behind her. There appears to be no alternative.

They wind their way through the large rock formations and down the far side of the hill. The girl lags behind until Clara is beside her. She slips her hand almost protectively over Clara's, gives it a firm squeeze.

At the bottom of the hill, two more figures emerge from the shadows. An angular woman with care worn eyes pulls the child roughly away, holds her against the folds of her long skirt. An old man in a large brimmed hat coughs into a ragged handkerchief, shifts his unlit lantern from one hand to the other.

The woman peers at Clara with guarded suspicion.

Clara clears her throat. "I . . . I didn't know there were wolves in this area."

"One," the woman says in a strained voice. "Just one."

The company moves on, Clara in their midst. She becomes two

selves, one looking out, barely able to see beyond the periphery of dark bodies, the other watching, following like a lens. One demands she turn around, run. The other, however, is in command.

They veer away from the lake, follow a faint path that winds over and around several smaller hills. Long grass brushes against Clara's ankles, hooded forms of bushes appear with increasing frequency on either side and, in the distance, dark tips of full-sized trees appear.

The child breaks away from her mother, dawdles for a few steps. When Clara reaches her, she takes Clara's hand again, moves in to match her adult stride.

"They want to kill him," she whispers. "They don't under-stand."

She must mean the wolf, Clara thinks. The whole thing is absurd. Besides, wolves travel in packs. They must know this. Ahead, the three long rifle barrels glint their absolute authority in the moonlight. Clara remains silent.

A tape recorder begins in her head. "You can't force me to come with you. I'm quite capable of looking after myself." The phrases are well spoken, definitive. It repeats and repeats but each time she opens her mouth, the words crumble.

A long mournful howl brings the group to an abrupt halt. A breeze twines its pine-edged scent into the plaintive tones. The old man bends down to light the lantern. The men fan out, barrels to the darkness.

The woman pulls her daughter away, more roughly this time. The girl flings herself into her mother's skirts, clutches at the rough fabric, sobbing. The woman hunches down, embracing the child, rocking her back and forth. Fear moves Clara closer to the pair.

"Her brother disappeared last time," the woman says. "He was only thirteen." She lifts the child up, turns from Clara towards the darkness of the forest.

Clara stares at the child's fingers twined together against the back of the woman's neck. What does she mean ... it was her broth-er ... her brother was killed by a wolf? Ridiculous. He ran away no doubt, fed up being with this strange obsessive family, acting out their grade B movie lives. The tape recorder clicks on again but it's fainter now, less insistent. Clara feels her life peeling back layer by layer. She can barely even remember the cabin.

The men have gathered driftwood, and one of the sons pulls strips of cloth from his pocket to bind the end of each piece. A battered oil can appears and they carefully douse each wick. Clara watches a massive blue orange flame shatter the darkness. Then another and another. The smell of oil burning on wood filters through the air.

The howl comes again, closer this time. Its mournful tones pull at Clara, and when she looks up, the child is watching her.

"Move on," the father snaps. "There's not much time."

Again Clara sees the macabre little torch-lit group through a lens. The flickering light elongates their clustered shadows tracking together. She no longer has any idea where they are. It has ceased to matter.

The hills are behind them now and they move into scrub brush. Most of the time, Clara keeps her eyes on the rooted path. She is acutely aware of the men behind her, their sweat, the swish, swish of pant legs and swinging arms. Even though her caftan catches on passing bushes, she keeps pace, holds her distance. Space is now her only protection.

The pace slows noticeably and Clara looks up to see the dark form of a building through the branches of tall trees. As they draw closer, she can make out a massive old clapboard house, obviously deserted. Pure Gothic — empty door frames, broken windows staring from its peeling white frame.

The men have thrust what is left of the torches into the sandy soil a few meters back. Their light diminishes into a pale smoky glow. They cluster around a cellar opening at the side. Clara feels light-headed, giddy. The old man holds the light towards the stairs; the woman and child disappear into the blackness below.

Clara stands rigid between the dying light and the black well. Her last vestige of detachment vanishes as she realizes where they intend to take her.

"I ... I can't go down there."

The howl is heard again. Clara finds it plaintive, almost human.

"Watch your step," the father orders brushing past her.

There is a momentary lull, a few seconds when Clara glances beyond the shadows of the two remaining males towards the far side of the house.

"Better hurry, Miss." Footsteps seal her exit.

The stairwell blackness is suffocating and a sudden dizziness forces Clara to lean heavily against the rough inner wall. Cobwebs collect on her arm; something crawls across the back of her neck. The young men are so close, she hears their breathing. Panic drives her forward and she misses the last step. A firm hand grasps her shoulder from behind.

"Bring back that light!" he shouts. Clara concentrates on staying vertical and, when the lantern appears in the stairwell, she shakes uncontrollably.

"Give her a hand," the voice with the light orders.

Numbness sets in and, as they follow the flickering path of flame, Clara is less and less aware of the five male fingers pressing into her arm.

They turn and enter a small windowless room, a root cellar or storage place. Clara's feet record rough cement becoming packed dirt. A mouldiness permeates. The group has assembled here, someone pulls shut the thick oaken door. Clara hears the rasp of a bolt pushed into place.

The lantern is set in the middle, blankets are distributed. Clara pulls the rough material about her, burrows into the safety of its aging dustiness. She watches everyone settle into seemingly prearranged places, cross-legged in a circle around the light. The child is restless, squats down, gets up, cannot settle.

The house is obviously old and long neglected. The wall opposite her is crumbling, the lantern highlights the labyrinth of cracks that zig-zag into blackness.

Clara leans against the back wall, waits in the oppressive silence for someone to speak.

"How long do we have to stay here?" she asks finally. "Won't someone explain . . ."

The woman looks up momentarily, stares coldly.

"Two others besides our son have disappeared," she says. "We brought you here for your own good."

The small vestige of reason left in Clara's brain questions this. Wolves do not kill people. It would be in all the papers. Besides, people disappear for other reasons.

The lens takes over again and the circle recedes until Clara feels completely detached from it.

A small warm hand on her arm momentarily re-adjusts the focus. The child motions towards the door, then moves back into the circle.

The air stifles Clara, she knows she must get out soon. On the far side, the old man silently lights a pipe. Its small red eye illuminates his wrinkled beaten face.

One small step at a time, Clara inches towards the door. The blanket slips, and as she pulls it back over her shoulders, her hand brushes against a surface of thick soft hair, animal hair. It's her own arm . . .

Her fingers feel closed together now and her legs hunch down. "Please," she tries to call. "Please let me out." The syllables implode into the circle. No one pays the slightest attention.

Clara presses against the door, fights tearing off the blanket. The need to flee accelerates with her heart beat.

The child is beside her again, quietly tugging at the bolt. She looks up. "Go," she whispers. Her eyes meet Clara's. "Go and be free." The child leans heavily against the door and a narrow crack appears. Then she flings herself into the circle, crashing against the lantern.

Clara lunges against the door, leaps through. The steps melt underfoot as she bounds on all fours out onto the sand. She hears them plunging up the steps behind her, shouting, calling. She crashes through the trees towards the first slope. The bushes reach out to her, the grass brushes against her belly.

A plaintive howl echoes through the soft dawn light. The tone is articulate, the meaning clear. She pauses only momentarily, then lifts her sleek gray head to answer.

17
James Bacque
DESIRE
AND KNOWLEDGE
IN KEY WEST

S HE wakes in the dark listening. Dawn lights the Renoir on the wall and she imagines him painting this nude young woman, fresh and glowing long ago. Now the woman is dead and Nina thinks with pain of the paintings she wanted to do when she was like this young woman, happy with hope.

The clock reads five a.m. She gets up wearing her dress, carries the heavy bag to the door of the living room, pauses, afraid of all the alarms they have in this house, the machine gun that waits beside Dade's bed.

She shuts off the sound-scanner and quietly opens the door. Damp from the ocean smokes in the air, darkening the red hibiscus by the door. Hitler wakes up and prowls towards her, his head down, sniffing her.

There is no bus in this part of Lauderdale. She has to walk down the street to meet a taxi. She feels free, the sun half a red ball over the mild gray Atlantic lighting her way between the shuttered and whirring houses.

Before she gets into the taxi she turns around looking for a car that she fears might be following her along the wide empty streets. She lies to the taxi driver, gets out at the Hilton, and takes a second cab all the way out to the airport. She has been so distrustful of them all along that she has never told them her address in Toronto, but she is still afraid to go there. She phones Catherine at her hotel in Key West. When the girlish voice of the woman she trusts comes on the line, she almost weeps. "Can I come down right now," she asks urgently.

"Right away," Catherine says. "I'll get a room." Nina hangs up quickly, feeling the heat of emotion starting in her choked throat.

She lies to the ticket man, saying she is going marlin-fishing. He looks at her tiny wrists and says with a smile, "Good luck." Her history so depresses her, especially the terrifying revelations at her father's funeral that most of what she says now to any stranger is a lie or a truth camouflaged by a flagrant hint that it is a lie.

She keeps truth hidden from men just as her father kept himself hidden from her. At his funeral three days ago, she discovered the source of his mystery. Leo was a bigamist with a second family of rich drug-runners in Fort Lauderdale. Or is hers his second family? Near his coffin hiding the final violent bruises under his skin blooming like pressed flowers red and blue, she met his two sons, her half-brothers Dade and Frank, and her father's other wife, Susie, a scared crazy woman full of Quaaludes. Susie took her into the guarded house and showed her the small Renoir that Leo meant her to have, the shining nude entitled "Woman Of Speracedes" which had hung over her bed that night.

"It's yours, take it," Susie said carrying it into the bedroom. "He bought it for you, you take it along with you when you go now, you hear now."

Every time she was embraced at the funeral by a new male relative or friend of Leo's with tears in his eyes and words about how wonderful and generous Leo was, she felt a hard lump of gun. Susie invited her to do a ganja run with them to Jamaica as if it would be a family picnic, running drugs past the Coast Guard. From the moment she got there, Nina planned her escape.

The concierge in the Pier House lobby actually gets up in alarm as she arrives. Nina walks collapsing towards Catherine who is opening her arms with affection that is already becoming sick dismay as they embrace. Nina whispers in her ear, "Don't let go of me, I'm falling down." She is held up until Pierre shoves her bag in behind her and sits her down on it while he gets a chair.

"I didn't think I was going to get out alive," she whispers up to Catherine. "I'm afraid they're following me."

Catherine is looking down at her with calm concern like a mother, but without predatory anxiety. "Have you eaten," she states reprimandingly, then brusquely orders orange juice from the reception woman, who swishes away to get it with a twitch of her flowered sarong expressing extreme doubt about this fainting arrival.

In their pale blue room overlooking the shining blue gulf, Nina sits drinking coffee, the haggard waif in the war-torn movie lacking only the broad-brimmed hat with the ribbons dangling over pigtails. Pierre says he is certain that if they were afraid of her they would not have let her escape.

"You don't know what they're like," she says. "I went to the ladies' room in a restaurant and a strange man followed me in. Dade came running in and shoved his gun into this guy's face and said 'I'm going to blow you away.' I said, 'Dade, put it down,' and he said, 'Don't worry, it's loaded.' He gave this incredible laugh like he was going out of his head right there and then. Oh, they're insane, he was zonked out on coke. The guy practically fainted, he got down on his hands and knees and crawled out."

Pierre, a big, very certain man, is staring at her, smiling. Finally he says, "They don't know where you've gone."

They put her to bed in the room next to theirs and she sleeps almost round the clock.

For three days she is a hermit. All her tiny meals are brought in to the room. When she comes out, she is behind dark glasses, under a wide-brimmed hat, skirted to the ankles. She sits with her back to the room. But bearded Alan Cohen, music teacher from Cincinnati, has veered from Pierre and Catherine to concentrate on mysterious Nina. Nina asks Catherine immediately, "How long has he been here?"

"Since we were."

"Then he can't be looking for me."

"Take a deep breath, hold it for ten seconds, then let it out slowly." Nina pretends to obey, but she is secretly scanning the edges of the garden from under the hat. It is at this moment that she begins to feel the whole thing is ridiculous. From now on, fear is a pose which she can not quite abandon.

Alan Cohen, seeing all her defences, thinks she is also pretending when she says she likes Scarlatti. "What do you like of his?" She looks at him in perplexity. She had said she liked Scarlatti because she knew Alan wanted her to like him. It was an answer that did not require proof.

"Oh those lovely jangly fugues on the clavichord." She takes a chance — "The Concerto Grosso" — because they all wrote one. Now she is riding a lie again, witch on a broomstick through the horn-mooned sky. Cohen looks levelly at her and she knows he is intending to straighten her out.

"Hey, it's a *menage à trois*, right?" Janice says, blurry with drink, her tooth painfully missing from her once-pretty face. Janice's husband Dave, steady Alan Cohen, and all the others look at her with pleased expectation. Everyone in the hotel has been guessing what goes on amongst Pierre, Catherine, and Nina. The physical affection among them makes it obvious that they are not normal. They kiss and they hug and they smile and hold hands indiscriminately. Janice insists on an answer with her "Huh, threesies huh?" Nina feels the smile of disaster on her face. What can she do but nod. She doesn't want to deny what they want to believe, that she and Catherine and Pierre have the recipe for the ultimate drug, sex with a friend. "It's a very special relationship," she says primly, preserving her mystery. No one is satisfied.

Many people think she is deceptive because they make wrong assumptions about her. She changes quickly because she feels, like her father, among the hunted of the world: in the open she must move quickly, repose is hers only in secret. Her last exhibition, which she titled "Paintings I Cut Out Of Dreams," was of doors ajar on rooms which people have just left, of boots falling over and dresses just taken off hanging warm and empty.

Alan studies Janice with sad distaste, an expression so overt he obviously doesn't know he has it. Janice chatters desperately in her pain, terribly drunk, her head falling forward. It is St. Patrick's night. Waiters break up a fight as several women yell encouragement to the flailing men. Nina stares at the men aghast, thinking that this society is out of control. Janice's husband David, beefy and jumpy, asks, "What are yew thinking?"

"American effusiveness is just optimistic hysteria," she says, then laughs at her own primness.

David looks at her with puzzled truculence. "That's the trouble with yew Canadians, you're all suh goddamn propuh." He draws himself up proudly and states, "I mean, I *believe* in Mom and the flag and apple pie and all that shee-it." Everyone laughs.

Janice leans forward to Nina obviously sure she has found a friend and says, "David's impotent. Oh just with me. We haven't done it for years." Nina nods, not quite surprised. In Janice's tone is an anxiety about more than impotence. "He doesn't mind if I fool around, I'm trying to lay Alan tonight." She nods as she says this. It is a conversation with herself. "It's not his fault, you know." She has tears in her eyes. "It was the way he was brought up, and then he was hurt in 'Nam. He's been married four times already and he's only thirty-one. He's violent sometimes but never cruel. I love him so, crazy man. Can you understand that?" She looks with open hurt at Nina who sees that suddenly all the Americans are looking at her. Janice has made an appeal beyond manners to their common humanity.

Nina suddenly throws off her Canadian reserve, feeling like a young woman undressing for the first time at a topless beach. "My first husband beat me so badly I had to go to hospital, my second was a suicidal drunk, I've been in analysis for four years, everyone knows what I need except my second husband Robert, who is the only one I ever needed, I've just been told my gallery has been cheating me for years, and now I find that my father had a second wife and family. At his funeral, I found out."

At the end Janice is actually cheering this dam-burst, saying "Yah yah, right on," and waving her fist, and Alan is slowly smiling, saying "Far out, far out." It's as if she has passed a barrier and became American. She realizes with amazement that for these people, citizenship is equivalent to despair.

Alan leans forward opening his eyes wide so they seem to flash, an effect she sees him practicing in a mirror. He says, "Come to bed, it'll do you good." Like most men she has known, he thinks that going to bed with him will be a general restorative like a sauna.

"Poor Alan wants to conquer me, if only he knew how many times I've been laid waste," she thinks to herself.

She tells Alan, "There's no pleasure in this restless search for pleasure." He stares at her distressed. She has just taken away his whole reason for coming to Key West.

Dr. Fleming questions her: "Are you afraid? Are you afraid of sex? Are you afraid of men?"

When she lies down with him, she is remote. "He's nice, he's high in the air above me connected to me by that spindly thing like a dragonfly, and how does it feel? As pleasant as a pina colada, not as moving as a toothache." She is fascinated by male intensity, her own remoteness. A few grunts from Alan, a grateful kiss on the side of the neck, and it's over again. All through Alan's experience she was discussing it with herself. "I'm like a soul migrating from a body," she decides.

She puts on a white nighty and tiptoes to the glass door onto the garden. Alan does not stir. She quietly closes it, taps on the adjoining door, tiptoes to the bed. Pierre sits up. She sits beside him, and he holds her close beside him. Catherine makes a comforting "mm-hmm" sound in her sleep. Nina holds Pierre's hand.

"I can't sleep. Let's go to the Wheelhouse and drink brandy."

Barefoot they cross the flowered central garden on the lighted path holding hands, and she feels the wicked daring of the schoolgirl breaking curfew.

It is two a.m. but the bar is full, loud with revelry. No one notices that she is wearing only a nighty. They find a table and they talk and watch a St. Patrick's night fight breaking out at the bar. In a far corner a man and young woman are seated on the floor by a table kissing passionately; their love-making grows ever more intense, clothes twisting off, legs twining with legs, hands going down over more and more sunny skin. She watches this amazed and excited, feeling that in this strange atmosphere with people acting so oddly, something is out of joint, there is a crack in the world tonight through which strange new things will erupt.

"I'm surprised that you bother with Alan," Pierre says.

"Everyone told me I needed to go to bed with a man, even Dr. Fleming. He says I'm sexually anorexic. Or maybe it was anaemic."

"Anorexic from him probably means your lack of his normal male desire."

"That certainly wasn't my problem with Robert. We were like those two there." She glances at the couple who are now nude under the table. "But I kept expecting sex to turn into something else, happiness or love or knowledge or something. I thought at least I might learn something, but desire makes no difference to knowledge. Or at least not to mine. I ended up feeling so stupid. Is desire love? Is friendship desire. I might as well expect making love to change my opinion on acrylic paints."

"It's mainly just friendly," Pierre says, looking at the struggling couple. "But you expect everything."

"I want to paint the best," she blurts out suddenly. "The best."

"You're doing fine," Pierre says with a sigh. He reinforces her opinion of herself a lot and sometimes it feels to him like a job. He has become her caryatid holding up her collapsing ego.

"It's nothing compared to what I want. I used to imagine these great paintings and new techniques and went for them but they're so hard, so difficult and I used to get them wrong a lot and then I'd have to do a painting all over, again and again and it was too hard, too expensive, so now I say 'It's too chancey, you have to earn a living Nina,' and I compromise to get the show done, I think, 'That's okay, that'll sell.' I always want to do the best and I always draw back at the last moment."

"It's the same with men?" Pierre offers.

"But then I despair because I don't want just an ordinary life. I want to give myself up to something wonderful and it's always love."

Pierre laughs. "Oh happy love."

"Love like a happy death," she says.

He thinks she is too sensitive for the violent mediocrity of ordinary life. He is touched by her plight. He looks at her with deploring affection, feeling huge with a strength that is useless to her. He takes her round the waist so she leans against him comfortably as they saunter along the path.

She takes her watercolors to the garden in the courtyard by the pool. As she walks by the security guard, he looks over her into the shrubbery on the far side of the garden, chatting into the dark box in his hand. She finds an hibiscus in bloom, sitting before it to paint in fear her trembling memory of the smoky red hibiscus by the door of Dade's house. As she colors in the background of oleander leaves, Hitler's eyes look at her from the shadows. Pierre is silent before the watercolor, then shakes his head, his hand resting on her shoulder.

"Amazing. Terrifying," he says in approval.

"It's called Hitler's Eyes," she decides.

She bronzes by the pool. Alan squats beside her, teetering on the balls of his bare feet, contemplating saying something to her. "Are you rich," he finally asks.

"Does he care about money," she wonders, then languorously looks into his cement-gray eyes. Cohen is wondering about something else.

"No. Why do you ask?"

"In the sense of, do you work. I can't afford this place, really." Suddenly she realizes that he is staying for her.

"Neither can I."

"Maybe we should move in together."

She laughs. "Or out."

At Freddie's Bar that night they dance among the men dancing with men, then stand in the darkened room among whispering shifting men watching *All About Eve*. Near the end tough George Sanders tells off chief bitch Anne Baxter: the room erupts with applause at the woman's punishment. A hand firmly caresses Alan's bottom. He looks at Nina who stares at him questioningly. Alan turns on the hand caressing him again, slapping it away.

"Tempting beast," says the man. He walks away.

She takes Alan's arm and presses her negligible breast against his arm, reassuring to be reassured. They walk home through warm dark to a police car standing in front of the hotel chatting to itself. Two cops in blue shirts bring out a small scared dark man between them. One of the cops is smoking a cigar. They shove the prisoner into the caged rear section and slam the door hard.

"You're in 603?" the manager says to Nina. "He was trying to get into your room. In fact the door was open. We'd like you to come and see if he took anything."

For a moment she is capable of swooning, but that would mean missing the next events: she must know why he was there. She runs out to the car which is just rolling away.

"Who is he? What's his name?"

The cop with the cigar says nothing but turns and looks at the man, who shakes his head mumbling, "Miguel."

Has she seen him before? Was he in Dade's club that night? Was he sent?

"Of course not," Alan says later, "how could they find you?"

"Check my credit card imprint from the hotel. If they don't own the hotel they own the bank, if they don't own the bank, it's the computer company. They find out everything, they traced a stolen boat from Majorca to the Turks and Caicos and collected from the thief, he was using it for ganja runs. One of them has a submarine. I'm going."

"But nothing is missing."

"They don't want anything. They want me. I'm going."

Before the sun is up she has packed and headed out to the airport in a taxi. The red edge of the sun shimmies up out of the sea as the little plane leaps up off the runway. She is in Miami Airport behind dark glasses all day watching the female narks in Guccis with lapdogs in their arms jostle suspects while the trained dogs sniff for drugs. Then she lands in Pittsburgh for three hours that seem like a week.

Toronto's night is so warm that her taxi driver opens his window as he cruises down her street to the apartment. He offers to take her bag up for her, but now she feels almost safe. She doesn't need anyone beside her up the dark stairs. She opens the door to her apartment alone, tired, a little drunk from the booze in the airports and on the flights, still humping her big bag alone.

She closes her door behind her and turns on the light, looks into the living room and screams "No." She puts her hands over her eyes, runs back to the door and pulls it open. She turns in her doorway and looks between her fingers back into the living room and again sees her father's Renoir standing on her mantelpiece.

18
Charles Wilkins

THAT'S THE ISLAND AND THESE ARE THE STONES

IN the autumn of 1973, I hiked the entire Appalachian Trail, from Halstead, Vermont to Truckey, South Carolina — twelve hundred miles, forty-seven nights in the wilderness.

One morning in Virginia as I crawled from my tent, I spotted a cougar, a mountain lion, looking down at me from a tree about twenty-five yards away. I stared for a few seconds then scrambled back into the tent and, crouching on my knees, pulled my four-inch Buck knife from my pack.

I considered screaming at the thing, trying to scare it off. I considered darting from the tent and climbing a tree, to have at least superior positioning should it decide to attack. I considered sprinting back down the trail to a lake I'd passed the evening before and diving in.

But I did nothing — just knelt there sweating, staring out through the netting in the tent flap.

I waited perhaps an hour and was about to take action when a middle-aged man and woman, Germans, came striding down the trail. My tent was set in such a way that I could see them through the small back window. When they were fifty yards away, the cat leapt from its perch and disappeared into the woods.

I crawled out and greeted the couple, anxious to tell them about the cat but not wanting to alarm them. I asked if they'd stop for coffee. "We've had our coffee," smiled the woman, and before I could tell them anything they moved on, and I quickly packed up and followed them down the trail.

Late that morning I stopped at the ranger station at Walford Peak and told the ranger about the cat. Above his desk was a plaque: "God grant me the serenity to accept the things I cannot change . . ." He listened to my story and said, "I been out here thirty-one years, pal, and I never seen a mountain lion yet — you sure it wasn't something else?"

"Like what?"

"Like a porky or somethin'?"

"No," I said, "it was a cougar."

He lit a cigarette and exhaled what must have been a cubic yard of smoke. He got up, walked to the window and stared out into a dense stand of spruce. A spot of sweat about the size and shape of a birch leaf had soaked through the back of his shirt. He turned and said quietly, "I'm no authority on wildlife, son, but one thing I know fer damn sure — there ain't no mountain lions around here."

I have done a fair bit of traveling, much of it alone. But for a few weeks in December of 1974 I traveled with four Americans, two men and two women, in their mid-twenties. I met them in Barcelona, and a few days later when they were about to leave for Costa Blanca they offered me a place in their van.

One of the women, Catherine, was from Cleveland. She was six feet tall and had an engineering degree from Ohio State University. She wore skin-tight jeans and was the only member of the group who didn't drive.

One morning in a campground south of Valencia she got up, made coffee, and brought me a cup as I lay in my sleeping bag. I had chosen to sleep outdoors in a picnic shelter to prevent crowding in the van. I slipped into my clothes and carried my coffee to where she was sitting on a ridge of grass that overlooked the sea. In her lap was a book, whose title was hidden from me. "Do you want to hear something strange?" she said. She flipped a page and read: "The eastward view from the Borros Campgrounds takes in a small treeless island, believed to be the ancient quarrying site of rust-colored pebbles once carried by Spanish sailors in the belief that they would ward off the evil spirits of the sea. The same stones were carried by the sailors' wives to keep their husbands faithful."

She closed the book and pointed across the water to a faint brown smudge on the horizon. "That's the island," she said. "And these are the stones." She opened her hand and showed me two tiny red balls, heavily blotched with grime. She put one in the pocket of my shirt and said, "Don't lose it."

That afternoon in the van, she caught me staring at her thighs; and by nightfall I had lost the stone.

In Calpé, we rented a villa next door to a half-dozen Americans who had gone to university with Catherine and her friends and who had planned to meet them here. When we arrived, a young man with a Farley Mowat beard leaned out the window and yelled, "Where the fuck were you?"

Every night for two weeks, we partied until everybody was either unconscious or too weary or sick to carry on. During the day we lay on the beach and made beer and wine runs to the bodega. We smoked finger-sized reefers of North African marijuana.

In no time, Catherine and I were up to our throats in a dizzying love affair — all of which took place in my head. We humped round the clock — in every possible position. When a dozen of us went skinny dipping one night, I followed her into the water, dove down and disappeared in the amniotic sea of slime and salt. When I surfaced, my forehead was within a foot of her backside. It was as close as I would get. She turned and said my name in mock dismay, as if I were a silly old friend, or a pet.

That night she made love to an Australian, an engineer like herself. I could hear their whispering and wheezing from where I slept on the couch outside her room. I saw myself crashing through the door, throwing the light on and dousing them with ice water. A ventilation fan squealed from the kitchen until I imagined its bearings were at the point of liquefaction. When I announced at breakfast that I was taking the bus to Madrid for Christmas, Catherine looked up and said, "Really?" Her friend, Dee, who had barely spoken to me since our arrival, sat down at the table and said, "Would you mind if I came along?"

"Not at all," I lied.

"Are you sure?"

"Positive," I told her.

She walked to her bedroom and called back, "When are you leaving?"

"Soon," I said.

"Have I got time to go to the bodega?"

As we jounced across central Spain, I suffered a longing for Catherine that I imagined was more or less proportionate to her apathy towards me. I reminded myself that I hardly knew her, that we hadn't even kissed. Which was certainly the larger part of my problem. I took a room near the Generalissimo's palace. Dee went to stay with a girlfriend who taught at the American school on the outskirts of the city. My bed had a deep concavity in the mattress, and my sheets had been laundered to the translucency of cheesecloth. A hangnail, an earring, a few minutes of brisk lovemaking would have torn them to bits. But they stayed intact. I thought about Catherine; slept with her; dined with her. I doused her in ice water.

On Christmas Eve I walked through a light rain to the Prado and found my way to a high-ceilinged gallery that housed a dozen or so El Grecos. My only company was a dignified old man, a kind of Prospero figure, with white hair and a linen-colored goatee. He wore a three-piece suit, and was examining one of the paintings with a magnifying glass. As I came up behind him, he turned to me and I recognized him as the gangster actor, Edward G. Robinson. I spoke to him, and he responded with a brief, exuberant lecture on the paintings around us. He was intrigued by a particular quality of light that he was unable to define. He used the words "dispersal" and "longing" but couldn't quite put them into context.

When I was about to leave, he said, "What's your name?" and I told him and he gave me his hand and said, "I'm Edward Robinson."

I told him I knew, and he nodded and went back to his magnifying glass.

I had Christmas dinner with Dee and her friends, and the next day the two of us left for Paris by train. As we rolled through the Pyrenees, she offered up a fulsome assessment of the writings of Simone de Beauvoir and Jean-Paul Sartre. She asked me if I'd studied existentialism, proceeding to define it as a belief that man's existence preceded his essence — all of this as dispassionately as if she were reporting the number of miles to the border. She looked at me smugly, and I realized the nature of our problem: we didn't really like one another. I told her I had no use for definitions, then, as if to dispel the foolishness of such a statement, launched a gassy commentary on the need for intellectual defiance.

We got to Paris around suppertime and by eight o'clock had taken a room in a crumbling hotel, the fourth-floor windows of which looked out on the holy shrine of the Sacré-Coeur. The man at the desk wore eye makeup and what appeared to be a brassiere underneath his shirt. On the wall of our room above the lone bed was a poster of a young David Bowie and a prominent spray of what were unmistakably blood stains. A sign said, THERE MUST BE NOT WASHING OF GARMENTS POSITIVELY IN THE SINK.

Sometime after midnight I got into bed and lay there, face to the wall. Dee went into the bathroom, and when she came out I glanced at her in the darkness and realized she was naked. She got into bed behind me, and, after a brief silence, I asked her if she had enough room.

"I'm fine," she said quietly.

I lay there, restless with her presence; I told myself there were a million men for her, men with Ph.Ds and Porsches and law practices ... and hearts bursting with love. What could I say, that I wanted her friend instead? I hoped, simply, that she wouldn't test the issue.

In the end, she didn't have to. I fell asleep, waking up an hour later with an image of her nakedness very much on my brain. I turned to her, surprised that she hadn't been facing me. I put my hand on her side, and she drowsily pushed it away. In a pathetic reprise of high school clumsiness, I tried again, then again. Ten minutes later we were holding tight.

Afterwards, she told me that as a seven-year-old she had founded an organization called Dolls are Real. She also told me that in her fourth year of university she had had thirty-three lovers, most of them men. I drifted into a precipitous anxiety. I dreamt of a man who had somehow lost his ribs.

Dee went to London; I took a train to Andorra where I paid a skeletal Arab sixty dollars for a six-hundred-dollar Rolex. I asked if it was stolen, and he looked at me as if I were an imbecile. On my second morning there, I bought the *International Tribune* and went into a restaurant for breakfast. On the back page of the paper, beneath an article on Sudanese politics, was a lengthy obituary for Edward G. Robinson. I read it, feeling faintly etherized, then read the sports page, the funnies and the lead editorial, all of which seemed to have been written by someone who viewed the world through the reducing end of a peepscope. That night I tore out the obituary and trimmed its edges with a pair of nail scissors. I stared at it for a few seconds and stuffed it in the pocket of my jeans.

By the time I got back to Calpé, most of the men had taken off. The Australian engineer had gone to Morocco. Catherine now shared her room with a woman from Montreal. On a mild morning in mid-January, a few of us walked to the beach to play football — no contact, four downs to the field. On the play that ended the game I ran a few feet into the water chasing an overthrown pass and ended up diving into the surf in my T-shirt and jeans. An hour later at the villa I pulled the soggy obituary from my back pocket. Edward G.'s picture was smudged to the point that his Homburg appeared to have lifted from his head. I carefully unfolded the wad of newsprint and plastered it to the stucco of the living room wall. A few days later it would be scraped off in bran flake-sized bits by a cleaning woman whom we'd hired to guarantee our damage deposit. But for now it clung, a graft, a reminder, last week's urgency half dissolved in sea water.

During the afternoon I walked down to the docks where I ran into Catherine who was carrying a plastic bag of tiny fish. We talked briefly and went out onto the breakwater where she asked me about my trip. A fleet of brightly painted fishing boats bobbed in the harbor. She asked about Dee and I told her what there was to tell.

We walked to the market and bought fruit and olives and wine. As we walked home she asked if I still had the little red stone she'd given me in the campground.

"Of course," I said.

In the early evening I went out on the veranda and lay in the hammock. A few visitors arrived, and before long the nightly drunk had begun. Someone had brought an Iron Butterfly tape, the sound of which poured out the door like exhaust from an overheated dynamo. If I raised my head I could see the greenish lights of the breakwater. Catherine came out and we made our way downhill and walked along the beach away from town. We sat for a while on the rocks, and she told me about growing up in Cleveland. She then told me about a marine scientist whose underwater sound equipment had picked up a massive, unidentified beat, a kind of heartbeat, at five miles' depth somewhere off the coast of South America. The beat had been recorded across a two-hundred-mile-square area, and over a period of two years.

I told her I liked the story but that I felt it was the work of a poet, not a scientist. "Maybe both," I said.

"No," she said. "It's true."

I agreed that it was.

As we walked back the moon sent meteoric runners of froth along the waves. She took my elbow, and I put my arm around her waist. We stopped for a minute and stared out at the breakers, then turned to one another and kissed. If we were factors in the unwieldy arithmetic of night, or of the tides or moon or the crashing of waves — or of the simple emergence of a fact from behind the endless curtain of endless possibility — I couldn't, then, have told you how or why. Nor can I at this moment. But we were.

We walked on, and as we got close to the lights of town, I began telling her about the time in the Appalachians when I had been cornered in my tent by a mountain lion.

19
Shelley Leedahl
SPADES

IT was not knowing that scared us. Things like that didn't happen in Jackfish, where everyone knew everyone else and it was relatively safe to walk the streets at night. It didn't take long for the cops to learn about our dare at the church and we were each brought into the station and questioned, but none of us knew any more than what we actually saw: Buck walking around the church. Once, twice, three times and he was gone.

It started out as one of those long lazy summers when, at fifteen and a half, I was too old and too cool to be dragged along on boring summer vacations with my parents, and too young to have a respectable paying job. My two older sisters had already graduated and left Jackfish. They broke Mom and Dad in, so that by the time I was in high school, they let me do pretty much what I wanted. I was rescued from the annual family camping trip on the strength of a half-assed babysitting job.

The grueling four hours I spent each afternoon with the Gillis brats, changing dirty diapers, refereeing fights, was my penance for the nights, when most of the kids I hung around with ended up at my place. Someone would smuggle beer from their dad's stash or maybe there was a little pot and we'd all sit around in the purple haze of my blacklit bedroom. The rock music was always too loud and the neighbors sometimes complained to each other but no one ever called the cops because it was a small town and Dad was a bank manager, a position which carried almost as much weight as parish priest.

Some nights we'd stick a candle in a bottle and play a few rounds of Truth Or Dare, but most of us were already getting too old for kissing games; we had real dates to experiment with, and besides, none of us girls wanted to get stuck with Buck. His real name was Bernard, but he'd been Buck since Grade Two when he was bucked off a horse and had his head stepped on, and although his misshapen face gave us girls the willies, the guys all liked him, or pretended to, because he scored them a lot of dope and was considered a little dangerous. His old man had done time in Prince Albert for fraud and his brother was at the prison camp north of town for a B and E. Buck's mother was the cheapest bootlegger in town. Kind of a hard luck family.

Like I was saying, Buck didn't do much for any of us girls. He had crooked rotten yellow teeth and long greasy hair he parted in the middle, and he wore his shirts open at the neck to reveal a few black hairs on his pimply white chest. His hands were permanently stained: yellow, from nicotine, and sooty black which made little roadmaps in the creases of his palms from puttering with the engine of his jacked-up Mustang. You know the type.

I didn't have much say when Brad, my boyfriend-of-the-month, showed up with Buck on my first night of parental freedom that summer. Mary Ellen and Jennifer knew I had the house to myself, so they came over, and I guess John and Michael and the others just saw the cars at my place and thought there was a party. Like I said, it was a small town.

Anyway, that night we were all sitting around listening to Pink Floyd and getting depressed when Buck said we should have a seance. We girls groaned and rolled our black-lashed eyes but the guys thought we should try it and they called us chicken so we slowly agreed, the way girls do when they want guys to know they're making a major sacrifice.

No one really knew what to do, so we just sat around in a circle on the floor and stuck a thick white candle in the middle, lit it, and took turns asking the candle stupid questions like "Is there a spirit in this room? If there is, the flame will rise."

At first the boys said a bunch of dumb things, like if John got any last night, the flame would drop, or if Michael had a hardon, the flame would rise. Nothing much happened that night except people kept blowing out the candle and then it would be even blacker in the room and a lot of "oooohs" would go up, but no one thought anything of it.

The next night we all got together again, eight of us, and this time Buck got us playing that old game, "He's sick, he's dying, he's dead." You probably played it yourself. One person lies on their back on the floor, another sits at his head with the victim's head in his hands, while the others each sit around the victim with their two index fingers underneath the body. The person at the head begins by saying "He's sick" and each person repeats this. The leader then says "He's dying", as does everyone else, and finally, "He's dead." Then the person at the head says "Lift," and if there haven't been too many burps or giggles and each person concentrates, the victim can easily be lifted above everyone's head.

It didn't always work. Sometimes someone would say the wrong thing or laugh and Buck, whose elongated head looked even more eerie in the candle's flickering light, would get mad and we'd have to start all over. But when it did work, and it often did, everyone was amazed and the room always felt different after, like someone was watching.

Buck was really getting into this and he insisted we play it night after night. He often sat at the head, which surprised us girls because it was more like Buck to take a strategic position, such as the hips or chest when the victim was female.

It was about eleven at night, Friday, two days before my parents were due back. We'd played the "He's sick" game for about an hour already when Buck pulled a worn deck of cards out of his jean jacket pocket and asked if anyone wanted to see the devil. Because we were afraid of Buck, we girls didn't say anything. Of course, the guys asked how. Buck swore that if someone walked around a church three times at midnight, holding the ace of spaces, he would see the devil when he finished.

I don't think anyone, even the boys, was too keen on heading out into the dark night to check out Buck's theory, but he persisted, and the guys didn't want to seem like wimps. After they said they'd go, Pam Dobson, who was sixteen and had earned the nickname handjob among the guys, said she was going too. The rest of us girls followed along, some because we were too scared to be left alone in the house, others, like me, because we didn't trust our boyfriends alone with Pam.

As far as churches went, there wasn't a lot of choice. There was the United Church, where many of us were baptized, and even though we thought it boring, we didn't exactly want to desecrate it; the Presbyterian church, a plain white stucco building in a lot overrun by quackgrass; the Faith Center, where we heard strange things like altar calls took place and which many of us considered to be a kind of religious cult; the Jehovah Witness hall, which, in a five to three vote, we determined didn't qualify as a church; and the Roman Catholic church, a huge sprawling brick affair, complete with bats that swooped down from the steeple towards our hair. Of course, no other church would do.

It was on the outskirts of town, a fair distance even in Jackfish, which also sprawled, as if the early residents weren't entirely sure they wanted to be part of the community. The strange thing was that we decided not to drive. A bunch of fifteen, sixteen, and seventeen-year olds with souped up cars and we chose to walk, like it was the last mile or something.

Buck led the way; the rest of us followed behind, a loose pack of disciples. And then we were there, huddling on the gray concrete steps beneath the massive oak doors. Buck pulled out his deck of cards, fanned it, then withdrew the ace of spades and swung it in front of the guys, daring them to take the walk.

No one moved. The wind has a funny way of coming up unexpectedly on the prairie and it chose that moment to rustle through the long grass and rush up our sleeves and down our necks. Buck broke the silence.

"Come on you guys. It's ten to twelve, it only works at midnight." Still, no one offered. "Okay, what'll you give me?" he asked, then took a long drag on his cigarette. "What do I get?"

The guys pulled out their wallets, we looked in our black or brown leather handbags, and together we came up with thirty-four dollars, which we offered Buck. He accepted, counting the wrinkled ones and fives in his grubby fingers, then gave me the money to hold.

There was no giggling now, only the rustle of old newspapers and plastic bags being swept against the church by the wind. Buck held the ace in his right hand and left us on the steps as he walked around the corner of the church into the enormous dark yard. It was five minutes before he rounded the other side.

"One," he said, and smiled, showing us his stained teeth. We shivered and didn't say much. Those of us who had partners shrunk into their arms.

The second time around, Buck must have walked more slowly, because it was ten or fifteen minutes before he jumped out from behind the corner and yelled, "Two!"

We may have felt like stopping him then, I know I did, but no one said a word and Buck walked past us again. Five minutes. Ten minutes. We thought he was trying to scare us and we waited, thinking Buck would come howling around that corner at any minute. Fifteen. Twenty minutes passed, and still Buck didn't show. Brad and Michael and some of the others starting cursing Buck, calling him a stupid S.O.B. and saying how they were going to ream him out when he came back. Mary Ellen said it had been long enough, too long, and we'd better go look for him.

It was a group effort. No one wanted to be alone, and we shifted together like a dark shadow around that massive church. Around the back, the rectory, the old sheds where we imagined chipped ceramic saints stood comforting each other in musty storage.

We called "Buck," softly at first, so the people in the wartime houses across the street wouldn't hear us, then more loudly as the night got older and we became more afraid. Louder, as if our own voices could be any comfort on that windy night in July.

By two o'clock we still hadn't found him and nobody thought it was very funny, his trying to scare us like that. Except for Tracy and Jennifer, who were supposed to be home at one-thirty, everyone else came back to my place. We sat around the television, flicking from channel to channel, with all the house lights on. I quietly thanked God that my parents would be home in a few days, and I didn't sleep until dawn.

On Saturday, Brad phoned to say that Buck hadn't shown up for work at the Co-op where they both packed groceries. Brad phoned Buck's mom, who told him Buck hadn't slept at home, and did we know where the hell he was and could we tell him to get his skinny ass home? That was when we really started to worry.

There weren't too many places Buck could go. We thought he might have planned a little escapade with Pam, but we questioned her and she pretended to be offended we'd think such a thing and swore on a Bible she didn't know where he was. On Sunday, the cops had an APB out on Buck and the whole town was buzzing. My parents had heard the news on the radio and I'm not ashamed to say I ran out to the car when they drove up. I broke down like a blubbering idiot, as if I'd really cared about Buck.

A farmer found the body five days later. It was half-hidden in a hollow near the river that runs north of town, a few miles behind the Roman Catholic church. Old Jake Waterman was fishing when he noticed a large raven circling high above him. The thing wouldn't go away, he told the cops. Circling like a hawk, but it was a raven, he was sure.

Waterman thought there must be a dead gopher or rabbit nearby, so he lodged his fishing rod into the sand.

It had been hot; the rancid odor led him to Buck's body.

You know how rumors spread in small towns. Waterman remained pretty quiet about the whole thing, so what can you really believe? Some say Buck's eyes had turned yellow and that one had rolled, or been pulled, out of its socket. Others say his hands were chopped off and forced inside his mouth. Last I heard he had been castrated and bled to death.

The coroner said it was a heart attack, and we might have believed him but someone must have dragged Buck out of the river and the police had no suspects, not one shred of evidence.

We bought flowers for the casket with the thirty-four dollars — Buck's money. Those of us who were at the church the night he disappeared clung together like conspirators in a dark secret, but there was no secret, except Buck's own, and he wasn't telling a soul.

20

Sharon Abron Drache

THE MIKVEH MAN

IN one of the oldest cities in Canada, considered for many historical reasons a city of firsts, lived Rabbi Meir and his wife, Bertha.
The couple had been the spiritual leaders of Kingston's only Jewish
congregation for almost twenty-five years. Indeed, the Jews were
very proud of what they thought was tangible proof of their stability.

Despite the fact that the majority were not observant, their synagogue had always been called 'orthodox'. As Boris Wolinsky, the
president once said, "I may not be religious myself, but when I go to
shul, I want to feel like I'm in a *shul*, not a church. If I wanted a
church, there are lots in Kingston!"

The reason small, Canadian communities had difficulty keeping their rabbis was that they were filled with Boris Wolinskys,
zealots for an ideal only. For example, when the hiring committee
met over twenty-five years ago to discuss the qualities their new
rabbi ought to have, the six members agreed that, although every
man was created in God's image, their rabbi must resemble *His* more
than any of the congregants.

At the time, Moe Greenberg declared, "That's idolatry."

"Unfortunately, it's the truth," sighed Irving Abelson.

Accordingly, they decided to hire a rabbi from an orthodox sem-
inary. However, the only rabbis willing to come were among the
new crop of graduates, who invariably treated the small town stint as
internship. Most of these men arrived with their pregnant (or soon
to be pregnant) wives to face a plethora of problems. The wives suf-

fered because they could not meet the social demands, and the husbands who strove for religious purity only got bogged down with synagogue politics. There was little Jewish education for the children, no *shoichet* and no *mikveh*. The poor rabbi had to pray for his daily quorum. As much as Kingston wanted an orthodox rabbi, no orthodox rabbi wanted it.

And that is why the six-member committee and the entire community was blessed when Meir Levy applied for the rabbi's job.

Rabbi Levy was born in Lodz. When he was seven he came to Montreal with his Uncle Benjamin. Both the rabbi's parents and his older sister and brother had been dragged away in a tumbril while Meir watched from a crack in the wood wall of the garden shed where he had been playing. A dozen Russian officers marched behind the wagon, whose wheels clacked monotonously, while Meir's sister screamed. The rabbi never saw his mother and father again.

Meir lived in Montreal until he was forty-five, except for the four years he studied at a New York *yeshiva*. He returned with *smicha* and a wife, Bertha, to take charge of a Montreal pulpit. There he served eighteen years.

Before reaching their decision to engage Rabbi Levy, the members of the Kingston synagogue argued:

"He's too old!"

"He'll have old-fashioned ideas."

Yet, they hired him, because, they said, "At least, he'll stay!"

"Sure, he's too old to move."

"Since when is forty-five old?"

But Meir and Bertha proved to be the most patient, understanding rabbinical couple the *shul* had ever employed. Being older, they didn't try to change the ways of their congregants. Rather, they accepted them for what they were, a bunch of *apikorsim*.

Willingly, the Levys endured the inconveniences of small town Jewish life. Every Monday, Bertha made her long distance call to Feinstein's, the kosher butcher in Ottawa. When Jake Feinstein brought the order on Thursdays, Bertha piled the meat as neatly as she could into her already crowded freezer. For the rabbi and rebbitzen had many guests for the Sabbath and other Jewish holidays. There were the university students constantly dropping in to talk about *life*. Of course, Bertha always invited them for a meal. Then, there were Kingston's established, not the Anglo-Saxons of longstanding repute, but the synagogue president and members of the board, the chairman of the UJA drive, the Jewish businessmen from Princess Street and their families, all frequent visitors to the rabbi's house.

Now, Rabbi Meir and his wife were older. They had just celebrated their fortieth wedding anniversary. Meir was seventy and Bertha, sixty-five. The *shul* executive got together to discuss how they could honor their faithful, rabbinical couple, the first to stay in Kingston for more than three years, in fact twenty-five! As usual, they could not reach a unanimous decision.

"How about a testimonial dinner in his honor and we'll use the money to plant a forest in Israel?" asked Sadie Swadrin.

"No," replied Morris Lithwick, "whatever we give should have something to do with the synagogue."

"A new youth room, next to the social hall," Pearl Cohen suggested.

"You think those kids would ever use it? A waste of money!" declared Sonia Reifeld.

Boris Wolinsky's wife insisted, "It should be a *personal* present."

The president moved they vote on the various suggestions but since everyone chose his own, they wasted their time. What they did manage to decide was to call the rabbi and ask him what he would like.

Merle, Boris Wolinsky's wife, was elected chairperson of the "Honor The Rabbi Committee." She phoned Rabbi Meir that evening but he was too modest to help her. She'd propose alternatives and he would answer only with silence. Finally, he said, "Ask Bertha." But Bertha, too, was indecisive. "I'll have to ask Meir first."

Bertha brought the rabbi his glass of tea with four strips of lemon rind and two spoons of sugar, hovering around his chair like a frazzled bird. "Isn't it marvelous, Meir, that they want to honor us? And so many beautiful offers. One of the gifts was free meat from Feinstein's, for as long as we stay here. Think of the money we could save — yesterday, I paid $2.80 for a pound of liver — I'm afraid to look at the bill . . . it's probably over a hundred dollars! The prices went up again because the Ottawa *shoichet* moved to Miami. Now, Feinstein has to order from Montreal. Meir, should we get free meat, what do you think?"

"I think ... I don't want free meat. I want something that will not only please us, but them, too. Do you know what I really want, dear Bertha?"

"What Meir?"

"A *mikveh.*"

"A *mikveh*? You're *meshuggah*! Who will use it? I'm too old and there are not three women in Kingston who are observant enough to visit the ritual bath."

"No, the women won't use it, but what about me? I could go with my *minyan* and a few of the university students before *Shabbos* and other holidays. Who can tell how many might follow? Remember my ancestor, the Ba'al Shem Tov? (Meir's cousin was married to the BeSHT's great-great-grandchild.) In Podalia, where the Hasidic leader lived, the *mikveh* became a custom for men."

"But this is Kingston. You can't turn those *apikorsim* into Hasidim."

"Who knows, Bertha?" he continued, full of enthusiasm. "This will not be an ordinary *mikveh*. I plan to call my cousin to make the arrangements."

"Which cousin is this?" Meir had cousins who did all kinds of religion-affiliated jobs, from synagogue beadles, to scribes, to ritual slaughters.

"Cousin Kalman from the Bronx. Not only is he a rabbi, he's also a Mikveh Man. He will make a *mikveh* that will do Kingston proud."

"You have to ask the board," Bertha insisted.

"I'll call Boris tonight."

"No, call Merle. But let me warn you, she'll explode when you tell her."

"That's why I'm calling Boris. A *mikveh* is a touchy subject. Besides, this *mikveh* is going to be for the men ... they have nothing of their own anymore!"

Bertha gulped, "Call ... but, call Sol Buchinsky, not Boris. Sol is Merle's co-chairperson."

When Rabbi Meir told Sol his idea, he immediately declared: "Impossible Rabbi, you ask the impossible. *Mikvehs* are more outdated than Bar Mitzvahs without parties."

"Sol, listen a moment. You never know what a *mikveh* could do for this community. It could inspire . . ."

"Forget it! The women would immerse themselves nude in Kingston harbor, before they would go to your *mikveh*."

"Look, I'm thinking of a different *mikveh* . . . a *mikveh* . . . for men!" The rabbi found himself saying, "This *mikveh* would be a sort of spiritual sauna." Then he kicked his knees together in frustration while he waited for Sol's answer. But, that's what he meant. A chance for the men to have a shared religious experience, separate from the usual synagogue prayer.

And believe it or not, it worked, because Buchinsky said, "What a rabbi we're blessed with! You win, Meir — don't worry, I'll convince the committee."

"You mean it?"

"I mean it!"

"Wait 'til I tell Bertha. She won't believe it."

"Meir?"

"Yes, Sol?"

"I don't believe it. . ." And he hung up.

The Mikveh Man arrived two weeks later, on a Friday at four in the afternoon. He wanted to celebrate the Sabbath with his cousin and his wife before he got down to business. Although Bertha had been rushing around all day, baking the challah, skimming the soup, roasting chickens, she went to meet Cousin Kalman at the station.

He got off the bus looking very shaky, dressed in a heavy dark suit, even though it was the middle of summer. He didn't scan the terminal for his family but instead stared at the floor while he teetered to the line of travelers, waiting for their bags.

Bertha recognized him at once because he wore the same black, straw panama Meir had admired years ago.

"Kalman," she called from the sidewalk near the bus, "It's me . . . Bertha . . . over here." The short rabbi (he was only five-feet-six-inches tall) looked up and made a pushing sign as if to say, "Patience, I'm coming."

With a red plaid valise in one hand, he approached her, repeating the same gesture as a greeting. She bowed, keeping a respectful distance.

"Excuse me, Bertha, I have a terrible headache. The air-conditioning on the bus was broken. It was stifling. Such a trip I wouldn't wish on my worst enemy — but tell me, how's Meir and Daniel?"

"We're all in good health, thank God. We'll fill you in tonight. But now, let's go home. You look like you could use a rest, even before *Shabbos*."

"Bertha, just a minute," Kalman sat down on a bench and she immediately followed suit. "What's the matter?"

"Is there a coke machine?" he asked, opening his suitcase. "I need to take an aspirin."

"Aspirin and coke? You'll get even more dizzy."

"Bertha!" Kalman replied, the mere utterance of her name serving as reprimand. She pointed to the coke machine and he waddled across the station. "Kalman's fix," she laughed to herself.

When they arrived at the rabbi's house, Kalman went straight to his room. Sundown approached. Still, Bertha did not hear a sound from upstairs. Soon Meir would be home from *mincha* and it would be time to put the finishing touches on the Sabbath table.

Bertha went upstairs to change her clothes. She always wore a silk or *shantung* dress on *Shabbos*. She liked soft materials. Tonight her dress was pale yellow. While she combed her hair and adjusted her necklace, she thought she heard voices coming from Kalman's room. She found herself crossing the hall, actually having enough nerve to pin her ear to his door. She knew Meir considered his cousin 'other worldly' because he was so pious. Now, in her own house, she was certain she discerned four separate voices. Three, in a dialect of Hebrew, perhaps Aramaic, while Kalman spoke what sounded like Biblical Hebrew. No sooner had she begun eavesdropping than the conversation abruptly ended, the door opened, and she fell forward into Kalman's moving body.

"Bertha!"

She stiffened, but still could not resist asking, "You had visitors, Kalman?"

"Yes," he smiled. "Visitors!"

"Where are they now — disappeared into thin air?"

"Sort of ..."

She looked perplexed while Kalman smiled, "Don't try to figure it out. The visitors are My Voices. They come and go, invited or not.

The situation is similar to yours, with your university students."

"Excuse me, Kalman, but what are you talking about?"

"My Voices," he repeated simply.

"Surely you're mistaken. You were talking to yourself."

"Never mind — now, I want to relax with you and Meir."

Bertha hesitated. "All right," she smiled. "Come, let's have *Shabbos*."

At the Sabbath table, Cousin Kalman spoke about his family in the Bronx. "We're so fortunate, Rose and I. The children and grandchildren live practically next door and only five blocks from *Bes Yankov*."

Meir inquired after Uncle Nachum, the most devout member of the family, a descendant from the *Datschlaver* dynasty of Polish Hasidim. They spoke of mutual friends, Benjamin Leipsig and Judah Weisberg, for they were the two others, who like Meir, left a big Jewish community to bring enlightenment to the Diaspora — for Meir, Montreal was Jerusalem.

Benjamin was a rabbi in Miami where the women wore sleeveless dresses to *shul*. Judah was in Detroit at an equally *treyfe* synagogue where they operated the bronze doors of their Holy Ark by remote control.

"Tell me, how are you two?" asked Kalman. "How do you manage here?"

"Uncle Benjamin's family is in Datschlav, just north of Montreal," Meir assured him. "Over two hundred families now. One day, they hope to have a separate town. They'll close the stores on *Shabbos* and other Jewish holidays.

"But, since Uncle Benjamin died two years ago, we haven't seen the relatives," confessed Meir. "To tell you the truth, they make me uncomfortable. They think Bertha and I are black sheep for living in Kingston."

"Take a look at them and you see who the black sheep are," Bertha signed, smoothing her *shantung* skirt.

Kalman changed the subject, "How's Danny?" (Danny was the Levy's only child.)

In a stream of praise Bertha rambled. "You know he and his wife Miriam went to Israel in '67. After the war, they settled on Kibbutz

Uriah, near Tel Aviv. Danny still paints. Several galleries carry his work, and Miriam, she sings in a Jaffe nightclub ... And Moshe and Micah?" Bertha answered her own question. "My grandchildren have ambitions — Moshe wants to be a teacher and Micah, *veysmir*, a mime! He idolizes Marcel Marceau."

"How old are the boys?" Kalman interrupted.

"Moshe is seven, Micah, six. Let me show you a picture." Bertha scurried to the living room mantle, returning with a gold framed photo. Proudly, she held the photograph under Kalman's nose.

"Beautiful — already they have plans, but the years pass and the plans change," said Kalman, thinking of the path his own life had taken. First a beadle in his father's *shul*, then rabbi, and now Mikveh Man! As a child he was a poor student but his teachers always took special interest in him because he had an extraordinary sense of the supernatural.

He would amuse them and his family and friends with endless stories about his Voices. One went like this:

> On the occasion of my Bar Mitzvah, My Voices appeared just as I was about to recite the weekly portion. They brought me a pair of golden wings, similar to the ones they wore. Standing before the Holy Ark, my body trembling, I feared I might crush their delicate present. My father asked: 'Why are you shivering, Kalman?' Of course I didn't tell him a thing. Not then.
>
> At home that evening, as soon as I counted three stars in the sky, I tried on my gossamer wings and flew about our garden.

After Kalman told this tale, he always related the following: "Every ten years, on the anniversary of my Bar Mitzvah, My Voices returned with another gift. On my twenty-third birthday I received three coral eggs. To this day, when I rub them, I cause unusual events to come about. At thirty-three, My Voices brought me two translucent turquoise eyes through which I am able to see all the good and evil in the world, simultaneously. At forty-three, I received a silver wand, capable of turning back time, and at fifty-three (nine years ago), My Dear Voices gave me a shovel!"

Such was the eccentric nature of Cousin Kalman. After chanting the final benedictions at supper, Meir could resist no longer. "Tell me exactly how you plan to make our *mikveh?*"

Kalman hesitated, "On *Shabbos?*"

"I don't mind," Meir shrugged.

"Very well," reaching into his vest pocket, he handed Meir a photograph. You and Bertha, take a good look — do you recognize the church?"

"It's the oldest in Kingston, built in the mid 1800s, I believe."

"That's where we'll find our *mikveh!*" Kalman nodded.

"What?"

"It's made of limestone!"

"Dear Cousin," Rabbi Meir insisted, "we can't find a *mikveh* in a church. Even if we could, how could we use it? A *mikveh* in a church is no *mikveh.*"

It was then that Kalman wondered if he should go upstairs to fetch his red plaid valise. He could display his Voices' gifts, show how he could accomplish the impossible.

But, alas, he knew the wings would be rusty, the eggs faded pink, the eyes dull blue, and the wand murky gray. Every Sabbath his gifts lost their powers. Even the shovel was deceptive. From sundown on Friday until Sabbath's end, this ordinary spade became a jeweled sceptre.

"Don't worry," Kalman said, "we won't leave the *mikveh* in the church. After we find it, we'll carry it away."

"And how do you propose to find it?"

"By digging for it, naturally."

"Kalman, we love you and we have great faith in your abilities, but we cannot agree to such a plan. The community thought I was crazy when I asked for a *mikveh.* If I tell them we have to dig for it in a church, they'll probably fire me."

"They want to honor you, not fire you," Kalman reminded. "Let me explain: the original church font was unusually large. In those days, they still performed baptism by immersion. Surely you have heard of the unceasing efforts of the local bishop with the Indians in the 1800s — he used to baptise two or three at a time in that font."

"Wait a minute," Meir interrupted. But Kalman paid no attention.

"That font has laid buried in the courtyard between the rector's house and the cathedral for years. And don't look so worried. The church has another font, much smaller than the old one, since today they baptise by pouring and sprinkling. I assure you they'll never want the old font back." Kalman's eyes gleamed. "They won't even know it's gone, will they?"

"How do you know?" Bertha inquired. But Kalman remained tight-lipped, got up, and went into the living room. She followed with his cup of tea and a plate with thick slices of honey cake.

"Bertha makes the best cake," Kalman said.

"The best," Meir agreed.

While they drank tea, they began chuckling and soon they were laughing so hard, tears came to Meir's eyes. "So Kingston will finally have a *mikveh* — when do we start digging, Kalman?"

"Immediately after *Shabbos*, we'll assemble at the *shul* — around nine. I hope to get to the church by ten. With luck, we'll hit the *mikveh* by three in the morning."

"I guess I'll have to tell the congregation tomorrow morning during services. I fear they won't agree to your plan."

"Don't tell them, until the last minute," Bertha suggested, totally caught up in the adventure. "Tell them you heard there's buried treasure in the churchyard and we Jews ought to dig it up and give it to the city."

Meir's eyes shone. "Part of what you say is true, a *mikveh* is a treasure." But he wondered why he clung to the old ways, as he summoned his strength: "I'm going to tell them the truth. I'll tell them we're digging for the *mikveh* in a churchyard."

"They'll hit the *shul* roof," Bertha said.

The next day, following service, Meir still had not made his announcement. He watched his congregation trickle out of the sanctuary while his loyal *minyan* stood around, chatting with Kalman. Rabbi Levy invited them to his study for a glass of whiskey, toasting: "Here's to the success of the Mikveh Man." The quorum drank. Everyone, in a slightly inebriated state, pledged support.

Meir didn't waste a minute. "Be back here tonight by nine. Bring your shovels."

It's difficult to describe what the line of men looked like parading with Kalman through the town. The solemnity of the occasion called for complete silence, each trooper with a shovel on his shoulders, on what Kalman called *the mikveh march*. He, however, did not carry his. Instead, he schlepped his red plaid valise.

The men dug and dug, resting briefly at one-hour intervals. At three in the morning, there was still no sign of the font, and the *minyan* was tired and disbelieving. Panic-stricken, Joe Lithwick cried out: "The priest gets here at six-thirty. If he catches us and this hole, we risk being shoveled into it."

"We'll just dig for one more hour," Kalman announced. "I'm sure we'll reach the font by four."

By the fourth stroke of the clock tower, one quarter of the churchyard had been dug up. Max was sweating. "We'll have to get this dirt back before dawn," he said to Kalman.

"Don't worry — I personally will take care of the dirt, after we find the font."

Throughout the entire evening, Kalman hadn't been participating. Instead, he sat on his suitcase, giving orders, where to dig, where to pile. Occasionally, he got up and poked at the hill of dirt beside the hole. Max said, "I suppose you're looking for the font. Surely, we should have found it by now, Kalman?"

But the little man from the Bronx only shrugged.

At five, the sun began to rise and the quorum was silent with fear. They threw down their shovels, refusing to dig deeper. Kalman paced the perimeter of the opening in the earth.

Before the astounded *minyan*, he opened his red plaid valise and took out his golden wings. He fastened them securely to his black, baggy jacket arms, leaped smoothly into the air, and flew about the churchyard, landing at the end of the hole near his suitcase. He carefully pulled out his three coral eggs, which he immediately winged to the bottom; then he flew back up, collecting his translucent turquoise eyes, which he positioned on top of the heap of dirt, so they could act as a telescope. He soared slowly over the opening in the earth, waving his wand, while the men stood by in a state of shock.

Kalman urged each of them to hold his wand over the hole and also to gaze through the two turquoise eyes. Reluctantly, they did as he asked. He took his ordinary shovel and covered the three coral eggs with exactly six shovels full of church dirt. Instantly and miraculously, everyone present thought he could see the font, big enough for the immersion of several people, adequate for a real *mikveh*, shining in the early morning sun.

If I told you the men lifted the font out of the hole and that they carried it to their *shul* on their shoulders, marching back over the same route they had taken to the church, you wouldn't believe me.

If I told you that Kalman transported the font singlehanded on his golden wings, back to the synagogue, you wouldn't believe me either.

But if I remind you that Kingston is a city of historical firsts, perhaps you'll concede that the first *mikveh* in town may have been created by a rabbi from the Bronx, in honor of the occasion of the twenty-fifth anniversary of the hiring of Rabbi Meir and his wife, Bertha, the first rabbinical couple to stay in Kingston for more than three years, in fact, twenty-five!

21

David Welham
WAITING FOR
THE ASSASSIN

A T 7:45 a.m. when Ben turned on his car computer the dream took hold. He saw himself back at the office. Like one of the managerial dinosaurs he walked slowly along the hall to the Executive Washroom with the *Financial Times* tucked under his arm. He felt safe in the end stall, reading his paper, finally relaxed. When he opened the door to leave, he was confronted by a tall man in a tailored suit. The man's face was covered by a ski mask. Only his eyes were clearly visible through the narrow rectangle of the mask. They shone with neon brightness. Framed in the black mask they looked wider than normal like the eyes of an innocent.

The brief case he carried snapped open with a loud click. In a continuous motion he pulled out a sawed-off shotgun, leveled it at Ben's stomach, and fired. The sound echoed around the bathroom until it deafened him. The scene then slowed as if viewed frame by frame. The force threw Ben backwards. The toilet tank exploded. For a moment he sat on the seat then fell forward. As he lay on the floor, he watched the pinkish water flow towards the drain in the center of the room. It twisted in a puddle before it went down the small holes. Ben turned his head to look up at the assassin. The man pulled off his mask — Robertson, the senior partner.

"Why," asked Ben.

"Cost effective," the assassin said.

"What?" asked Ben.

"You die by misadventure, the insurance company pays. If we let you go we have to pay. It's business. Nothing personal."

The assassin then put the mask into his briefcase along with the shotgun. As he turned away Ben said, "But I'm management!"

The assassin stopped and stared over his shoulder at Ben, the eyes grew even wider.

His car computer beeped as his daily schedule came on screen. Ben came out of the dream. He could feel a trickle of sweat move from his armpit to his waist. When he leaned back into the driver's seat, his shirt stuck to him. His hands fumbled with the cassette case as he took out the motivational tape to put in the car's deck.

The cover of the cassette had a drawing of a crouching samurai. The title was *Steps to Power and Control*. On the back the liner notes explained that the author had adapted the process for North-American businessmen from an oriental system called the Five Rings.

"Waiting for the Assassin," said the narrator in a deep, almost sensual voice. "Are you just waiting for him? In business today, if you're sitting comfortably in your office, doing what you've always done, then you're waiting for the assassin. He knows exactly what you're doing, when, and how you're doing it. He'll be there first, waiting for you. Why are you waiting for someone to just come in and take it all away? This is the information age. Information moves. If you don't reach it first, your assassin will. That makes you the target."

Ben stopped the tape. He'd listened to it many times, and every time there was something new to absorb, something new to think about. Lately he'd play little snippets, turn it off, and then meditate on the idea while he drove. That's when the ideas really flowed. Often the ideas of the tape chilled him with their applicability to his situation.

Ben reviewed the day's schedule. Two years ago he'd turned his car into a mobile office. His computer and printer were fixed on the passenger seat. The copier was secured to the floor. In the back seat he stored the extra paper and supplies he needed. He also had a travel bag with two complete sets of clothes in it.

While he reviewed his schedule, he made his daily call to Heather, his secretary, before she left for work.

"Heather. I'll be in this afternoon after I meet with the new client. He's promised me the project schematics for today. What I want you to do is get a contract ready so we can represent him. I'll fill in the name and the technical information.

"Something else. I did a search at the Business Name Registry. I came across a new company called Matsu Futronics. Spelt like it sounds. The business is listed as mind technologies. With the meeting tonight with Randcorp, that's too coincidental. I checked the city business licence office. They're registered as a R&D brokerage firm. But I couldn't find out anything else; every search led to another dead end. I think I have some serious competition.

"So I want you to phone around. Use your office contacts. If the data base is closed maybe we can tap the human one. Someone has to know."

"Okay" said Heather. "If you're coming in, Harris is going to corner you. You've been ducking him for a month. He's pretty edgy about it. But I could arrange a late lunch."

"Hum." Ben paused as he thought through his strategy for Harris. "Yes. Set it up. Have Dino's deliver their lunch special. Make sure there's two bottles of red wine." Ben knew that after Harris had a couple of drinks he'd be easier to deal with. "Make sure you tell him personally. No memos. Get him talking and coax any hidden agendas out of him. Fax me the information.

"And phone the company lawyer and gauge his readiness for tonight's meeting with Randcorp. Tell them I'll have the technical information to them by five."

"Fine. Is this meeting in town?" she asked.

"No. Just north of town," said Ben.

"Oh," she said. "The secretary network says Will Howard lives out there?"

Her voice sounded inquisitive to Ben. The question made the nervous sweat collect under his arm. The dream of the assassin was still fresh in his mind. He felt a throbbing constriction around his temples and with his free hand rubbed at them gingerly.

"I heard that too," Ben replied, "but I haven't been in touch for awhile."

Ben had no qualms about lying to Heather for the time being. Lying, after all, thought Ben, is just being elusive for the moment. He assumed Heather was loyal. Their relationship went back to when he was a junior partner with the firm. He had taken her with him as he was promoted. He'd also been responsible for her computer expertise. But she also worked for two other partners and had ambitions of her own. Everyone was a team player until their own career was threatened; then it was every man and woman for themselves.

His expertise ensured his continuation in the company; the tape had given him the business sense to make him a power player. After a decade in the firm he'd seen many of the senior people become redundant. That's when he accepted the prophetic nature of the tape — its universal application. The assassin had come and they'd been unprepared. In some ways a literal death would've been better than being made redundant in your late forties or early fifties. What chance did they have to survive? They were corporate dinosaurs; in their case murder would be more humane, he concluded — survival of the fittest.

Ben started the car and pulled out onto the frontage road; he checked his watch — a few minutes behind his normal schedule, he thought. The recognition of a regular schedule made him wince. The first lesson on the tape went on in his head: "Regularity is a threat. Terrorist groups always plan around the expected pattern." He entered a note on his daily plan reminders that he should review his day plans for the last month to see if there was too consistent a pattern. "Assassins will exploit such a weakness. That is called a window of opportunity. Learn to see where you create them. If you can recognize them, then you can open them to your own advantage."

Ben used his phone modem to access the main frame computer at the firm. Because the system's design was his own, he'd built in an override access for himself. He called up the code words to get into his associates' latest entries and also checked on Harris's projects. Ben scanned for any evidence that someone else had started into mind technologies. It wouldn't surprise him that Matsu might be a front for someone at the firm. The whole process took only ten minutes and showed no connection.

In the background the tape played into Lesson Two: Unity — Opposition. "Get to know your opponent. It is common for enemy commanders to have a picture of their counterpart to study. Real opponents know they are alike. Do not think of him as separate from you. That is fragmentary western thinking. Think of him as part of a struggle you are both involved in. Both pieces that complete the same puzzle. That is knowing the full picture. Know his face. If he is a worthy opponent he knows yours."

Ben prided himself on the knowledge about not only his competitors but also his cronies. He could identify all the other mobile executives. To prove it to himself he reviewed them all, seeing the faces fall one after the other like a stack of ID cards. He knew that at a stroke of a key he could scan their files and see their strategies as clearly as if he stared them in the eye.

"Change the power of the fear into a transforming energy you can use. Emotion prevents clear thinking." So Lesson Two advised.

Heather's fax came in just before he reached Will's. It read: "Meeting at 2. Harris anxious. Knows you've got the meeting tonight with Randcorp. He wants to know about what."

Harris will be no problem, thought Ben. In his mind he visualized a window opening. He would present his decoy plan and then proceed to the evening meeting with what Will had designed.

Ben and Will had been in high school together and had been hackers; cyber punks they liked to call themselves. Will had even gotten him a job at the firm, talked about what a great company they were.

Will could've been rich by now, high up the corporate ladder, but he'd been glitched by Harris. Ben still remembered the morning that Will came in all excited. He'd made a breakthrough on an accounting program he'd been working on. "It'll change everything in that department," he'd said to Ben proudly just before his meeting with Harris. When he came out he looked shaken. Over lunch, Will told Ben how Harris had saved him from making a career blunder. Harris had told Will that the program was too complicated and therefore costly to implement; Harris would bury the plan for Will until the timing was better. Will expressed how relieved he was that he had someone looking out for him. Three weeks later Harris presented the program to the board as his own and was promoted to head the reorganization. For Ben, it had been the object lesson of his pre-tape days. For Will, however, the theft was too much — he became unproductive and was forced to resign. No benefits. Will had retreated to the country. Now he made his living designing computer adventure games. Whenever Ben needed advice on the latest developments, he always talked to Will. Will's hacking skills were unimpaired; in fact, thought Ben, the introspection during his recovery may have made him better. Will could have been a formidable player, made a real come back. Ben just couldn't understand why Will preferred his garden like some monk who had withdrawn and only took on the projects that held some special personal interest.

When Ben drove the car into the yard, Will's dogs ran out as always and jumped up on the door barking until they recognized him. Then Will came out and called the dogs. They went bounding to him. With a sigh Ben got out of his car and checked the door for scratches. Will waved him over.

"You should come and see the garden," Will said. "I've developed a new program so that the entire irrigation system and sprinklers are computerized. The program is humidity sensitive. I'm working out the last of the variables now."

"Just think what you could do with that for the green lawn buffs in the burbs," said Ben. "You could clean up."

"I don't know," said Will. "I just made it to make sure the plants got the optimum moisture."

Ben rolled his eyes. "Look," said Ben, "make me a hard copy of the plans. I think this has real practical use."

"Sure," said Will. "You want to see it in use?"

"Let's take care of business first. I'll look at the garden later," said Ben as he followed Will into the house. All that talent, thought Ben, and all he's worried about is vegetables.

Ben leaned back against the kitchen table while Will made him some coffee. "I was reading the latest issue of *Advanced Tectronics*. There's lots of coverage about Virtual Reality."

"I'm aware of it," said Will as he sat down and indicated with a wave of his hand that Ben should too. Ben continued to stand.

"The theory is well known now. Still lots of research going on. Espionage too. There are even a few programs in existence. Mostly sports things like handball. Nothing sustained. And no one has developed a working portable proto-type." Will smiled up at Ben. "Until now."

Ben did not try to hide his surprise. "You've done it!" he shouted. The dogs jumped up at the noise.

"Yes," said Will still smiling widely with a proud father look on his face. "And the software."

"You know how big this is, don't you? A portable computer that creates a 3-D reality around you. Pre-packaged reality. Most people won't ever have the time or the smarts to create their own programs. What a market. They'll be like compact discs. And think of the money in memory expansion!"

Ben paused for a moment, breathing heavily and licking his lips. He realized that he was preaching to the converted. Still his enthusiasm kept him talking.

"This is ground floor stuff. We can create industry standards. I can make us both rich." In his head Ben was already thinking of promotion; he would get Harris's job like the guy was sitting still. That would make Will happy. This could be a major coup; maybe he'd become a full partner.

"Let's see it," said Ben. "I want to try it."

Will got up. "You'll have to sit down." Then he left the room. In less than a minute he returned carrying a brief case. He placed it on the table and opened it up. "As you suggested I tried to keep the machine as user friendly as possible. It's really quite simple. You put on these glasses." Will handed Ben what looked like sunglasses except that they were wired to the computer in the case. Next Will gave Ben a pair of gloves to put on. These too had wires running back to the machine. "I'm working on a way to eliminate the wires, work it on a transmission system, like your beeper.

"I've created a program sampler from the programs I've been developing. Literally all you have to do is turn the machine on, punch in the program of your choice and you're away."

"What are the programs?" asked Ben eagerly. He now wore the glasses and gloves.

"Youth, Sex, Nature, Nostalgia, Sports, and Adventure. Each has several choices to let you narrow your category. So what do you want to try?"

"Youth," said Ben. "While I'm on, why don't you get that sprinkler information together."

"Okay," said Will, "I'll make you a teenager again. The program will run five minutes."

Ben was sixteen again behind the wheel of his father's car. There was no loss of the present and yet he was back in time and experiencing the road. The kitchen had become an expanse of highway.

The steering wheel had substance in his hands. He felt his foot press down on the accelerator. The car responded by shooting forward. Ben had forgotten how sensitive the car was. The sensation of the speed of the car came over him. There was nothing but open road ahead of him. He held his foot to the floor until the car raced full out. Exactly the rush that Ben loved. Then the program stopped. Ben was back in the kitchen. "That was too much," he said.

"There's only one hitch," said Will. "Someone has been trying to break in. Someone knows."

Ben sat up stiffly, all the relaxation from the program gone. "Have they been able to extract anything?"

"No. But they're persistent. And they're good too. I haven't even been able to track them. At first I thought it might be you."

Ben shook his head. Inside his heart fluttered and his mind raced with probable suspects. He finished the rest of his coffee in one gulp. He needed to get to his car. For an excuse to leave he looked at his watch.

"Time to fly. I'll check the garden next time. Keep me posted about the intruder. I want to know the next time he tries to get in. The precise time.

"Under the circumstances, I think I should take the prototype. This'll prove to the investors that we're the company that's ready to go."

Will walked him to the door. Ben shook hands with him. "This will really blow Harris away," said Ben. "Trust me. When I finish with this deal you'll have everything you want."

"I have that now," said Will. "Would you like some fresh green beans. They're just starting to come in."

Ben laughed. "Will, when have you known me to cook at home? Thanks but they'd just go to waste." Maybe, thought Ben, he does have what he needs but it was still hard to believe.

As he started his car, Ben looked in the rearview mirror. Will stood on the porch, one dog on either side. Who would ever guess that this guy had just made history. He looked down at the briefcase. There are lots of firms that would kill to get their hands on this technology. He switched on the tape deck. "What you need is objectivity, foresight and symmetry. These qualities will provide the basis of success."

Once he entered the freeway he pulled into the far left lane. The physical rush he had felt from the machine had gone beyond the emotional high of driving fast. Because the program took control, he could concentrate all his attention to the thrill. The adrenalin rush made him feel invincible. As far as he was concerned the program had him driving for that five minutes — scenery flashing by in a blur of colors. That's how information moves too, he thought. As he passed other cars he felt like he was picking off competitors one by one, consuming them as he consumed the roads. He smiled with pleasure to see them fade in the rear view mirror. No competition he thought; but as the tape had taught him, and practice had shown, the ones that come up from behind are the ones to watch for. That meant technology as well as people.

The tape resumed with Lesson Three: Becoming Your Assassin — You Are He. "When you have studied your opponent long enough you can start to think like him. This means that you can feel his strengths and know his weaknesses. Fear makes him a demon with a blank face. Your knowledge allows you to imprint your image on him. You are he."

The traffic slowed to a crawl near a major on-off ramp. Ben immediately felt annoyed. He hated to lose the flow. But he remembered the tape, "Nothing happens without purpose." Ben looked around to see if there was something he was supposed to see. In the dividing ditch between the lanes he saw that the purple flowers were blooming. Interesting but not important, he thought. He looked at the cars near him, again nothing interesting. So what was he supposed to see or discover, Ben wondered impatiently? In his rear view mirror, he saw a silver Jag. The car was a classic XKE type. The tinted glass made it impossible for him to see anyone inside. He'd seen the car yesterday on the road north of the city when he'd finished his meeting with his contact from Randcorp, about production and distribution. "There are no coincidences," he heard the tape say. He remembered saying the same thing to Heather. That meant they knew about Will. Ben saw himself flung backwards into the bathroom stall.

Ben stayed in the slowest lane. The Jag maintained its distance. Even so, he got the license number. In a moment he'd tapped into the Motor Vehicle Branch. The car was registered to a new company.

Ben traced the company. For the moment he was glad the traffic crawled along; the electronic trail became complex, with lots of dead ends. Finally, when he tracked the parent company, he was not surprised to see "Matsu" appear on the screen. "Don't react with emotion," he remembered the tape saying. "It may only be a trap. Don't jump at the bait lest you end up in a trap." Ben watched the Jag planning his reaction.

When the traffic started to move again, the Jag followed him at a discreet distance. Fifteen miles from the city center the Jag closed the gap. Ben stayed in the fast lane; the Jag moved up on his bumper. Ben increased speed. The Jag kept pace. No way, he thought, are you going to force me into the slow lane. He kept the Jag boxed. Better than Parchesi, Ben thought; you're not in my league yet. The game lasted for five minutes until Ben pulled over to take his exit. The Jag pulled up beside him, but Ben was away on the exit. The tinted glass was an advantage he hadn't considered. Ben thought there was more honor in letting them know your face. The blackness inside the Jag was as bad as talking to someone who refused to take off his dark sunglasses. Ben knew they were reappraising him, even photographing him for all he knew.

As he drove up the exit he heard the tape again. "At some point you'll even have the same dreams."

Don't get nervous he told himself; that'll just result in mistakes — turn you into your own worst enemy. Instead, he knew he should be rehearsing for his meeting with Harris.

In the elevator all the way to the twenty-third floor Ben felt claustrophobic. The elevator was too much like the washroom stall; the dream was still vivid in his head. As the doors opened on the reception area, he closed his eyes. His stomach churned. He heard the steady clack of keys. Ben opened his eyes to all the composure, order, and civility that he knew hid the real agenda of business — to win. That competition gave him the same rush as an open highway. Yet he shook his head at how backward they were in their thinking — they used computers as fancy typewriters. His car experiences had taught him that modern business had more in common with highways than office blocks. Computers had created a world of electronic highways that were never closed. How could he have worked here for years and never seen the horror of the place? The scariest thing was that if he was promoted again, convention would insist that he move into one of the main offices. That would be one of the things he would change.

Some of those secretaries had more of an idea of the power of those machines than their bosses did. Heather was a good example of that. As Ben came towards her she didn't notice him because she was focused on the screen. "What's on line?" he asked, making her jump and turn to block the screen, then relaxed when she recognized Ben.

"I was just finishing the contract," she said.

"Good," said Ben, "and I want you to prepare a second one. This one will be farmed out to our subsidiary, Ampex."

"So your meeting went well?" asked Heather.

"Yes," said Ben, "and I decided to visit Will. He's got a new sprinkler system that's computer controlled. I think Ampex would do well with it."

"And you too, as his agent?" asked Heather, with a sly smile.

"Diversify," said Ben. "Business is a matter of survival."

"Did you manage to find out any more on Matsu Futronics?" asked Ben his voice dropping.

At that Heather's face became tense as her forehead wrinkled and her lips became tight. "I couldn't get anything. I tried everyone. Nothing yet. Though I'm still waiting on two more sources."

Then she lowered her voice. "Are you involved with them?"

Ben looked at her hard to see if she was covering up anything. From what he could read of her body language she was telling the truth. Ben felt flattered, then annoyed. He had a mental flash of the washroom, felt the cold tile pressing against his face, the slow burn in his stomach slowly giving way to numbness, and the frustration that his legs wouldn't work. With the discipline from the tape he pushed the emotion back.

"Any more on Harris?"

"No. And I even got into his computer files to check," Heather smiled proudly at the achievement. "There's nothing there. And I know his secretary isn't good enough to hide anything or plant traps."

"Okay," said Ben. "That means that I'm still in control of this." In spite of the presence of the Jag, he said to himself. "Give me the contract you're working on and start the other one for Will Howard. I'll deal with them in the Board Room while I'm waiting for Harris and drop them off on my way out so we can fax them to the lawyer."

At first Ben walked round the room to feel it out. He performed the same ritual every time he came in. He tried to visualize the meeting with Harris. As he walked around he thought about the Matsu challenge. Had they discovered the scope of the deal with Randcorp? More importantly had they started to move in? Ben concluded that the Jag signaled the overt challenge. For the moment he knew he would have to wait for their next move. He forced himself to sit down and focus his energy to the documents Heather had given him. As he skimmed them he filled in the detail Heather couldn't. She brought in the second contract, and he completed the information about the sprinklers from Will's specs. All the while, in his subconscious, he tried to become Matsu so he would be ready.

Harris came into the Board Room two minutes later. The food was laid out. Ben waited for him with the papers piled in front of him. He kept straightening them, tapping the edges until they were perfectly aligned. Harris sat down across from him. He poured himself a glass of wine.

"So what is this big deal you've got cooking?" he asked Ben.

Ben helped himself to the pasta salad.

"Well," he started, "Will Howard has developed . . ."

"Howard!" exclaimed Harris. "I remember him. He worked here when you were just starting. Had the business sense of a tomato. I'm surprised you're still hooked up with him. I thought you had more brains." Harris scooped the pasta onto his plate. "So what has he developed?" Harris's voice was now inquisitive.

"A new sprinkler system," said Ben.

Harris drank his wine and then slowly said, "Sprinklers?" Then he poured himself another glass.

"I think it's a good idea," said Ben.

"Sprinklers are for Woolco. We deal in high tech. We create systems. Move information. And market those products. You don't spend a month on sprinklers. I can't believe you'd piss your career down the drain for this. That hippie must've given you some heavy dope 'cause you're not thinking. I thought you were a shark. But if you go ahead with this you're dead in the water."

Harris stopped, emptied the glass, and refilled it. Ben slowly ate his pasta salad. While he held his face passive, he saw Harris becoming obsolete technology.

"The board'll go crazy when they learn how you wasted the last month," Harris continued. "And I'm not going to take the fall for this. You know what business is like today — you're only as good as your last deal. And I don't think Randcorp. is going to be too impressed with sprinklers either."

Ben interrupted. "I think this is a good deal."

Harris stood up. "If you want to go ahead with this you're on your own."

"Don't you even want to see what he's developed?" asked Ben.

"I already saw what Heather put together," replied Harris as he refilled his glass. "You don't think I'm that dumb do you?" He stood up still holding his glass. He drained it and set the glass down carefully. Then he pushed his plate towards Ben. "Thanks for lunch," he said sarcastically, turned on his heel, and left the room.

Satisfied, Ben smiled and slowly finished his lunch while reviewing the contracts.

When he was finished he buzzed for Heather to join him.

"Is everything all right?" she asked.

"Yes," said Ben. "Why?"

"Well," she stopped not sure how to proceed, "Harris came out of here pretty upset."

"Harris isn't the concern at the moment. What else have you found out about Matsu?"

"One source was able to tell me that they're monitoring any firm that's developing mind machines. Also that they've got a lot of money behind them. My other source told me that they've also been approaching individual firms about marketing a device that could produce images like a big hologram. No one's really taking them seriously at this point."

Ben listened and thought about the assassin. He didn't want to make Heather suspicious so he tried to be as calm as possible. "If you find out any more about Matsu contact me immediately. So keep phoning around. Here are the files. Make sure they get registered via our patent branch before you leave." Then he left the office.

On his way to the elevator, Ben struggled to keep his concerns under control and to rechannel the energy as the tape had instructed. His fingers drummed his thigh and his right hand clutched the briefcase so tightly it started to ache. As he stood in front of the elevator doors he felt an urge to run for the stairs. When the elevator stopped and the doors were about to open, Ben stepped just to the side so that he wouldn't be visible. The elevator was empty. Ben ducked inside and didn't relax until the doors closed and he started his descent.

As Ben stood on the street corner waiting to cross to the car park the Jag drove by; it slowed as it reached the corner. For a moment Ben imagined the window opening and the shotgun emerging. He wedged himself back into the crowd feeling vulnerable and exposed, clutching the briefcase. When the light changed he stayed in the middle.

When he reached his car he felt safe again. He knelt down beside it pretending to check a tire. As he did he felt the wheel well for devices. He repeated the check for each wheel. Then he stood and opened the hood. Everything seemed the same. Ben couldn't help looking over his shoulder, expecting to see the Jag at any moment.

Still nervous he opened the door and eased himself into his seat. He closed his eyes and turned the key in the ignition. The engine turned over and sounded normal. Ben let his breath out slowly.

On his fax were the signed contracts from Will. Ben turned on his computer and called up his calendar. He made a note to have his mechanic check the security devices on his car. Then he called up his private log. He wanted to make some notes on the meeting he'd just had with Harris. On file he found a message from Will. "Was out gardening. Break-in happened around three. Discs stolen. Didn't get master discs but could put together proposal from info. taken. Dogs were tranquillized by darts but should be okay. Advise."

Ben thought he should be surprised but he wasn't. If anything, he was angry with himself for failing to anticipate the move. Now he had to consider priorities. For a moment Ben thought about calling Heather but decided she couldn't really help. There was no point calling Will either; the Jag had been monitoring him all along. No, thought Ben, the first thing is to deal with Randcorp. — be ready for the meeting. After that was settled he'd go out and see Will; he owed him that much. To psyche himself up he put on his tape.

"Lesson Four: Beyond the Assassin — A way of Life. Now that you've internalized the process, it can apply in whatever situation you need to recall it. As the warrior understands that the weapon is but an extension of his arm, you must develop so that your sense of power becomes an extension of yourself. There will be no conscious break between the ability and the execution. You have now internalized recognition. Anticipation. And prevention. You will expend fewer resources if you deal with the assassin now."

He was only five miles away from the hotel when he got a call from Heather. "Bad news," she said. "They've called off the meetings."

"Why?" Ben asked immediately.

"They said they need to check the technicals further. A possible infringement problem because of a new proposal they received."

Ben didn't have to ask who'd got to them. He knew it was the Jag — the arm of Matsu. Instead of turning back, Ben knew the moment for prevention had come.

"Okay. Get them on the phone again and press them. Ask them if the Matsu group is involved? Get back to me."

Two miles from the hotel Ben saw the Jag going the other way on the freeway. He floored the car to get to the next exit. "At the end of the chaos of conflict lies the restoration of peace."

Ben knew that when he caught the Jag he'd have to rely on instinct. He thought through the sections of the tape for something that might help him. He rewound the tape to Lesson Two. "Visualize your enemy in defeat. See yourself move. See yourself act. Establish the reality of his defeat in your mind. When you meet you will only be acting out reality. Repeating the established pattern. Visualize your success."

In the first image that came to mind, Ben had cut the Jag off and headed up the ramp as he had done the last time. He saw the Jag skidding off the highway, brakes locked. It flipped, traveled through the air, and then struck one of the support pillars of the overpass. After a loud whump, there was a moment of silence before the Jag burst into flames.

The tape concluded: "With every victory, security. With every successful visualization another step to realizing reality."

As he sped up the exit ramp Ben watched the Jag; the event occurred as he had visualized it but with more terrifying detail. Even from the top of the ramp he could hear the shriek of metal on pavement alternating with the dull thud of impact. Finally came the sound of glass shattering and metal twisting as the Jag hit. He couldn't stop watching the flames, all movie glow red and yellow, in his mind. No one got out.

Ben idled his car at the top of the ramp until the black smoke all but obscured his view. He heard his own voice telling him to get going before someone came. He drove away towards the first truck-stop restaurant he saw. Ben thought he should try to relax until the call came. Even though he went through his deep breathing exercises the image of the burning Jag stayed with him.

After gassing up the car, he went into the restaurant. He ordered coffee and apple pie with ice cream. As he ate his pie he thought about the machine in the briefcase. Maybe a program could help him forget the past few minutes or at least ease the nervous energy that made his fingers tap the table. If there was time maybe he would listen to another program. Then he realized he should call Will. He paid his bill and went out to his car.

Will's answering machine picked up his call. "If you're screening calls Will, it's just Ben. The problem has been solved. I'll come out and see you tomorrow. I'll have some good news."

Ben chose the Nature program. Maybe I'll figure out what Will sees in this. When the program started Ben found himself at the edge of a forest. Behind him, he could feel the wind of passing traffic. The ground trembled slightly. Ben walked into the forest. The path led him past a waterfall, through a glade, and finally to the top of a knoll. He decided to sit and wait for the program to end. He meditated on his actions and the Jag; it was obvious that only time could dull the image of the flames. The accident was virtually the way he'd pictured it. Virtual Reality, thought Ben — the tape taught me to create my own reality. Ben turned his attention to the meeting he knew was coming in an effort to calm himself through the rest of the program.

Ben had just put away the machine when his phone rang. The call was from Heather. "It's back on."

Ben said nothing.

"Ben. It's on. The competition folded. How soon can you get to the hotel?"

"Half an hour, forty-five minutes," said Ben. He visualized the meeting going smoothly.

"Great. I'll tell them an hour. I'll call the lawyer for you."

All the way to the meeting Ben kept checking his rear view mirror for signs that he was being followed again. Every time he checked he glimpsed into his own eyes. They were clear, white, and shiny.

Every few seconds he checked the mirror just to reassure himself. Nothing followed him as far as he could tell. For that moment longer he stared at the mirror as he focused on his own eyes. When he looked away he was sure that the mirror went dark.

Yet in his peripheral vision, something seemed to be there. At first he told himself that it was only the memory of the burning Jag, yet he kept glancing up until he realized he was only seeing his own reflection. Because of the constant checking the reflection was already there, opening its eyes to stare at Ben, waiting for his next move.

22
J.J. Steinfeld
PENALTY
FOR MISUSE — $20

HE WAS on our side, Barzole the psychologist used to say, and it was that damn expression that finally alienated me, made me want to put fear on his face. I was the only one to make Barzole look frightened, really frightened. It was an achievement, believe me. Barzole had worked with some of the most hardened cons our god-fearing country hides away and had developed a fearless exterior that would be the envy of the toughest cop. Fearless or not, he was still effusive — this was a man who overflowed with ideas, and used the word "creative" with more emphasis and frequency than any word deserved.

Barzole would have been ecstatic that I am writing this piece for *Contemporary Prison Life*, a fancy journal he helped establish back in '78, had I not, should I say, put the fear of God into the man. He would be shaking with approval, patting me on the back and saying, "Ah, flex your creative muscles . . . Creativity is the embrace of the gods . . . Don't abuse your creative gifts." He believed I was the most sensitive and creative inmate he had worked with in ten years of probing the criminal mind. Problem was, Barzole didn't know what was in my heart, what made me tick and got me in the joint in the first place. He only knew the cold facts in my extremely thick file.

Barzole was always coming up with ways to retrieve and rehabilitate us — after all, *he was on our side*; the way he said that you'd think he was our father or something, though he couldn't have been over forty. Creativity Therapy was the foundation of his masterplan to reshape the incarcerated. Through creativity, he wrote in an article for *Contemporary Prison Life*, he believed the hardest, toughest, most anti-social con could be reached and transformed. He used to apply his theories to us, then I'd read about our therapy group in an article, except that it would be Prisoner A or Prisoner B or Prisoner C. I always seemed to be Prisoner F and was his favorite, the creative soul at battle with the criminal mind. You'd think I was a maze-bedazzled rat he was doing meticulous experiments with.

The chain of events leading to Barzole's encounter with fear started harmlessly enough. After telling us it was his birthday — "But don't ask me my age, guys, one should never ask a practicing psychologist his age" — Barzole wrote on the blackboard in our meeting room: "Describe the moment when you went down the criminal path. Write down your thoughts — those of you who can write — or tell your story from the heart. Be creative!" He read the instructions to us as he wrote, then read them twice more for good measure. From our heartfelt stories, Barzole was going to put together a play about our lives: *Doing Time*. The bastard already had a title before we opened our hearts a crack.

Barzole had a theory — he didn't shit without a theory — that we were great actors who used our innate thespian talents in the wrong direction, that is, on the street instead of on the stage. He proclaimed in true Barzolean style, waving his puffy hands, pacing around the room, tapping at the back of our stiff institutional chairs, that he was going to write *Doing Time* and shape us into a reputable and dynamic theatre company. First we would put on plays in the prison, learn about our craft, polish our natural talents, then when we were all out of the joint, he would take us on the road, from St. John's to Vancouver Island. In the beginning we all laughed at the idea, but his damn enthusiasm and persistence won us over; he had us believing we could actually be great actors. Us being the seven sweethearts in his Thursday afternoon therapy group. The prison groups he supervised were divided into specific categories based on either sentence or type of crime. Barzole was a stickler for categories and order. Despite his reputation as a prison reformer, he enjoyed telling us that prison was an orderly universe, more orderly than the world outside.

Barzole had literally built his career on crime. When he told us he wanted to take us on tour — a bunch of ex-cons being nothing more than a traveling freak show — I began to question his motives:

who did he really want to help, Barzole or the cons? I'd have loved to have seen his curriculum vitae and how many of his listed accomplishments he had done at our expense. He was using us, like everyone else.

Barzole was encouraged that a few prison art shows he had organized had done well and he was ready to expand his creative empire. Beneath that psychologist's skin was an impresario wanting to engulf the country with con talent: art, drama, prose, poetry, the works. He was going to merchandise us like Snoopy dolls. I have to admit, I wasn't aware of Barzole's deviousness right away. The air in the dungeons of Kingston isn't always conducive to clear thinking.

But I've got to hand it to that slick dude, he thought my little story about when I realized I had criminal impulses was brilliant. The other cons talked about ripping off stores or boys-will-be-boys vandalism on Saturday nights or kicking ass for the fun of it. But not me. I have, as dear Barzole was fond of saying, a literary bent. That profound assessment got me the nickname "Benty" in the joint. I wrote "PENALTY FOR MISUSE — $20" for the great Dr. Barzole, the least I could do since we both had attended the University of Toronto, except he finished with much distinction, and me ...well I'm sure the alumni and Board of Governors would rather forget me. My adroitness as a thief will never get me invited to reunions or asked to speak at commencements. I specialized in works of art, but I often stole for the sake of stealing, accepting my identity as a thief without question or apology. Yet my criminality was developing long before I carried away my first Eskimo carving.

In the large gray room where we had our weekly meetings, a concrete room that could have doubled as an abattoir, I stood in front of my chair and read my little story to Barzole and my mates in captivity. It was just like being back at the good old U of T:

"'PENALTY FOR MISUSE — $20' by Prisoner/Recidivist 7367 ... I remember so clearly the sign, PENALTY FOR MISUSE — $20, that I would read morning after morning as I commuted to classes. 'Post No Bills' and 'Keep Off The Grass' signs always gnawed at me and while I rarely violated their commandment in those obedient days, the desire to trample grass with tarantellas of rage stirred restlessly within me. I was fairly straight then, pursuing my education, living out the respectable fantasies of my parents and grandparents. But I was sick and tired of being obedient — I must have been a mutant at heart. I had fantasies about being a fugitive or bomb-planting revolutionary, even grew a Zapata moustache and Castro beard against my father's wishes.

"If I pulled the forbidden emergency handle, I used to speculate, I would be arrested, put in a dark cell on bread and water, subject to a grueling and scandalous trial at which the enraged public would clamor for my privileged neck. Such outlandish speculating interested me a hell of a lot more than the economics courses I was taking. I had had it with Kondratieff cycles, Keynesian gobbledygook, and the flushing of micro- and macroeconomic toilets.

"That senseless, pestering urge to pull the handle — to forfeit the twenty dollars and embark irrevocably on a life of crime and degradation — would not relent. I wanted to see how the authorities would treat me, what my law-abiding, Q.C. father would say and do, how a product of privilege and wealth like me would thrive in the sewers. That handle — and the unpredictable consequences it would trigger — was one of the mysteries of life that, if unravelled, could offer the sort of blinding insight only ascetic holy men or psychotics can get.

"Besides, I thought with the logic of the trapped, pulling that handle was the one way to keep out of law school, out of my father's and grandfather's firm. Their dream of three generations of lawyers in one firm I found obscene. That handle was important to me those dull mornings I rode to classes. In those scholastic days, busting my balls for A's and useless knowledge, I didn't believe I had the guts *not* to go to law school. The best law school in the country had a cell waiting for me unless I could do some fancy footwork.

"The first time I became intrigued with the handle remains vivid in my memory. I moved to a seat near the alluring, summoning handle, the magnificent instrument of gray steel and grayer sin. Sure I was overreacting, sinking my teeth into hyperbole, but I was a dreamer caught in the shell of one doomed to a life in the law, another link in an endless chain of legal minds bearing the same last name. Grandfather, once one of Canada's sharpest legal minds, was already talking about me siring a lawyer son, a 'Ripley's Believe It or Not' four generations under one plush roof. By the time I was at university, grandfather was allowed to deal with only the simplest divorce cases.

"In that subway car an excited rhythm ruled my heart. I stared at the handle and read: EMERGENCY — PULL TO STOP TRAIN. The instructions — or perhaps divine orders — were clear, even a moron without the benefit of higher education could follow them: *pull to stop train*. What would be the forbidden sensation? Would the passengers be tossed violently about? Would steel and bone meet in crashing and cracking symphony? Oh how I longed for the twin joys of exploration and discovery. Oh how I needed to bite from the Apple. Try to understand, my life had been blueprinted for me, I was an Old Boy at birth. You had to see the opulence and anesthetizing security I was embedded in. My one act of protest in those days was to take the subway to university and leave at home the Porsche my father had bought me when I was still at Upper Canada College. Maybe my mother accidentally looked at an accursed hunchback when she was carrying me; something sure as hell derailed me.

"With an assassin's ardor for his targets, I studied the others in the subway car — the regulars and the irregular riders — feeling I could influence each and every one of their lives with a single pull. One pull and the world would rumble, the world would shake. PENALTY FOR MISUSE — $20. What a paltry sum for such a monstrous tampering with the scheme of things. I imagined God sitting before billions of gray handles, pulling feverishly away.

"The passengers appeared as if they were protecting something valuable; locked within their fleshy armor was treasure not for touch or sight. What a dedicated crew of automatons. I always imagined the worst of people in those days of confinement.

"PENALTY FOR MISUSE — $20. It wouldn't be misuse; on the contrary, it would be a noble deed. I had one tiny gray handle and God had billions of handles, was that fair? God didn't have to be a lawyer. His son merely had to die for the sins of humanity. I certainly smashed my head against outrageous images those days, simply because I felt so absurdly trapped. But against the images in my mind was the reality of that gray handle. If I acted, the passengers would be expelled from their trances, forced to react, even if only with cries of surprise and inarticulate complaints.

"If I pulled the handle, maybe the deed would be recorded,

spread near and far. How I loved to see my name in print, the encasing of rushing history, the halt of devastating time, the illusion of permanence. LAWYER'S SON — AND LAWYER'S GRANDSON — MISUSES EMERGENCY STOP — CANADIAN GOVERNMENT APPALLED. And if some unsteady morning rider unfortunately should be maimed — or, perish the thought, killed in his rumbling steel coffin — then perhaps the evening news and the front page of the *Globe and Mail* would be mine. Only twenty dollars for disrupting the lives of ten commuters. Only twenty dollars for immortality served up on a silver platter, what a bargain.

"An eleventh and twelfth blank face boarded the subway car, not suspecting the thoughts of the lurking coveter of the *verboten* handle. Maybe on New York subways people feared for their lives, but not in the tranquility that was Toronto in 1972, the best of all possible times. Twelve souls were now under my power. TWELVE MEET THEIR GRISLY DOOM AS MANIAC, FORMER UNIVERSITY OF TORONTO ECONOMICS STUDENT, PULLS THE HANDLE — PRIME MINISTER SENSES AN INSURRECTION AND IMPOSES THE WAR MEASURES ACT TO SAVE OUR SUBWAYS. *Twenty-dollar fine protested as exorbitant. Famous defence counsel says ex-scholar victim of society, the glorious Canadian Dream gone amuck.*

"I stood, bringing my body nearer the handle. Just as I was about to defy the Establishment gods, a woman, squeezing a fat shopping bag and seeming one with her subway seat, looked asquint at me. Could she be a mind reader, blessed with extrasensory gifts? The evil eye swelled in her triangular and reproachful head. Would she attempt to stop me, to appropriate the glory that was my due? Would she be lauded in the papers, over the air waves?

"I lifted my miracle arm and reverently touched the gray handle, a lover's gentle touch. The woman squeezed her shopping bag tighter, a passionate sexual squeeze. Some got off, others got on, such is life, on-moving, never-ending, one long subway ride full of screeches and folly, signifying nothing. Damn you silent readers, I'll set your tongues flapping, I thought.

"Suddenly mortified, paralyzed by my foolish thoughts of consequences, I lowered my miracle arm — the woman sighing the repeal of her curse — and gazed at the subway car's exit doors: DO NOT LEAN AGAINST DOORS. I approached the firm, inviting doors,

then leaned against them, waiting for my stop, ashamed of my Zapata moustache and Castro beard. I left the subway car, unscathed
and temporarily denied access to the flowered halls of heroes. Odin
would have to wait for my bonhomie. But I had glimpsed my salva-
tion, my way out, and I promised myself that I would pull that
damn handle before I really believed that Keynesian theories
worked, before I got my degree from the U of T."

Barzole applauded but the others didn't understand what the big
deal was. My images and words threatened them. Rick, a bungling
break-and-enter man who had more tattoos than fingers, had read a
story before me about the first time he raped a woman, how he
couldn't help it in the front seat of a '53 Chevy. Then, like a cornered bully, he barked out at the group that he had never had a
chance in the straight world. He capped his performance with a
solemn confession that he screwed up everything he had ever tried
to do. The man could do marvelous TV commercials for manic-
depression. The other cons thought Rick was on to something good
and let go with a spate of enthusiastic comments.

My story was more elusive to my fellow prisoners, but not to
Dr. Barzole. *Irony, satire, crisp Swiftian and Shavian insights*: Barzole
saw it all there in my humble tale. The touch of signing my story
with Prisoner/Recidivist and my number he found a deft stroke. He
also saw the core of his play in my heartfelt outpouring.

Barzole put his arm around me as the other cons whistled pruri-
ently and he told me to rewrite my brilliant story because he was
inviting some theatre people from Toronto to Kingston next week.
He then further embarrassed me in front of the cons by launching
into a gushing paean to my creativity and sensitivity, reminding
everyone that Oscar Wilde and O. Henry had also served time in the
slammer.

The next Thursday, after the other stage-struck cons did their
little histrionic numbers, I read my revised story with an avalanche
of feeling and foreboding mystery. Then these theatre types from
Toronto lectured us about the "freeing" aspects of acting. One fat-
faced dude had actually studied with Lee Strasberg in New York and
pointed that out more times than I could count. They all agreed we
had the makings of a first-rate play and an exciting theatre troupe.

"*Doing Time* is going to free us all," Barzole shouted and began walking around our chairs. Getting higher and higher on his dream, our dear, effusive psychologist told each con how much he was on his side, how working together would produce vibrant, vital, creative theatre. When he came near me, I grabbed the bastard and pulled a shiv out of my notebook. I had the blade at his neck before any of the theatre types or my fellow prisoners could blink. I was on center stage, the way I liked it — *defying the script*. That's when I saw fear on Barzole's face for the first time.

I wasn't going to hurt Barzole — that would have been too easy, like punching an assistant professor when you hated the educational system or killing a cop on the beat when you knew there wasn't a cat's ass of justice in the world. I patiently massaged Barzole's jugular with my hand-crafted knife. One of the theatre types wanted to negotiate, and another told me to keep calm, I was jeopardizing my theatrical career. The fat-faced dude who had studied with Lee Strasberg didn't make a peep. The cons had all seen hostage takings before. My little impromptu performance was relieving the monotony of their lives and they were thankful: *this* they understood in their guts.

"*Why?*" Barzole finally whispered. It was a beautiful word from such a damn cocksure bastard. Again, "*Why? Why? Why?*" I waited a good long dramatic time before I spoke and then I let Barzole have it with all the conviction of a Stanislavsky graduate.

"Because I never pulled that goddamn handle when I had the chance," I told my fearful captive.

I allowed another minute to pass before speaking again, studying everyone in the large gray room, the subway rumbling along as always.

"You didn't understand my story, did you, Dr. Barzole? You believed all that crap you learned at the U of T."

I gave up my hostage after an hour, bored with the whole ordeal, and without so much as a nick to Barzole's smooth, theory-stuffed body. I got an extra eighteen months for that one-hour escapade, another eighteen months to write my stories, to find gray handles to pull.

23
Don Bailey
REMEMBRANCE DAY

THE clerk at the temporary-help agency tells me I'm lucky.
"We've been watching you," the guy says.

"Yeah," I reply. I don't feel very lucky. Lining up every morning with 300 other guys, most of them still drunk from the night before. All of them desperate for a job that will get them through another day. Just enough for a room and a bottle. Maybe some smokes. Eating is a luxury.

The clerk writes an address and a name on a slip of paper.

"Don't screw this up," the guy says. "The last man we sent got over three months' steady work."

"What happened?" I ask. I know it's the wrong question. Actually any question is the wrong one. Behind me I can hear someone pounding on the counter and loudly demanding to see the manager. Probably has the place confused with his favorite bar.

The clerk lights a cigarette. Doesn't offer me one. But blows the smoke my way. I don't like guys like this. Sitting behind a desk. Answering telephones and taking the work orders. Acting like there was something magic about the whole thing. Charging the customer six bucks an hour and paying slobs like me four. And wanting to be thanked. I worry about getting chapped lips from all the ass kissing. A hernia of the lips caused by too much puckering-up. And back strain from an overabundance of genuflecting. Work-related wear and tear, but I doubt the Workers' Compensation Board will entertain an application for recompense.

"What's your interest?" the clerk asks.

"I'd like to get something steady. Maybe this other guy did something that upset the customer. Something I could avoid."

"Client," the clerk corrects, pulling out the bottom drawer of the desk and propping up his feet. He smiles. Nice teeth. Probably has a dental plan.

"What you're saying right now is why I'm sending you and not one of these other walking-wounded types."

"I appreciate it," I say. Humility goes a long way with these guys.

"You're an intelligent guy. Not that this job takes any brains. Yard work. Taking care of the grounds. Putting up the storms. Taking them down. Cleaning the pool."

"The pool?" I'm impressed.

"The client's a widow. Lives on her own. There's household help. A cook and a maid, so none of that domestic stuff falls to you."

"Is this a live-in situation?"

The clerk shrugs and stubs out his cigarette. A huge butt, but why put my balls in his hand when he's already got a good grip on my throat?

"That's between you and the client. The last guy did and that was his downfall."

"How so?"

The clerk laughs. His laugh has the auditory charm of a toilet flushing.

"He got it in his head that he was the man of the house. Tried to exercise his conjugal rights."

"She's young then?" I'm not so far gone that the idea of working in close proximity to a young woman still doesn't hold a certain allure. Especially one that's rich.

"Don't even think about it," he says. The expression in his eyes discourages flippancy. He wears the grim, grilled look of the natural keeper. If he wasn't here, he'd be running a zoo someplace. Or herding kids in a day-care center and drumming respectable nursery rhymes into their impressionable psyches. A guy born to the responsibility of keeping us undisciplined types in line. When Alzheimer's finally claims him, he'll be awarded his own school crossing somewhere. They'll bury him with his stop sign nestled reverently in his still hands.

The world needs keepers. I've always had one. First my mother. Later a bunch of teachers, Boy Scout leaders. Then summer-job bosses. Girlfriends. Loan managers. Full-time employers. My dentists. And finally a wife.

I don't mind most keepers. They know their place. I know mine. They keep. I'm kept. But a guy like this is a frustrated catcher. He should've joined the police force. But he doesn't have the nerve.

"Does she pay me?" I ask.

He smiles again. The right button. He likes practical questions.

"The agency," he says. "She doesn't get her hands dirty with money. An accountant handles it all."

I nod knowingly.

"If I work out and she decides she wants me steady does the agency still rake off their two bucks an hour?"

His cute grin reminds me of a goldfish with teeth.

"Contract you signed runs two years," he says.

"Well, thanks," I say with as much irony as I figure he'll misunderstand.

Then I get up and leave.

I head over to the Good Shepherd Mission and pick up my stuff. I've been flopping there off and on for the last three months. Out of all the take-a-dive-for-Jesus joints in this town it's the most humane. The staff know they've got us by the shorts and don't keep yanking to prove their point. No drugs or booze. Chapel before meals and you're in. A lot of other places want you to take bible-study courses or attend AA meetings. For people who profess a deep faith in the human spirit they need a lot of proof of a guy's good intentions.

I collect my bag. It contains a change of clothes, a toothbrush, a razor and a small photo album of my family. The old doll on the desk looks worried as she hands it over.

"Pastor Friezen is in his study," she says. "If you want to speak with him I'm sure he won't mind me interrupting."

"I'm leaving for a job, not a binge," I say.

"That's wonderful," she says. Her smile has the power to hem frayed pants, sew on loose buttons. Invisible mending. In their quiet way, they keep track of us here.

"It's a handyman situation," I say. "Comes with a room."

"Our blessings," she says.

I like that. Not God's blessings. Or Christ's. People who speak only for themselves.

It's a long jaunt to my new job, but that's okay. I like walking and we're having a mild Winnipeg spring. It's May and the snow has melted. Believe me, that's a gift.

Walking for me is a process of taking inventory. Some people I know like to walk so they can observe the birds in the trees, smell the newly mowed lawns and generally make a big deal out of their environment. Good for them. Personally, I ignore all that. I'm a city person and long ago accepted that such gathering places of humanity are crowded, noisy, dirty and aesthetically unpleasing. Why pretend otherwise? So instead as I trudge along I count my blessings and go over my complaints.

The truth is, I've got a lot to be grateful for. I've been off the booze for close to two months. It's been hard because I have an inclination to buffer myself from anything painful going on around me. When I'm sober and I read a newspaper story about something tragic like child-abuse, I get upset. So I drink and when I'm blotto the story blurs and is forgotten. What I overlook is that period when I'm just drunk. If I happen to be out wandering around when I'm in this state and come across a parent in a Safeway parking lot giving their kid a smack I want to get a baseball bat and crack open their skull. The booze fuels my rage before it extinguishes it. I always forget that. It's landed me in jail several times. Nothing serious. Minor assaults. During my respectable days I paid a lawyer to defend me and got off with a couple of fines. Since then I've served a bit of joint time. Money does make a difference.

My biggest complaint is this gnawing desire to regain respectability. I know the whole thing is a fraud but I want to believe I'm as good as the next guy. It's hard to maintain that belief living in missions or waking up in an alley half drowned in a puddle of your own puke.

The thing I like about the life I have now, especially when I'm sober, is how much time I have to remember things. Or to daydream. To imagine my place in the world in a way that nurtures me. Makes me feel affection for myself. How many people do you know who would proudly proclaim a liking for themselves? When I was respectable I didn't know anyone like that. Including myself.

I don't remember much about my early boyhood days. A shrink would probably say I'm repressing something. Most likely. Memory begins for me when I was nine.

My mother and I were walking along Bloor Street in Toronto.

The city of my youth. The place where most of my history took place. A war veteran stepped out from a store entrance and blocked our path. He was wearing a blue blazer over a huge beer belly. He had two rows of ribbons and medals on his chest.

"Poppy," he said.

My mother opened her purse and took out a two-dollar bill, which she jammed into the money-box on the tray of flowers strapped around his neck. Two bucks! That was eight weeks' allowance.

The vet pinned a poppy to the lapel of her coat. He smiled at her and she began to cry.

"My husband . . ." she stammered.

The man reached out and embraced her awkwardly. The tray was in the way and it tilted. Several of the poppies fell on the ground. I picked them up and kept one for myself.

"I'm sorry," the man said. I marveled at the ability of adults to talk like this. Total strangers exchanging hardly any words and yet seeming to know exactly what was meant.

When he released her she was still sniffling. She began to rummage in her purse for a Kleenex but before she could find one, the vet handed her a clean, white hanky.

"Keep it," he said. It was the first and maybe the last act of genuine chivalry that I ever witnessed.

Later we were sitting in Fran's Restaurant down on College Street. My mother had allowed me to order a grilled-cheese sandwich and french fries with gravy even though she believed I'd get an instant case of pimples. I could tell from the expression on her face that she was traveling the back roads of her own memories.

"You thinking about Dad?" I asked.

"Remembrance Day," she said. "November the eleventh, 1945. That was the day I got the telegram. An army officer delivered it. Missing and presumed dead."

"Maybe he's still alive," I said.

"No. Two years later I got the official death notice. It took another six months to get the pension. Thirty-seven bucks a month. Big deal."

"What was he like?" I asked. He was overseas when I was born so I never met him.

"He was hard to nail down," she said. "His attention was always drifting off to something else. So for a while he had a little carpentry business going. I kept the books and we were doing fine but one day he came home with one splinter too many in his hand and he just packed it in."

"Did you love him?" I asked.

She laughed.

"Whatta you know about that?"

"I know I love you," I said.

She took my hand and there were tears in her eyes again.

"As well you might," she said. "We've only got each other."

"Tell me more about him?"

"I adored him," she said. "He wasn't a prize to look at. Sort of homely looking. But when he turned those big blue eyes of his on you it felt like someone had put another log on the fire. All a person could think of was to snuggle up to the warmth."

"Would he have liked me?" I asked.

She laughed again but her eyes looked sad.

"He woulda piggy-backed you around in his heart," she said.

I've always remembered that expression.

"What else?" I asked. She so rarely talked about my father.

"He had a way of believing in you that made you believe in yourself."

"Like what?" I asked.

She took a sip of her cherry Coke, her expression dreamy.

"I told him once that I'd always wanted to play the piano but when I was a kid my family didn't have money for lessons. Two weeks later a truck pulled up with a piano on it."

"The one we have now!" I said.

"The same," she said. "I never figured out how he paid for it. We could barely meet the rent. And then one day this old lady with arthritis in her hands appeared and told me he'd paid her to give me ten lessons. I was furious because if we had any spare money I wanted to buy curtains for the bathroom. We were on the main floor and anyone passing could look in and see their fill. But instead I took piano lessons."

"And learned to play good," I said.

"Yes, but I never would've on my own."

Memories are like movies. The story runs its course and the picture and sound dissolve into blank silence. The credits roll. Just as well. I've arrived at my new place of employment.

The place is a sprawling two-storey brick affair. Another thousand square feet and it would qualify as a mansion. It has the mandatory pillars framing the entranceway. The wood trim has been painted recently and the masonry has been sandblasted. Some kind of hedge surrounds what must be an acre of front lawn. Lots of work here for idle hands. I decide to go around to the rear. My instincts tell me I'll get a warmer welcome.

I follow the paved driveway to the back. There's a triple garage with a small, sporty car parked outside one of the closed doors. A Honda, I think. Off to my left is another acre of lawn leading right down to the river. But set in the middle is a cedar enclosure. About thirty feet square. The entrance gate is open so I decide to check it out.

A slender woman in her fifties is lounging on a deck-chair next to an empty swimming pool. She is wearing a black one-piece bathing suit, a wide-brimmed sun-hat, and dark glasses. Beside her is a small table that holds a bottle of wine, cigarettes, a lighter, and an ashtray. She has a glass of wine in her hand which she tips to her mouth and drains when she sees me.

"You the guy they sent to get my pool operating?" she asks.

"Names Raymond Blake," I say.

"Oh yeah, Rick from the agency said he was sending you over. Know anything about pools?"

"No ma'am, I don't. But I can figure it out."

"My name's Cherl Anderson. I like to be called Cherl. I've been a widow for two years and when people call me Mrs. Anderson it just reminds me of my loss. My husband was, is irreplaceable. You drink?"

She fills her glass and since it's the only one in sight I wonder if she expects me to drink straight from the bottle if I accept the offer of a nip.

"I do but right now I'm on the wagon."

"What happens when you fall off?"

"I don't," I say. "Occasionally I leap off but it's never an accident."

"When you leap, what happens?"

"I've been known to be unpleasant."

She laughs and the sound is like a callused foot being dragged across unfinished concrete.

"So what do you do in this unpleasant state? Torch buildings? Piss on people's flower beds? Lust after ground-squirrels?"

I laugh and point to an empty chair.

"You mind if I sit down?"

"Help yourself," she says. "But I want an answer. This is the interview."

I ease myself into the chair and take a couple of deep breaths. I've got a bad habit of breathing shallow when I walk long distances. She lights a cigarette while she waits for me. She offers the pack to me and I take one.

"Mostly I go to my room and bang my head against the wall," I say.

"Why's that, Ray? It okay if I call you Ray?"

"Sure. My mother did."

"Tell me about her in a minute. Explain the other first."

"When I'm drunk I get pissed off with the world. But then I get pissed off with myself for being so stupid. Nothing I can say or do is going to change the way the world is."

"Amen to that!" she says, holding up her glass to the sun. "Here's to you, Barney!"

She downs half the glass and puts it on the table. She notices me giving her a close look.

"Barney was my husband," she says, "Made himself a bundle in the reinsuring business. Know what that is?"

"In the bookie business it's called laying off bets. Same thing. Spreading the risk around."

"You don't look half as smart as you talk," she says. And then she frowns as if I've presented her with a puzzle. She takes another sip of the grape. It's at least ten in the morning and the stuff is probably full of vitamins.

"A lucky guess," I say to reassure her.

"I don't like stupid people," she says. "The last man the agency sent had his brains dangling between his legs. Harmless enough except when he got a drink in him. Then he got thinking and this woke his brain up, if you get my drift."

I nod and try not to smile.

"Nothing worse than an erection with more intelligence than the man it's attached to. He got it in his head that the lady of the house needed some roto-rooter work done on her. The thing is I was married to a good man for thirty years and he left me a lot of good memories. He also left me a wine cellar with over 3000 bottles. Some of it pretty rare stuff. Thirty years of collecting. Every bottle catalogued. I'm fifty-six years old and I plan to drink two bottles of that wine every day until it's all gone. Or I'm dead. Whichever comes first. You know why?"

"No, but I suspect you're going to tell me."

She picks up her glass, drains it and then holds it empty against her thin chest. I see a single tear dribble out from under the lens of her glasses.

"I'm sorry," I say.

She brushes her arm across her face and I feel her glaring intently into my eyes.

"I don't mind a little friendly razzing," she says. "But when it comes to Barney I won't be laughed at."

"I meant no disrespect."

"I can see that," she says and then holds her lighter out to my unlit cigarette. "The thing is that Barney worked too hard. That's what killed him. Running here and there. Making more deals. More money. And the little bit of free time he had was spent on his wines. He thought of them as the children we never had and when he was told about the cancer he asked me to start a wine museum after he died. But I didn't. And every day his precious wine is enjoyed by me. It's spiteful of me but it gives me pleasure. In some way it makes me feel closer to Barney. In the morning I read his handwriting in the catalogue and sometimes there's a little story in the margin of how he tracked this or that bottle down. There won't be another man in my life until every last drop is drunk. Only then will Barney be truly gone."

We sit there in silence for a minute, both of us smoking. Thinking our separate thoughts. I suspect we're both of us a little envious of the other.

"So tell me about your mother," she says.

"Is this part of the interview?" I ask.

"The most important part," she says.

I don't know if she's being sarcastic or is just sloshed. I rarely talk about my mother. I had so little of her that I'm selfish about whom I share her with. But then Cherl takes off her glasses and it's like being exposed to the sight of a nude child frolicking on the beach. Intimacy, innocence, and vulnerability all jostling for tender attention. Her eyes are a deep blue. The sunlight ripples in their depth. There is the promise of warmth in those eyes. And the evidence of pain.

"My mother was a practical woman," I say. "When my father was killed in the war she decided her main task in life was to raise me properly. That meant earning a decent income. But men were coming home from the war looking for jobs. The only work available to women was menial and didn't pay much. So she went into business."

Cherl fills her glass. The bottle is empty. She studies the label and nods with satisfaction. Another rare vintage bites the dust. She looks at me expectantly.

"So what did she do?"

"She hired herself out as a housekeeper."

"Tough way to make a buck," she says, sipping at her wine.

"Yeah, except she had her own little wrinkle that made it pay real well. I didn't twig to it until I was fourteen and I saw the *Globe and Mail* bill for an ad she ran. It had the copy with it and even after I read it I wasn't sure. But there was something strange about the ad."

"What did it say?"

"Reliable housekeeper available by the day. For single gentlemen only. That was the thing that got me. Why just single guys? So I asked her."

"What was her answer?"

"She told me the going rate for cleaning house was $12.50 a day. Didn't matter if it was a four-bedroom home or a bachelor apartment. When she first started she got roped into working twelve, fourteen hours a day for families. They wanted their laundry done, the ironing, the silver cleaned. All for the same money. But then one day she got a call from a guy who said she'd been recommended. She went to his apartment and the place was immaculate. It was a tiny joint and while he showed her around she realized his problem had more to do with the bulge in his pants than dustballs under his bed. She was a forthright woman and decided it was worth the risk to draw his attention to her observation. She was out of there within an hour. With her $12.50."

Cherl looks stunned.

"You mean she . . ."

"When I finally figured it out she told me that sex was a bodily function that demanded relief. Particularly for men."

"That's amazing. How did you feel about it?"

"I admired her for what she did. She made a good life for us. With her three or four clients a day we never wanted for anything."

"Didn't it make her hard?"

"No."

"Did she ever meet anyone that she . . . fell for?"

"I don't think so. She never said and she never brought a man home. When she went to bingo she took me. She liked to dance but she waited until I was twelve so she could take me to the Legion socials."

"She sounds wonderful," Cherl says, "but lonely."

"For my father."

"Where is she now?"

"She died twelve years ago."

"Happy?"

I smile at this question. My mother always appeared happy but I always wondered if that wasn't just one of her rules.

"She told me in the hospital that she dreamed all the time of my father. She said that in the dreams they were young again and just beginning. They did their favorite things together. All her happiest memories were in the dreams. She thought maybe that's what death was, a place of dreams and memories. She was glad to be going there because eternity wasn't long enough to relive all the things she remembered and imagined . . . I think she was happy."

"What about you?" Cherl says. "Are you happy?"

"If I've got a job."

"I see you brought a bag. Planning to live in?'

"I'd rather."

"Com'on then," she says getting up. "I'll show you your quarters."

I am living in a garage. The walls have been insulated, dry-walled and painted a soft pastel yellow. There is a thick gray carpet on the floor. I have my own washroom complete with shower and the galley kitchen has every conceivable appliance. I want for nothing. The bed is firm. The television comes with cable and there is a sound system I still haven't figured out. I've even got my own phone. The back wall has been removed and replaced with glass patio doors that allow me to look out at the river.

This morning I sit drinking my coffee and watch a canoe glide by with two young women paddling. The birds are chirping in the trees and the sound is not unpleasant. My chores have been done and today is my day off.

Suddenly Cherl appears at the door. She is carrying a bottle of wine. I get up and let her in.

"Burgundy," she says holding up the bottle. "A very special bottle. You want a taste?"

"No thanks, Cherl, but I'll get you a glass."

She flops down in the easy chair and the robe she is wearing over her bathing suit opens to reveal her dark tan. When the sun shines, Cherl is at poolside pursuing the task of demolishing her late husband's wine collection.

I give her a glass and get myself more coffee. We both light cigarettes and then she raises her full glass in a toast. I click my coffee cup against it.

"A month today," she says.

"I didn't know you were keeping track."

"It's working out well," she says. "I wasn't sure you'd ever get that chlorine mixture right. You put so much in the first time I thought my bathing suit was going to dissolve."

We both laugh.

"You're good to have around, Ray. Good company."

I feel embarrassed. I've seen Cherl at her worst. Plenty of nights I've carried her inside and put her to bed. I wish I had a recipe for healing pain. I'd be glad to share it with her.

"You've been real generous with me, Cherl. It's like an oasis here. I called home last night. Talked to my wife for the first time in over two years."

"I'll bet she was thrilled. You're some kind of mystery guy. Got kids too?"

"One. John. He's twelve. She wouldn't let me speak with him. Can't blame her."

"You just walk out?"

"Yeah. Went for the proverbial loaf of bread."

"How come?"

"I let my wife become my keeper."

She stubs out her cigarette with angry energy.

"You're going to have to explain that, buster! My opinion of you is dropping."

"It's simple, Cherl. I was so much in love with Brenda that I couldn't fight with her. She'd say my boss wasn't treating me right and I'd quit my job. She wanted a bigger house so I bought it. She'd say friends were using me so I dropped them. We had to have a baby even though I didn't want one. After a while I gave up on my own ideas, opinions. Dreams even."

"Love isn't giving in," Cherl says.

"I know but sometimes it's easier."

"So what now? She order you home!"

I laugh.

"What're you so mad about, Cherl?"

"I don't know. But you're right, I am. Maybe it's just that I don't want to see you messed around. You're like ... a friend."

"Thank you," I say and I take her hand for a second. She grips mine tightly and the coldness of her skin makes me feel afraid. I withdraw to light a cigarette.

"She's involved with some other guy. It sounds pretty serious. I agreed to a divorce as long as I can stay in touch with John. She doesn't want me to see him but I thought I could write to him. There are things I'd like him to remember. When I taught him to swim. A fly-in fishing trip up north when he was eight. I want him to have those memories."

I stop because I realize Cherl is crying. She gets up and walks to the door with the bottle in her hand. At the door she turns to me.

"You going downtown?" she asks.

"Yeah. The Bay has a sale. I'm going to buy some clothes."

"You want to take the car?"

"No, thanks. It's a lovely day for a walk."

"Yes," she says, "I suppose it is."

As she leaves I regret I cannot enter the gate she has left open for me. I am forty-three years old but emotionally speaking, I'm still playing in the sandbox with my pail and shovel. Maybe knowing that will help.

When I return in the evening there are four police cars in the driveway. Also there is an ambulance. I watch two attendants carry a blanket-covered body and load it in the vehicle. A couple of uniformed policemen spot me and hustle over. The face of one is contorted with rage.

"You Raymond Blake?" he demands.

"Yes. What's . . ."

But before I can ask what's happened, he punches me. I know something horrible has happened. The pain in my face brings tears to my eyes. It's as if my nose is on fire and the tears are trying to put it out. I'm too stupid to fall so he hits me again and I feel several teeth break off and my mouth fills with blood. I can't keep my balance. I topple over and one or perhaps both begin to kick me.

"Let's drown the sonofabitch in that pond of booze in the basement," one of the cops says. "He probably busted all those bottles."

"Too good for this turd," the other says as he lands a heavy boot to my ribs. "I say get the rake he used on her and shove it up his ass. See what kind of expression his face takes on."

A few more kicks and I lose consciousness. But not before I know I'm in serious trouble.

Later, in lock-up, a doctor comes to the cell.

"Resisting arrest," a detective says.

The man of medicine cleans me up and gives me something for the pain.

In court a lawyer is assigned to me. He explains that I am charged with capital murder in the death of Cherl Anderson. The murder weapon has my fingerprints on it. The motive is robbery since all her jewelry is missing. Except for one diamond earring that has been found in my living quarters. I explain that Cherl often visited me. It probably just fell off. The lawyer assures me the Crown's case is shaky. He advises me to be optimistic. I assure him that I'll try.

But I'm convicted. The morning of sentence I am taken to a small room where Brenda waits. She stands when I enter and looks at me with distaste.

"I was against capital punishment before this," she says. "But now if they hung you publicly I'd bring John to watch."

The two guards smile.

"You believe I'm guilty?" I say.

"Yes," she answers. "I guess I'm just lucky it wasn't me you decided to kill."

"Why are you here?" Suddenly I hate her because I know what she is going to say. I can't remember ever hating anyone before.

"I burned all the letters you sent John. As far as he's concerned, you're dead."

"You can't make him forget his father."

"I can try," she says. "I've requested that you not be allowed to write to him from prison. Just in case one slipped through. They've agreed to co-operate. So forget him, Ray. Him and us. And this world."

Her face softens for a second and I see a brief glint of the person I once loved.

"Love him well, Brenda. For both of us."

Her face hardens again and she turns and leaves.

In court I receive the mandatory life sentence with no parole consideration for twenty-five years. I feel very afraid. Not of the sentence. I cannot imagine such a long time. Prison itself is just another place. Run on a rigid routine. Boring but bearable. I think my fear stems from a growing belief that I deserve this. I should have been a better person. A better son. A better husband. A better father.

My first day in prison I was released into the main population. Some young guy walked up to me in the yard wearing a big grin. I thought for a second I knew him but then he pulled a sharpened screwdriver from under his shirt and stabbed me in the stomach. I can't describe the pain.

After I was released from the hospital I was put into disassociation. This is a range of cells for stool-pigeons, child-molesters, and anybody else that the other inmates have decided is an undesirable. The guards see that we stay alive. They protect us from our peers. But we remain caged twenty-four hours a day. Pacing back and forth like disoriented animals. I've been here nine months. But today I'm leaving.

The keeper, Mr. Helson, stands in front of my cell bars as I pack. He is head of security and is unhappy with my decision.

"This is suicide, Blake," he says. "You leave here and you're signing your own death warrant. Put in for a transfer to another institution where they don't know about your beef. Or even hang in here another six months. Pretty soon they'll be busy thinking about somebody else."

I pick up my photo album and a diary I've been writing. I hand them to the keeper.

"Will you put this in with my personal property?"

"I could stop you, you know," he says.

"For a week maybe," I say. "Until I got my lawyer to file a writ."

He sighs and begins to thumb through the album.

"Don't you wanna keep these pictures for company?" he asks.

"I've got them all memorized. I want them safe. In case something happens."

"You got someone in mind? I don't recollect you having any visitors."

"My son," I say. "He's only a kid now but some day when he's grown up he might get curious about me. I wrote down a lot of stuff about the people in the pictures. Things he might want to know."

"Who's this?" he asks pointing to the only photograph I've ever had of my father.

"My father," I say.

"Good-looking man. Deceased?"

"World War Two," I say.

"Too bad," he says. He closes the album and then as he places the key in the lock to free me he continues. "It's always seemed to me there was plenty of wars to go around but never enough fathers."

"Amen to that," I say.

The grill swings open and I move out to the corridor with my blankets in my arms. The keeper steps in front of me and begins to walk along the gangway. I almost have to run to keep up with him.

I know I'm not a brave man. But I have a dream. In this dream my son is with me. Riding piggy-back. In my heart.

24
Jake MacDonald
BECOMING

THE blizzard hit at mid-afternoon.

Later in the day, with darkness descending on the city, Nimitz realized he wasn't going to get away clean. It was just before supper-time and he had turned off all the lights in his apartment; he heard footsteps coming in the outside hall. They were heavy footsteps, creaking, stealthy, and he was in the broom closet, peering through the crack, when they kicked the apartment door in.

One of them was a heavyset, bleary-eyed man. The other was a woman, mid-twenties, attractive, carrying a tape recorder in her right hand and a microphone in her left. Her lips were moving as she held the mike. The big man stepped past the splintered door jamb and beckoned for the young woman to follow. He gestured for absolute quiet. They moved down the hall towards the bedroom and out of Nimitz's line of sight.

His heart pounded in his ears. He was torn between anger, pure rage that they would barge into his apartment like this, and an intense embarrassment that at any moment he would be discovered. Then suddenly they were coming.

They walked right up Nimitz's cluttered hall and stood in front of the broom closet. The fat man planted his hands on his hips and shook his head in disgust as he looked around. "I don't know what to tell you, ma'am. The crazy guy, he could be anywhere."

The big man was Nimitz's landlord. He always paid his rent on time but nonetheless his landlord seemed to hate him. It was not unheard of for the landlord to go around kicking doors in. He was a selfmade man, a rumoured millionaire, and often declared that he hadn't worked his ass off all his life so that people could tell him what he could or couldn't do. Accordingly he often browsed through

Nimitz's mail, and often could be heard at strange hours of the night, squeaking down the outer hallway with his guard dog.

The young woman, carrying the tape recorder in the crook of her arm, moved down the hall and studied the big color posters he'd taped to the walls. Nimitz watched. She paused in front of the beautiful Kodachrome blowup of the fan coral, his favorite too.

"He certainly does like the sea, doesn't he."

The landlord tossed a hand. "Aw, summabitch. He's a nutcase, eh? All I know is, he's going to the ocean to become a fish, he shoulda give me 30 days notice."

The landlord fingered a rip in the wallpaper where Nimitz had taped the photo of a hammerhead shark. The hall window ticked, betraying a windblown gust of sleet. Nimitz's luggage was still piled in the hall, where he'd hurriedly abandoned it after hearing their approach. The young woman, who in her black leather coat, tightly pinned hair, and red lips looked vaguely feline and untrustworthy to Nimitz, eyed the luggage and glanced casually at the broom closet door, slightly ajar. "Well, I'd certainly like to talk to him anyway," she sighed. "I, uh, don't want to disturb this young man's privacy but I think he has a most interesting idea . . . a very clever advertising gimmick. Don't you think so? I mean, with these awful prairie winters . . . what an original promotion scheme!"

Nimitz was gritting his teeth, jammed into the closet, standing on one leg. Curses, he thought to himself, I should never have rented that billboard. Now, I've even got reporters after me.

With the last dregs of his bank account he'd commissioned a billboard at the corner of Stradbrook and Main, showing him in his fish outfit, bidding Winnipeg adieu with a lifted fin. SO LONG WINNIPEG — the caption read — I'M OFF TO THE OCEAN TO BECOME A FISH. And he'd signed his name. This public statement, which he'd intended strictly as a sincere farewell, had backfired horribly. The billboard company, after charging him $400, erected the message a day ahead of schedule and caught Nimitz unprepared. He'd hoped to be well underway, jetting his way south to the Caribbean by the time the billboard went public, but the phone had started ringing by early afternoon and hadn't stopped. He'd been beseiged by relatives, family, employer, neighbors, each demanding, no doubt, an explanation. But each time he'd taken to the broom closet. So far it had worked.

His landlord ground coins in his pocket, impatient. The lady reporter kept exploring the apartment, lifting, poking, spinning the fat papier mâché fish that hung on threads from the ceiling. Her head shook slowly, a tight smile played on her mouth.

"I got to get back to my hockey game," said the landlord. "It's Gretzky," he explained.

"Well thank you very much for showing me his apartment," the young woman said. "I hope he's not out wandering around in this blizzard tonight." She glanced at the broom closet. Her eyes were unfocused, abstract, her lips parted as she wedged the card in the door jamb, her face perhaps six inches away. This woman, Nimitz thought to himself, has taken advantage of men before.

Nimitz caught a cab to a hotel near the airport.

The storm was at its height. The streets were empty. It was suppertime, but dark as a wild eerie midnight. Nimitz sat in the back of the cab, clutching a huge stack of paraphernalia on his lap — mylar fins, ribbed with old car aerials, a scaly skin fashioned from an old body stocking, and large sequins, spiny dorsals, sheet-metal gills. The cab wallowed and skidded through the snow-clogged streets. Occasionally snow ploughs would lunge across the street in front of them, their disaster lights spinning crazily.

"You're going to a masquerade party on a night like this?" the cab driver remarked.

"No . . ." said Nimitz quietly, the lights of the city playing over his face one last time. "I'm going to the ocean to become a fish."

The cabbie nodded. "Sorry I asked."

At the hotel door the cabbie sulked, refusing to help Nimitz unload his gear. Nimitz paid him with a $5 tip, his bare hands freezing in the bitter January wind, and then carted his equipment to the brightly lit aquarium of the hotel entrance.

He stood at the front desk, his fins piled beside him, and rubbed his hands together for warmth. Bits of snow melted in his tousled hair.

"Mr. Uh . . . don't I know you?" the desk clerk asked.

"I doubt it," replied Nimitz. "I'm on my way to the ocean. I'd like to rent a room for a few hours until the airplanes are flying again."

"Of course, sir."

"And I'm expecting a call from the airline regarding my reservation. Other than that I want privacy, all right? No visitors — I want to get some rest."

The desk clerk's palm hit the bell. "Yes sir!" A bellhop materialized at Nimitz's side.

"You take the suitcase, I'll take the fins," said Nimitz.

The bellhop led him down the hall.

He wasn't in his room for more than ten minutes, testing the shower, testing the color television, ripping the sanitary band off the toilet seat, when a key sounded in the door and the lady reporter came into the room. "I'd like to introduce myself," she said.

Nimitz was speechless.

The girl said her name was Kate Mathews, freelance journalist, down on her luck. She said, "At a hundred bucks a story do you think I'm getting rich?" She was already sitting on the edge of the bed, but there was a resigned look on her face, as if she expected to be expelled from the room as quickly as she came in. Her leather coat was unbuttoned, and she didn't have a light for her cigarette. Nimitz didn't smoke.

"I'll talk to you for five minutes," Nimitz relented. "No tape recorder, and nothing published until I leave town."

"Okay," she said. "No sweat." She was still looking for a light for her cigarette. She found one, lit it, and slipped out of her leather coat. She was wearing black slacks, a fawn sweater and a silk scarf knotted around her throat. Nimitz appraised her bosom. This is one thing I'll miss, he thought to himself. A female trout or salmon is gorgeous, admittedly, but the female human isn't that bad either.

Settled, with her knees crossed, her Benson & Hedges aloft, her hair loosed and shaken down, she glanced at Nimitz and smiled. "Now . . . What's this about becoming a fish? Is this another one of these Fly-to-the-Sun promotions?"

Nimitz explained that he was serious. He showed her his fins, his weight belt, his underwater topographical maps of various ocean regions, all tucked away in waterproof pouches . . . his scaly outfit, designed so that other fishes would accept him, and most important of all, his solid-state rebreather. He laid all the gear out on the bed, explaining the function of each, and told her that he'd test the outfit one more time to make sure he hadn't forgotten anything.

Kate Mathews watched him with a look of disbelief as he stripped down to his jockey shorts and climbed into the fish outfit. In a matter of minutes he was fully dressed, in silver scales, rattling gills, and a great quivering array of gaudy fins. From around his neck, in the manner of a French cavalier, hung a lacy ruff of quills. He waddled carefully to the mirror, studying his image with narrowed eyes. "I put a lot of thought into this. You know, your average person would think I was crazy. They'd say 'Nimitz, you're crazy. Why not become a dolphin if you're going to all the trouble?' But that's just their own prejudice coming through. Dolphins share a lot of similarities with human beings, so naturally we think that they're wonderful. And nobody mentions that the Japanese slaughter them by the thousands, so there's a real risk involved. And not only that ... dolphins breathe air and I don't want to have to go up to the surface all the time. I've had it with that."

He stood sideways, glancing at himself in the mirror, and awkwardly adjusted one of his ventral fins. "I finally settled on the rooster fish. I'm one of the most grotesque creatures in the ocean, in a sort of flamboyant way, and also," he added with a modest smile, "I'm deadly poisonous."

Kate Mathews stared at him for a long moment. "This is a joke," she said flatly.

Nimitz shook his head. His gills rustled. "You don't have to believe me. You don't have to stay here, either. You asked me, and I'm telling you. Which part do you think is funny?"

"Well you can't just become a fish!"

He sat on the edge of the bed, crossed his fins patiently in his lap. "Well yes, actually, I can."

She stared at him, as if making some quick appraisal of his sanity, and he stared back. There was the faint sound of winter buffeting the outside walls. "You see," he began, "it's a well established principle of modern physics that mind can change matter. There's all sorts of people around who can stop their hearts, walk on fire, raise objects by looking at them ... it's all old hat. There's even some physicists nowadays who will tell you that there's no such thing as matter. It's just something we've invented, for convenience. That tape recorder, for instance, exists only insofar as we agree that it does."

She nodded sourly. "Heavy."

"So if all of this, my humanity, this room, this city, this world, is just an idea, then I'm changing my mind, that's all. I'm just changing my mind."

"If everything is just mind power, why are you bothering with all those flappy fins and so forth?"

"Well, I don't have the mental power of a yogi or somebody like that so I have to cheat a bit. I have to create a mood. I don't expect to turn into a fish just by snapping my fingers. I'll probably be down there concentrating real hard for weeks before I get any results."

She nodded, shook her head. "You can't do this. You can't take these philosophies and apply them in real life, they're not meant for that. Where will you live when you're down there? How will you swim with all that crap on? What will you eat? How will you breathe?"

Nimitz smiled benignly and displayed his solid-state rebreather, which was a black steel and rubber device resembling a harmonica. "With this I can breathe underwater just like a fish. It's good for up to two years. Cousteau designed it years ago but suppressed it because it would have ruined the SCUBA industry, which he earns millions of dollars from. Not many people know about it. I had to buy the plans from this Florida drug runner I know, and it cost me plenty."

She examined it dubiously. "This little thing?"

"Sure. It works just great. You just pop it in your mouth and breathe through it. It separates the H_2 from the O. Hydrogen bubbles shoot out those little vents on the side and oxygen flows in through the mouthpiece. It'll have to do until I get my gills working." She peered at his gills, several layers of clinking sheet-metal with meticulously handpainted scales. "But . . . where will you live? You can't just swim around like a fish with that monkey suit on."

He unbuttoned the gills at his throat and smiled. "Of course not. I'll tend to settle down off reefs in about forty feet of water. I tend to prey on crustaceans so you'll find me where there's a steady run of shrimp or squid or lobster. Give me some clear, clean water, a sand bottom and maybe a bit of riprap or coral nearby and I imagine I'll do very well."

"Really," she said. She was regarding him with unwavering fascination. "And you really think you can get away with this? You don't work for some goofy ad agency?"

He stared back at her, his eyes equally intent. "No I do not."

"And you think that mouth-organ thing will let you cruise around down their indefinitely?"

"Oh yeah, I just have to keep it filled with baking soda."

"You've got to keep it filled with . . . baking soda?"

"Yeah — the baking soda makes the bubbles. Along with the H_2O. Here, let me show you. I should test it anyway."

Nimitz stood up, clumsy because of the way he was bound by the fish skin, and wiggled into the bathroom. He heard her coming behind him, but couldn't see with the ruff of fins around his neck. He bent over stiffly, turned on the bathtub tap, and spoke loudly over the water's roar. "My name is Nimitz, by the way," he said.

"I know . . . your name is on the billboard, remember?"

"Yes, but I'd like to forget. I hadn't intended to become a notorious figure so early but my plans fouled up."

She was turning over the breathing device in her hand, looking up at him expectantly. He was taller than her but not by much.

"Allow me," he said. He shut the tap off and took the rebreather from her hand, paused for a moment and gazed down into the half-tubful of swinging water. Bright lights from the ceiling, reflected on the bath water, moved like thought on Nimitz's face. He clamped the rebreather in his mouth, looked at her, waved goodbye and then plunged his head into the water.

Seconds passed, and more seconds, and then she thought she detected a queer tremor in his shoulders. She seized him by the gills and dorsal fins and wrestled him bodily from the bathtub. He fell backwards onto the floor, she falling in a tangle beneath him, and as he gasped and coughed violently she scrambled onto one knee, pinned him to the floor and prepared to administer artificial respiration. Nimitz coughed and floundered and the more he struggled the harder she pinned. "Easy . . . easy," she soothed. "You're not going to drown."

"I know I'm not going to drown!" he protested, his voice nasal from the thumb and forefinger clamped to his nose. "I was doing fine. There was no problem! Didn't you see the bubbles of H_2?"

"No I didn't see the H_2," she retorted, mimicking the quack in his voice. "If it was working so well why is your face purple?"

He sat up, straightened his fins. "Excitement, I guess . . . I don't know! You try it, if you don't think it's exciting to be breathing air under water, man's oldest dream."

She made a cynical snort.

"Looks like I spilled a little water on you," Nimitz said.

She nodded, looking down at the water splotches on her slacks, the thin sweater drenched and clinging to her bust. "I guess I got excited," she said. She gave him a crooked smile.

At that moment the telephone rang. Nimitz flopped and wriggled on the floor, struggling to stand up.

"Here, let me help," she said.

"Get the phone."

Nimitz lay on the floor and listened as she answered the phone. Water, his element, soaked in through the fish skin and established a chilly presence in his undershorts. "It's the airline," she called out. "There's some flights starting to operate again. There's a flight 203 to Denver leaving at 10:40, a flight 515 to Toronto leaving at 11:15 . . ."

"All I want is to get to the sea!" he blurted. "Anywhere on the sea! Doesn't he have anything, tonight, going to the sea?"

There was a long interval and Nimitz listened intently to the voice in the other room. Her voice was calm and pleasant considering the circumstances; Nimitz was beginning to think that she was a little strange.

"There's a Skybus to Vancouver at midnight. It's leaving on time and there's still two seats left."

Nimitz struggled to his feet. "Yes! I'll take it."

Kate Mathews cooed into the telephone. "Wonderful, we'll take both of them."

In front of the airport there were taxi cabs clustered like predators, their lights flashing in ominous synchronization. The cab containing Nimitz and Kate Mathews slid to an icy halt in the loading zone. Nimitz paid the cabbie and exited clumsily. Still in his fish outfit, having chosen to never again remove that freely chosen badge of identity, he slipped on the ice and bent one fin against the taxi door. Kate Mathews exited from the cab behind him, carrying a luggage bag and taking his arm as they slipped and skidded across the road. "It's only a caudal fin," said Nimitz. "I'll hardly ever need it. Anyway . . . maybe it'll heal."

"I'll get some tape somewhere," Kate Mathews said.

Overhead, above the streetlights, the cloud cover had torn off and the sky was clearing. There were several stars, tiny chinks of light, visible in the huge dark emptiness but the wind still blew, swirling chips of ice into their faces, and they both exclaimed aloud as they rushed towards the door. Kate Mathews, her own clothes thoroughly soaked from the debacle in the hotel bathroom, had changed into an outfit assembled from Nimitz's suitcase. As she expected, his clothes were somewhat too large and consistently fish-oriented, with "Save The Whales" shirts and "Miami Dolphins" football sweaters, but she had nevertheless managed to put together an outfit she thought reasonably anonymous. Wearing wool breeches, an old British army khaki shirt, canvas vest, straw creel hung over one shoulder as a purse, she thought she could pass for someone marginally normal, perhaps even chic. However, as they entered the cavernous light of the airport terminal, aswarm with strangers, she drew near to Nimitz's fin. "I feel a bit conspicuous," she whispered, as they walked to the ticket desk.

"How do you think I feel?" he retorted.

Nimitz paid for their tickets. "I won't need money where I'm going," he sighed. There was a $2 bill in his hand. "This is it. The last money I have as a human. Should we blow it foolishly?"

She shook her head.

They secured their tickets, checked their luggage, and walked to the boarding gate. Nimitz went through the metal detector first. A female security officer, smiling as if she was overjoyed to see him, ran a hand detector up and down his body. Nimitz, at first concerned that his fish outfit would cause consternation at the security gate, saw that amongst the other passengers lined up for the Vancouver flight — ageing hippies, painted ladies, seven-foot-tall Rastafarians, radical nuns, skeletal drug addicts — he was barely noticed. They walked down the hall and down the long umbilical tunnel into the plane. They sat, waited, there was a whine, the engines staggered thunderingly alive and they began to roll, bouncing like a carriage, across the concrete ramp towards the runway. Nimitz pressed his forehead against the window and mentally photographed all those things he would never see again — lights of the city, crawling headlights, cold pavement swept by even colder snow. A moment later the landscape swept through an abrupt 90 degree arc and the jet braked to a stop. There was a long moment, a total silence inside the gloom of the aircraft.

Nimitz looked at Kate Mathews. She was pretending to look straight ahead, but he had the sense that she was studying him. She seemed sneaky, but in a constant and predictable and playful way. The trout fisherman's hat was perched on her abundant hair in a roguish tilt and she was twiddling her thumbs. As if reading his mind she whispered to him from the corner of her mouth. "I saw your picture on the billboard and that's why I'm here. I'm not really after a story, I'm after you. I know what kind of a man I like and the face on the billboard sparked my interest. And then I found out that you're probably crazy and that was two strikes. And then I found out that you're going away so you're completely unattainable, and that's three strikes and I'm out."

She proffered her hand, palm up, as if they were making a deal.

Nimitz took her hand, profoundly moved. He hesitated, as if searching for the proper words. "If you were a rooster fish," he finally whispered, "I would like to spawn with you."

The jet was on its takeoff roll. With the thunder of engines they were being pressed deep into their seats. Kate Mathews squeezed his hand. "That's the nicest compliment I've had all winter," she said.

It was like a hell-bound plane, Nimitz thought to himself. A full moon slanted in through the heavy plastic portholes as the plane bucked and swooped its way westward. At one point the pilot announced that they were flying into a one-hundred-mile-an-hour headwind, hence the buffeting, but though he changed altitudes the bouncing continued. Their departure time from Winnipeg was midnight, the same as their estimated arrival in Vancouver, and as they rocketed westward, locked in time, the strange-looking passengers who hulked up and down the gloomy aisle, or brayed drunkenly throughout the airplane, seemed like oddities of the human form, living exhibits in some doomed menagerie. Nimitz, with a leaden despair for his own species, studied the plastic mouldings, vinyl seat backs and mysteriously patterned rivets around him and tried to read some clues as to why his own civilization had come to this squalid end. Personally, he suspected that things had begun to go wrong as soon as the first amphibians crawled out of the sea.

Finally the plane began to descend. Kate Mathews, who had been sleeping with her head on his shoulder, stirred drowsily and he patted her knee. He felt like they were married. "We're going down."

She leaned across him, her elbows heavy in his lap, and peered out the porthole. "Oh look," she said. The lights of Vancouver, like a kingdom under the sea, glittered from the darkness below.

They landed at Vancouver International and picked up their bags. Even inside the terminal, teeming with crowds, they could smell the damp west-coast air. They went outside and it was raining lightly. The ever-present cabs idled at the curb and a tangle of roads, black and shiny as oil under the streetlamps, all led towards the lights of the city. "What now?" Kate Mathews asked.

"This way," Nimitz said. "I used to know a guy."

They walked down the road for half a mile. When they were out of sight of the airport entrance Nimitz went down into the ditch and spread the barbed wire fence. "Hop through," he said. He was shivering. Already the rain had leaked through the hand-sewn scales of his fish skin.

"What gives?" she said, as they began to slog across the muddy field.

"This is actually an island, Sea Island. When they built the airport there were some people living on this island but they kicked them all off. I know a guy who's sort of a hobo who lives in one of the old houses up here. He's a good guy, we used to work the tow boats together. Anyway, maybe he'll put us up for the night. He's thinking of becoming a fish too."

Soon, a dark row of houses, with not a light on, loomed ahead. The wind seemed to be picking up and Nimitz moved boldly through the yards, hurrying against the quickening rain. "It's this one," he whispered loudly. "But it doesn't look like he's home."

Around the back door, which was piled with fresh-cut firewood, there were many signs of occupancy — dog dish, rubber boots, swede saw. Kate Mathews spied a note on the door. "Look."

"DEAR STRANGER," the note read "COME ON IN AND HELP YOURSELF, BUT PLEASE REPLACE WHAT YOU USE. SPLIT WOOD IF YOU GOT NO MONEY. PERSONAL FRIENDS IGNORE THIS SIGN. I'M

SHANGHAIED TO RUPERT — CY".

They went in the door and Nimitz groped through the kitchen, locating a lantern and a wooden match. The lantern flared alight. The cabin had a kitchen at one end, a fireplace halfway through the room and an old double bed at the far end. "I want a coffee," Kate Mathews said.

"Me too, I'm cold."

"Take off that fish outfit, you must be soaked."

"I'll take it off and light a fire. I don't mind going human tonight, since it's my last evening as a *homo sapiens*."

Nimitz lit a fire and took off his fish skin. His shorts were also wet and he removed them, hanging everything by the heat of the fire. His torso, hardened by years of traveling and outdoor labor, was sculpted in shadow by the firelight. He was not ashamed to be naked in front of a woman he barely knew. It was his preference for basics that convinced him to become a fish in the first place. He got into the bed and pulled the blankets to his chin.

"Hurry up," he said with a shiver. "I don't want to warm this thing up all by myself."

"Warm what thing up?"

She came to the bedside with two steaming mugs of coffee. Nimitz watched her undress. He decided that she was undoubtedly the most straightforward, witty, and nubile woman he'd ever had the pleasure to watch disrobe. She climbed under the heavy quilts, shivered wildly from the cold, and wrapped herself around him. "Oh my . . ." she said. "Oh my . . ."

Afterward, in the total dark, with the fire down to only crawling embers, she stirred her sleepy warmth against him and kissed the side of his neck. "Nimitz . . . are you still awake?"

"Of course," he said.

"Well, what's that strange noise outside? That thumping, windy noise? It wasn't there when we first went to sleep."

Nimitz smiled; she could tell by the movement of his cheek. "What . . . didn't you realize? No, I guess you wouldn't have noticed in the rain and the dark. That thumping sound is the tide coming in. We're only about 40 yards from the sea."

Dawn broke stormy and dismal. For hours, as wind and rain slapped the windows, Nimitz and Kate Mathews dozed under the covers. Occasionally they would waken, nuzzle like cats and ease their limbs into some new model of entwinement. Outside, the sea growled patiently.

Finally, after sleeping all of the morning and much of the afternoon, Kate Mathews opened her eyes to sunlight in the window. She rolled over to tell Nimitz but he was already awake, staring at the ceiling. "When are you going?" she asked.

He looked at her. "Soon, I guess. I was going to go early but I hate to go swimming when it's overcast."

They rose from the bed and dressed. Kate Mathews wriggled into Nimitz's old fisherman's sweater and moved about the kitchen making coffee, her hair a luxuriant mane. Nimitz, strapping on his gills, gazed at her fixedly. His eyes were soft but the muscles of his jaw twitched with determination. Finally he moved up behind her and placed a fin on her shoulder. "Kate," he said.

She sobbed and threw her arms around him, "I don't *want* you to become a fish!" Her tears ran onto his scaly chest.

"Kate, Kate . . ." he whispered. "It's not what you want, or what I want, or what anybody wants that's important. It's bigger than that, it's the survival of a species. There was a time we crawled out of the sea, now it's time we realized our mistake and went back . . . don't you see?"

She nodded.

They drank their coffees and went outside.

It was a brilliant day, the sky blue as a flag. The sea was a darker purple, redolent with salty breezes, and across a line of dunes, drift logs and cane grass the surf dumped lazily on the beach. Nimitz walked boldly through the sand, his ostentatious rooster quills shivering colorfully in the wind, and seagulls swerved overhead, screaming.

There was a rowboat on the beach and together they pushed it into the water. "Do you know how to row?" he asked.

"Shut up," she said.

She rowed and he sat in the rear of the boat, going over his maps. "I'm going to swim out to the end of the Strait of Juan de Fuca," he told her. "And then hang a left and head south down the edge of the continental shelf. If I keep traveling I should make the Coronado Islands in four or five weeks time. There's lots happening down there, the waters are literally teeming with life. I'll take it easy for a while, rest up, prey on the plentiful crustaceans, then . . . head out. I got 7000 miles of Pacific Ocean to cross, not to mention what lies beyond, like the Great Barrier Reef, the Sunda Straits, the South China Sea."

She stopped rowing. They were fifty yards from shore, bobbing gently. Her chin was propped on her hand and she wasn't looking at him. And then she looked up at him and was focused, bright. "Good luck, Nimitz," she said.

He shrugged. "As long as I don't get speargunned by some tourist or netted by a Russian trawler I should be all right."

He pulled the fringed collar and fish hood up over his head. The glassy eyes, large as saucers, stared at her unseeing. "Next time you're at a fancy cocktail party," he said, his lips flapping, "take a good look at the seafood hors d'oeuvres . . . it might be me."

She nodded. Off in the distance a DC8 was lifting noiselessly, glinting in the sun. When she got back to Winnipeg, she thought to herself, the storm would be over and it would be 30° below. She stood up and opened the huge lips and took one last look at the human face inside. She kissed him, he kissed her. "Goodbye," Nimitz said.

He stood on the gunwhale and vaulted into the sea. Water exploded around him, flashes of colored light. Jeez it's cold! He was going to shout but realized with his weight belt he was already sinking. He breathed deeply through the rebreather, once, twice, and a rapture began to flood into his brain. Below him he saw the spiralling depths coming up to meet him, the sun winding down like a staircase of gold.

NOTES ON THE AUTHORS

MARGARET ATWOOD is the celebrated author of such works of fiction as *The Edible Woman, Surfacing, The Handmaid's Tale*, and *Cat's Eye*. She lives in Toronto.

JAMES BACQUE is the author of *Other Losses* and *Just Raoul* as well as *The Queen Comes to Minnicog*. He lives in Toronto.

DON BAILEY is the author of many books of fiction and poetry, including *Sunflowers Never Sleep* and *Homeless Heart*. He lives in Winnipeg.

WADE BELL is the author of *The North Saskatchewan River Book*, a collection of fiction. He lives in Calgary.

SILVER DONALD CAMERON is a renowned playwright and author whose most recent book is *Wind, Whales and Whiskey: A Cape Breton Voyage*. He lives in Halifax.

BILL DODDS has published short stories in several Canadian and Australian magazines. He lives in Vancouver.

SHARON ABRON DRACHE is the author of *The Mikveh Man & Other Stories* as well as the novel *Ritual Slaughter*. She lives in Ottawa.

DONNA GAMACHE has published stories in *Western People, The Toronto Star*, and *Canadian Christmas Stories*. She lives in MacGregor, Manitoba.

GAIL HELGASON is the author of several non-fiction books, including *The First Albertans*. She lives in Edmonton.

DAVID HELWIG is the author of such works of fiction as *A Postcard from Rome, Old Wars*, and *Of Desire*. He lives in Kingston, Ontario.

SHELLEY LEEDAHL is the author of *A Few Words for January*, a collection of poetry. Her stories have appeared in *The Fiddlehead, Grain*, and *Fireweed*. She lives in Saskatoon.

JAKE MACDONALD is the author of *Indian River, The Bridge Out of Town*, and *Two Tickets to Paradise*. He lives in Winnipeg.

SCOTT MACKAY is the author of the espionage thriller *A Friend in Barcelona*. His stories have appeared in *Ellery Queen's Mystery Magazine*, *Descant*, and *Tesseracts 3*. He lives in Toronto.

LINDA MANNING is the author of two children's books, including *Animal House*. She lives near Cobourg, Ontario.

HELEN PEREIRA is the author of the novel *Magpie in a Tower*. She lives in Toronto.

TED PLANTOS is the author of nine books of poetry and fiction as well as the children's book *At Home on Earth*. He lives in Toronto.

STAN ROGAL has published poetry and fiction in several Canadian, American, and European literary magazines. He lives in Toronto.

HELEN J. ROSTA is the author of the collection of stories *In the Blood*. She lives in Edmonton.

CAROL SHIELDS is the author of such acclaimed works of fiction as *Various Miracles*, *Small Ceremonies*, and *Swann: A Mystery*. She lives in Winnipeg.

J.J. STEINFELD is the author of the novel *Our Hero in the Cradle of Confederation* and four short story collections, including *The Apostate's Tattoo*. He lives in Charlottetown.

FRASER SUTHERLAND is the author of nine books of poetry, fiction, and non-fiction, including *In the Village of Alias*. He lives in Scotsburn, Nova Scotia.

ANN WALSH is the author of three books for young people, including *The Ghost of Soda Creek*. She lives in Williams Lake, British Columbia.

DAVID WELHAM has published his work in various Canadian magazines. He lives in Winnipeg.

CHARLES WILKINS is the author of five books of non-fiction, a novel, a stage play, and a book of children's verse. He co-authored the travel book *Paddle to the Amazon*. He lives in Dundas, Ontario.